Prai

"Adrian has a gift ... deeper into the amazing w

Fiction

"With an Adrian ... ity of dangerous thrills and passionate chills."

–RT Book Reviews

"Nothing beats good writing and that is what ultimately makes Lara Adrian stand out amongst her peers . . . Adrian doesn't hold back with the intensity or the passion."

—Under the Covers

"Adrian has a style of writing that creates these worlds that are so realistic and believable . . . the characters are so rich and layered . . . the love stories are captivating and often gut-wrenching . . . edge of your seat stuff!"

—Scandalicious Book Reviews

"Adrian compels readers to get hooked on her storylines."

—Romance Reviews Today

Praise for Lara Adrian's books

"Adrian's strikingly original Midnight Breed series delivers an abundance of nail-biting suspenseful chills, red-hot sexy thrills, an intricately built world, and realistically complicated and conflicted protagonists, whose happily-ever-after ending proves to be all the sweeter after what they endure to get there."

—Booklist (starred review)

"(The Midnight Breed is) a well-written, action-packed series that is just getting better with age."

—Fiction Vixen

"Chocked full of action, suspense and romance, Adrian's Midnight Breed series is a winner . . . patent edgy characters, action-packed storylines, and smoking hot romances."

—*Smexy Books*

"Fantastic! We recommend to anyone who loves action packed, intense reads with gripping characters and spectacular storylines woven into a phenomenally crafted world. If you haven't started the Midnight Breed series yet, we highly suggest that you bump it up to the top of your list. "

—*Literal Addiction*

"If you like romance combined with heart-stopping paranormal suspense, you're going to love (Edge of Dawn)."

—*Bookpage*

"The Midnight Breed series is one of the consistently best paranormal series out there.... Adrian writes compelling individual stories (with wonderful happily ever afters) within a larger story arc that is unfolding with a refreshing lack of predictability."

–*Romance Novel News*

"Crave the Night is stunning in its flawless execution. Lara Adrian has the rare ability to lure readers right into her books, taking them on a ride they will never forget."

—*Under the Covers*

"Adrian has set up a really interesting and exciting plot arc that will hold strong for many more books to come."

—*The Book Pushers*

"It's official. Lara Adrian is brilliant."

—*Yummy Men and Kickass Chicks*

The 100 Series

For 100 Days
For 100 Nights
For 100 Reasons
For 100 Forevers *(forthcoming)*

Run to You
Play My Game

Other books by Lara Adrian

Midnight Breed series

A Touch of Midnight
Kiss of Midnight
Kiss of Crimson
Midnight Awakening
Midnight Rising
Veil of Midnight
Ashes of Midnight
Shades of Midnight
Taken by Midnight
Deeper Than Midnight
A Taste of Midnight
Darker After Midnight
The Midnight Breed Series Companion
Edge of Dawn
Marked by Midnight
Crave the Night
Tempted by Midnight
Bound to Darkness
Stroke of Midnight
Defy the Dawn
Midnight Untamed
Midnight Unbound
Claimed in Shadows
Midnight Unleashed
Break The Day
Fall of Night
King of Midnight

Midnight Breed Spinoff

Hunter Legacy Series

Born of Darkness
Hour of Darkness
Edge of Darkness
Guardian of Darkness

Historical Romances

Dragon Chalice Series

Heart of the Hunter
Heart of the Flame
Heart of the Dove

Warrior Trilogy

White Lion's Lady
Black Lion's Bride
Lady of Valor

Lord of Vengeance

FOR 100 DAYS

A 100 Series Novel

NEW YORK TIMES BESTSELLING AUTHOR

LARA ADRIAN

ISBN: 978-1-939193-42-1

FOR 100 DAYS

ISE-2404

www.LaraAdrian.com

Available in ebook, trade paperback, and unabridged audiobook editions.

For 100 Days

ACKNOWLEDGMENTS

Avery and Nick have been living in my head for a few years now, waiting (not so patiently) for their turn on the page.

I have to thank my husband, first and foremost, for listening when I first told him about these characters and their story over lunch in a Paris café while we were on book tour there in 2014. What we'd planned to be a day of museum-hopping instead turned into a full-on plotting session that was even more fun. This book, and the rest of the trilogy, would not be what they are now without John's input and ideas all along the way.

My deep appreciation, also, to my copyeditor, Judi Fennel, and my dear friends who read the manuscript in draft form and offered thoughtful critique and encouragement. Thank you, Patricia Rasey and Liz Berry! I'm so grateful for your support and insight.

No list of acknowledgments would be complete without a note of thanks to my readers. Thank you for embracing my characters and story worlds—from medieval knights to modern-day vampires to alpha billionaires. Because of your amazing support, I have the privilege of following my muse wherever she leads. I hope you continue to enjoy the journey along with me!

1

Cold afternoon rain needles my cheeks as I emerge from Grand Central Station with the rest of the crowd fresh off the subway. I wince and tug the hood of my jacket a little farther over my face as I push forward in the drizzle and try to ignore the chilly, late April gust that sweeps through the city's skyscraper canyons on a low, banshee howl.

I swear, it seems like New York has been trying to spit me out and blow me back home to Pennsylvania almost since the day I arrived.

By now, I should be used to sudden shitty turns in the weather, and I curse myself for not taking the time to zip the winter liner back into my jacket before I left my apartment in Brooklyn. I'd been too preoccupied and anxious as I got ready for work, feelings I'm still carrying with me now as I head away from the station.

The restaurant where I tend bar six nights a week is up on Madison Avenue, several blocks away. Shivering as the rain starts to soak me, I walk briskly toward my destination, eyeing the other people around me with envy as they huddle under the shelter of their umbrellas. I should have brought mine too. Maybe I would have if half of its spines weren't mangled from battling other storms. Maybe someday I'll get around to replacing it.

Right. I practically snort at the idea. Considering the nasty-gram my landlord left taped to my door earlier this week, broken umbrellas are the least of my worries.

Unprepared and underfunded. The definition of my entire existence lately.

More than once in the past year and a half, I've been tempted to lie down and let this damn city win.

But not today.

Today, I have something I haven't had in a long time.

Hope.

It surges through me, sharp and bright and warm, as I reach the smoked-glass double doors of Vendange and my phone rings in my jacket pocket. I've been waiting for this call all day—ever since I got the voicemail from my friend, Margot, that she had news for me and didn't want to leave the details in a message.

Patience has never been my strong suit. Especially not when everything I have is riding on the outcome. I'd called Margot back immediately, but her assistant informed me she was tied up in gallery meetings at Dominion and couldn't be interrupted.

That was hours ago.

In the time since, I'd gone back and played her message at least a dozen times, trying to read clues in her voice, but there was only measured control and professionalism in her tone. And why not? She and I are friends, but I'm also her client—albeit, not a very profitable one. I can only wish that's about to change tonight. Hell, I'm praying for it.

I can hardly breathe from anticipation as I slip into the restaurant to get out of the wet and cold, my heart racing, chilled fingers fumbling inside my pocket to retrieve my ringing phone.

Although it's early in the evening, Vendange is packed with corporate and creative types from the surrounding area. Dark suits mingle with high fashion and Boho chic at the tight clusters of tables in the dining area. At the long, sleek bar, one of my coworkers, Tasha Lopez, is pouring drinks and flirting shamelessly with a group of male patrons who have no idea the curvy spitfire is a happily married woman with a young family at home.

Tasha spots me coming in the door and sends me a nod in greeting as I bypass the new girl at the hostess stand and the line of customers that's already starting to form at the front of the house. I've got a few minutes before I have to clock in for my shift, so I hurry for the employee coatroom to answer the call.

When I finally have my phone in hand, my heart sinks. On the display, the area code reads 570, not 212. Pennsylvania, not New York.

"Shit." The word leaks out of me on a quiet sigh.

This isn't the call I'm waiting for, and even though conversations with my mom never last more than fifteen minutes, I tell myself I can't afford to tie up the line even that long as I mute the ringer and decline her call.

The truth is, I can't deal with talking to her right now. Not today. And not here, where I have to put on a cheerful smile, make conversation all night with strangers as I serve them overpriced cocktails and pretend the rest of my world isn't the train wreck I know it to be.

None of that lessens the guilt that pricks me when I think of her disappointment on the other end. Keeping in touch is important to my mother, I know. It broke her heart when I moved so far away. She didn't make a secret of that, but I think she understands that I had to do it. Finally, I had to do something for me.

With a frown and a deep exhalation I can't hold back, I set my phone to vibrate mode and slide it into the back pocket of my black jeans. Employees aren't supposed to carry their phones while they're working, but I hope the hem of my untucked black shirt will hide it during my shift. It's not like I'll be able to concentrate on anything unless I keep it close tonight anyway.

"Hey, girl!" Tasha comes up behind me in the coat room as I'm hanging up my wet jacket and gives me a quick hug. "Thanks again for taking my shift last night, Avery. You're the best."

"No problem," I tell her. And it wasn't. I needed the extra night's tips, and even if I didn't, I wouldn't have said no. I know Tasha would come in for me on her day off, too, if I ever asked the favor of her.

She watches me as I take off my flats and trade them for the black heels in my purse that complete my uniform for the bar. Tasha's arms are crossed over her breasts, which are generously displayed in the low-cut V of her black top that's very similar to mine—another part of the Vendange dress code that I despise. "I mean it, Avery. You're a lifesaver. Joel said he was gonna dock me for a full day if I left without making sure the bar was covered."

I roll my eyes at the mention of the restaurant's oily manager. "Joel's a dick. How's Zoe doing today?"

"Much better. Just a passing stomach thing, but my mother-in-law panicked." Tasha shakes her head, sending her soft brown spiral curls swaying against the coffee-and-cream smoothness of her cheeks. "It's been a long time since Inez has taken care of a four-month-old and Zoe tends to fuss. But I know she's in good hands. Plus, it doesn't hurt that Inez is free child care now that she's living with us."

I smile, hearing the relief in her voice. "I'm glad everything's okay."

"Yeah, me too. FYI, you've got paint on your chin."

"I do? Dammit." I rub my face, then fish for the compact mirror in my purse. The smudge of dark plum acrylic stains my chin like a fading bruise. "I'm almost finished with one of my pieces," I tell her as I scrub the paint smear with the pad of my thumb. "It's not perfect yet, but I'm working on it. I want to have it ready to show Margot soon."

"Margot from the gallery?"

I nod, unable to hold back my grin. "She's supposed to call me tonight with some news. Her voicemail this morning said she wanted to tell me personally."

"Holy shit." Tasha's eyes widen. "Avery, that's awesome. You must've sold another painting."

She says it as if my art sells with some kind of regularity. It doesn't. Aside from one painting that sold almost immediately after Margot got me placed at Dominion more than a year ago, it's been a long, arid dry spell ever since.

Maybe that first sale was a fluke. I've often wondered. Dreaded it, really. People have told me I have talent. God knows, I love painting more than anything. It's always been my outlet, my refuge. But maybe passion isn't enough. Maybe I should've stayed in the hometown and saved my money to finish art school instead of running away to the biggest city I could think of as soon as I had the chance to break free and chase my dreams.

The truth is, I wanted to escape. I wanted to disappear. I wanted to become someone new. Someone different from me.

Someone better.

I wanted to live. For me, not for my mom or all the things she wants for me. Not even for my grandma, whom I'd looked after back home until her death from emphysema two years ago.

If I fail now, I'll be letting everyone down.

Fuck, who am I kidding? I'm already failing, and unless Margot calls to tell me she's sold my entire portfolio, the odds are I'll be back on the bus to Scranton before the month is out.

I stow my purse in an employee locker, then start gathering my blond hair into a long ponytail at the back of my neck, finger-combing the damp tangles into some semblance of order.

"You better go," I tell Tasha. "I have to clock in and you need to get behind the bar before Joel docks both of us."

She makes a face. "Right. Meet you out there." She starts to leave the coatroom, then swings back to point at me. "The second you hear from the gallery, I want to know. The very second, got me?"

"Yeah, of course." I nod, and now my smile seems forced as doubt crowds in to diffuse the hope I'd been carrying with me most of the day. "I'll be right behind you."

She leaves and I can hear her greeting one of the customers on the floor outside with her bubbly, easygoing warmth. I lean against the lockers and take out my phone to type a text to Margot.

Please call as soon as you can. I'm dying here. I need to know what's going on.

I hit SEND before I can change my mind and delete the desperate sounding message. I hate appearing weak or out of control, and the realization that I am both right now puts a sick feeling in my stomach.

I push the feeling away and slide my phone back into my pocket.

Then I step outside to the bustling restaurant to begin my shift, my mask of confidence held rigidly in place.

2

We're so slammed at the bar that nearly an hour passes before I can even think about the fact that I still haven't heard from Margot. I pour a glass of Pinot noir for a well-dressed strawberry-blonde at the far end of the bar and walk it over to her. Despite being model gorgeous, she's seated alone and has been preoccupied with texting and making phone calls since she arrived fifteen minutes ago.

I place the red wine in front of her without comment. She glances up then and meets my gaze, her elegant brows pinched.

"Can I get you anything else right now?" I offer.

"No, thank you." With a frustrated sounding sigh, she sets her cell on the bar and shakes her head. "I'm supposed to be meeting a friend here before I have to leave to catch a flight." She checks the sleek watch on her left wrist and frowns. "Evidently, she's running late."

"Okay. I'll check back in a few minutes," I tell her,

even though I doubt she's listening. Before the words are out of my mouth, she picks up her phone again and starts frantically tapping out another text.

I pivot away to take drink orders from a trio of thirty-something suits who've just swooped in to grab newly vacated seats at the other end of the bar. They request single malt Scotch, then make half-assed attempts to flirt with me as I retrieve the bottle and set up three neats of the twelve-year Macallan.

I know the game I'm supposed to play behind the bar to bolster my tips, but I can hardly pretend to be interested in faking a little playful banter right now. I'm still edgy and anxious, wondering how long Margot is going to keep me in suspense.

Just when I think I can't take another second, my phone begins to vibrate in my back pocket. It's all I can do not to drop the whisky bottle as I return it to the shelf in my hurry to get to my call. Heading toward the back of the bar area, I pull my phone out and covertly check the caller ID.

It's her.

Finally.

"Cover me?" I mouth to Tasha when I see her glance my way from across the bar.

She nods and holds up crossed fingers. Taking a deep breath, I slip off to the ladies' room with my phone in hand. "Hey, Margot. How's it going?"

I'm amazed at how casual and calm I sound when I answer, considering my heart is pounding about a hundred miles an hour.

"Long day," she says. "The gallery owner came in for meetings with me and the rest of the staff. I just got out about five minutes ago and saw your text."

I cringe at the reminder of my moment of weakness. "Yeah, um, sorry I missed your call this morning. I was working on the new piece and I guess I didn't hear the phone. Anyway, I can't wait to show this one to you. I think you're really going to like it."

"I'm sure I will. You know I love your work," she says. "And I'm the one who should apologize. I probably shouldn't have left a message at all. I wouldn't if I'd known how hectic things were going to be here today. I didn't mean to keep you hanging like this all day."

There is a hesitancy to her voice that makes my mouth go dry. I drift to the farthest empty stall and close myself inside for some privacy, and to try to muffle the noise. There is a steady flow of chattering restaurant patrons coming in and out of the restroom and music from outside in the main house vibrates the restroom walls.

Margot hasn't said anything more, and I realize she's not calling to give me good news.

"Something's wrong," I murmur, trying to guess how bad the blow is going to be. Normally, she'd be pressing me for details about my work and how soon before she can see it, but she's holding back. "You won't be taking the new painting, will you?"

She's silent, then she sighs quietly. "I'm really sorry, Avery."

Her apology hits me like a physical blow. For a moment, I'm just as stunned as if I'd been slapped. "No, it's okay. I understand. You've got a lot of my work already. Maybe we can talk about it after another piece sells, or—"

"Avery," she says, her tone going even gentler now. "Like I said, the owner was in today. We talked about implementing some changes in the gallery collections. We're going to be freshening things up a bit, clearing space in a few of the current displays to make room for some promising new artists that the owner feels strongly about . . ."

And I'm not one of them.

I don't make her say the words. There's no need. I know this conversation can't be easy for her. Hell, it's not easy for me, either.

I sag against the brick wall of the toilet stall and close my eyes. "How soon before you need to remove my work?"

She blows out a short breath. "Shit, Avery. You know I hate this, right? I wish the decision was up to me, but—"

"It's okay. I understand. You don't have to say anything more."

My words are clipped and quiet, but not from anger. Not at Margot, anyway. She's the only reason my work made it into the gallery in the first place. Dominion is one of the smaller galleries in the city, but it's got a reputation for quality and vision. It's also known for a willingness to take risks when it comes to the artists they showcase in their small, but respected, Fifth Avenue location.

Margot Chan-Levine is both the manager and the principal curator for the gallery. I didn't know that when we met for the first time a year and a half ago, nor could I have imagined that she would like my work enough to acquire some of it for sale at the gallery.

Unfortunately, it seems her instincts were off when it came to me.

"Sundays are my only free day right now," I tell her.

"Or I can come by one night before work this week and make arrangements to pick up my stuff."

"No, don't worry about that," she assures me. "We've got a lot of events going on at the gallery right now, so honestly there's no rush. I can keep your pieces in storage for a while until you're ready to take them. I realize this is a total blindside, and I feel awful about that. Besides, I know you don't have any extra space at your apartment. Let me at least do this for you."

Her offer to help stanch this new hemorrhage in my life should be a comfort, but my old defenses kick in, urging me to refuse. I can't stand the thought of asking her to do anything more for me than she already has. Except she's right about my furnished one-room studio having no room to spare. It's small even by New York standards, but that's not the worst of it. In a couple more weeks, I won't even have that meager roof over my head.

My building was sold a few months ago and is going condo. I've held out as long as tenacity and the law will allow, but my time is almost up now. I've got the eviction notice to prove it.

"Say something, Avery. Are you going to be okay?"

"Yeah. Sure I am. I'm fine."

My mouth is on autopilot, my head spinning while my stomach feels ready to revolt. I've got a lot of decisions ahead of me—most of which I'm not eager to make. Right now, I just need to get through the night and get home so I can start figuring out what I'm going to do. And in the back of my mind, I know this conversation has just solidified the fact that I'm also going to need to get busy packing up for . . . somewhere.

I feel the walls crushing in on me the longer I stay on the line. I need to be moving. I need to be busy or

I'm going to scream.

I clear my throat. "Listen, we're really slammed over here tonight. I've got to get back out to the bar."

"Oh, of course. I thought I heard restaurant noise in the background. I'm on my way home now, so if you need anything tonight—if you just want to talk some more—give me a call, okay?"

"I will," I lie.

"Avery, I'm really sorry."

"I know. I get it, and it's all right." I feel awkward and inferior, and I can't deny that I'm also more than a little heartbroken to hear that my art wasn't good enough for Dominion's owner. And I'm pissed at myself for actually thinking it could be. "I gotta run now. I'll call you in a few days. Thanks, Margot. For everything."

I hit the end button, then tip my head back against the wall and exhale a curse.

What the hell am I going to do now?

3

When I head back out to the floor, Tasha doesn't give me as much as a second to regroup before she's bee-lining my way. "So? Tell me! What'd she . . . *Oh, fuck.*"

My face no doubt tells it all.

"Oh, honey. Come here." At twenty-seven, she's only two years older than me, but she slides effortlessly into nurture mode, looping her arm around my shoulders and steering me away from the busier area of the bar. "Tell me what happened."

"I lost my spot at Dominion. They're bringing in some better artists and they need the space, so I'm out."

"What?" Tasha doesn't hold back her outrage, and to my chagrin, about a dozen people seated at the bar glance in our direction. "That's bullshit. You're an amazing artist, Avery. You deserve to be there as much as anyone else."

I bark out a brittle laugh. "Apparently the gallery's

clientele don't feel that way. Neither does the owner."

"Well, they're wrong." Tasha's dark eyes study me with a deepening concern. She puts her hand on my forearm, forcing me to hold her gaze. "Fuck them, Avery. They're all wrong."

I shake my head and withdraw from her comforting touch before her tenderness makes me crack. "It's no big deal. In fact, I knew this day was coming. I've only sold one piece all this time. Margot believes in my work, but she's not running a charity. And God knows, kindness never paid my rent either. Which reminds me, I've got customers to take care of—"

Tasha steps into my path to block my escape. "Are you all right?"

"Yeah." I hold her concerned, too-wise gaze then shrug. "Believe me, I've survived worse. I'm fine."

She doesn't move. Doesn't release me from her stare. Behind her, one of the servers calls to her with an incoming drink order. Tasha holds up her finger to him in response, all of her focus on me. "I'm your friend, damn it. Don't piss me off by acting like I'm not. Are things that bad for you right now?"

I want to deny it outright, but the words don't come.

I never can seem to hide much from Tasha, and her expression tells me that I wouldn't be fooling her even if I tried. But as well as she's come to know me since we've been working together, there are still things she doesn't know. Things no one knows about me. Not here in this new city, this new life I'm trying to make for myself.

And as much as I'd like to keep my current personal problems a secret from Tasha, she's obviously not about to let me shut her out right now.

"My building's being turned into condos and I'm getting evicted from my apartment." I blurt it out without taking a breath. "I have two weeks before I have to either buy my place or move out of it."

"Jesus, Avery. A couple of weeks? What are you going to do?"

"The only thing I can do—move out. I can't afford to stay and even if I had the money I wouldn't want to buy in that roach-infested building."

"Shit, honey. Where will you go?"

"I don't know." It's the truth. Even though I can feel Pennsylvania tightening its grip on me where I stand, I'm not ready to admit total defeat yet. I'm not ready to give up.

Tasha nods, contemplation churning in her caring eyes. "If you need someplace to stay while you figure things out, Antonio and I can make room for you at the house. We don't have a spare bedroom, but there's a sleeper sofa in the living room that's yours for however long you need it."

"No." I'm touched by her generosity, but I can't impose on her like that. Her house is full enough with her new baby and a mother-in-law who recently moved in. I shake my head. "Thank you, but no. I won't ask that of you—"

"You didn't," she points out. "But then, you never ask anyone for anything, do you."

It's not a question, so I choose not to answer. "I'll manage. I've been taking care of myself for a long time. I'll get through this too."

On the other side of the bar, another server arrives and calls to us with a new order.

"Be right there," Tasha shouts over the din of the

restaurant. Her soft doe eyes study me for a long moment, a sad kind of understanding in their depths. "You know, it's okay to let people help you once in a while. It's okay to let people care about you."

I can't tell her that I agree. I can't even give a weak nod to appease her.

I learned a long time ago that help never comes without a price tag, hidden or not. And even the people who claim to care about you the most can turn against you in the blink of an eye.

She walks away to fill the incoming drink orders from the dining room, and I get busy bringing fresh rounds to the people seated at the long bar. I notice the woman at the far end is still alone and waiting. Her glass of Pinot is untouched, and her cell phone sits next to the drumming fingernails of her left hand.

As I approach to see if I can bring her anything else, she glances at her phone and picks it up to read what I assume is an incoming text. She frowns, then her jaw drops open in a look of utter exasperation. "No . . . Oh, for the love of fuck! You have *got* to be kidding me."

Evidently, I'm not the only one dealing with disappointment tonight.

I'm not the type to pry into other people's business, so I let her outburst go unmentioned. "Do you need anything else right now?"

She huffs out a heavy sigh and lifts her thick-lashed green eyes to me. "How about a miracle?"

"Excuse me?"

"Never mind." Tossing her phone into her purse, she shakes her head. "I was counting on a friend to do something for me, and she just cancelled. Now I'm totally left in a lurch."

"I'm sorry." I can see that she's visibly upset. I also recall that she's supposed to be catching a flight at some point tonight. "If you're ready to cash out, just let me know."

She takes a sip from her glass, then glances at her watch. "I don't need to leave for a few minutes. I'd much rather stay here than wait around at JFK any longer than I have to. I'm Claire, by the way."

"Nice to meet you," I reply. "I'm Avery."

"I know."

I tilt my head. Maybe I'm gaping a bit, too, because she immediately winces and lets out a little laugh.

"I'm sorry. That came out a little stalkerish, didn't it?" She waves her hand as if to erase any unease. "We haven't met. I come in from time to time, and I've heard some of the other bar staff talking to you."

"Oh." I shrug it off with a brief smile. "No worries."

She's not someone easily overlooked, yet I can't say that I've noticed her in the restaurant before. Then again, New York is full of beautiful people. I had to train myself early on not to gawk at every celebrity, athlete, and supermodel who crossed my path.

"I have an apartment a few blocks from here," she volunteers as I pick up a bar cloth and start wiping down a vacated spot a couple of seats away from her. "To be honest, though, I'm never in any city long enough to claim I'm a true resident. I just flew home last week from a gig in Paris. Tonight I'm off to Tokyo for a few months to shoot some commercials and a game show pilot."

"Sounds exciting." I'm still small-town enough to feel a twinge of envy at her jet-set lifestyle and glamorous career.

"It's never boring," she admits before taking a sip of

her wine. "But I don't like leaving my apartment empty for long stretches while I'm gone. The friend who stood me up tonight was supposed to stay at my place while I'm in Japan. My poor plants just got a death sentence."

I grimace. "That sucks."

"Tell me about it. I don't suppose you know of a good house-sitting service I can call? One I can hire for the next four months on zero notice?"

She needs a house-sitter for four months? That desperate part of me I don't want to acknowledge practically groans at the irony of this situation. I'm soon to be homeless and this woman—Claire—has more living space than she can use.

Even though I'm sure her question was meant to be rhetorical more than anything else, before I can answer, Tasha's voice sounds from behind me.

"Avery, why don't you do it?"

Until that moment, I didn't even realize she was nearby. I swivel to look at her, my eyes wide. *What the hell are you doing?*

I know she can read that demand in my face—in my mortified glare—but Tasha being Tasha, she's completely unfazed. She smiles at me as if I'm not fuming and speechless at her interference.

"Think about it," she says cheerfully, and more than loud enough for Claire to hear. "The timing couldn't be more perfect. You told me just today that your place is being renovated soon and you can't stay there once the work begins."

Renovated? I give a tight shake of my head. "I didn't say—"

"Yes. You *did*." She speaks slowly and gives me *that look*. The one I'm sure makes even her six-foot-four husband stand a little straighter. I have to admit, it's working on me right now too.

But I can't do this. It wouldn't be right. I'm a stranger to this woman. I can't imagine she would even consider—

"Is that true, Avery? Do you need someplace to stay?"

I turn to face Claire. "Yes, it's true, but . . . you don't even know me."

She sets down her wine glass and studies me for a second. "How long have you worked here?"

"Almost a year and a half."

"So that tells me you're responsible enough," she points out.

"And reliable," Tasha adds. "Six days a week, Avery's here. Sometimes, all seven. Never missed a shift, not even a single sick day in all this time."

"Impressive." Claire nods as though her mind is already made up. "You'd be doing me an immense favor. I can't even tell you how grateful I'd be." She glances at her watch, then sucks in a breath. "Shit. I have to go or I'm going to be late. If you can do this for me, Avery, I need your answer now."

Tasha stares at me expectantly while I glance between her and Claire, uncertainty gnawing at my stomach. I don't believe in luck or cosmic favors, but it seems like the universe is handing me a life line right here. Can I really afford to refuse it? With my apartment being sold out from under me and the odds of making some money off my art anytime soon being next to nil, I don't exactly have a lot of options.

"I'll pay you, of course." Claire discreetly takes an envelope out of her black Birkin bag. "Five thousand for the four months. That's what I was going to pay my friend." She holds the cream-colored envelope out to me and keeps her voice low. "It's in cash. I hope you don't mind."

My mind sputters at the idea. Maybe people like Claire can toss around five grand like it's nothing, but, to me, especially right now, it's a small fortune.

No, it's miracle money.

With the added bonus of a four-month stay of execution on my homelessness situation.

The reality of this incredible twist of fate is so overwhelming, I can hardly form words. "I, um . . ."

"She'll do it," Tasha interjects. "You'll do it, right, Avery?"

I think I must have nodded. To be honest, the next few minutes pass in a blur. She gives me her full name—Claire Prentice—and jots her address on the back of her business card before handing me a key to her apartment. She takes down my name and cell phone number, then pulls a twenty out of her wallet and places it on the bar.

"That should cover the wine." Smiling, she slides off the bar stool and pulls on her coat. "I'll check in with you from Tokyo after I get settled to make sure everything's good at the apartment, okay?"

My head bobs automatically. "Ah, okay." I'm not about to argue. I don't think she would have waited around to give me that chance anyway.

With a hurried thanks, Claire Prentice sails out the door and ducks into a taxi that arrives at the curb.

I stand there for a moment, dumbstruck, processing everything that just happened.

I have five thousand dollars cash in my hand. On the bar in front of me is a Park Avenue address. Beside that, a gleaming brass key that will grant me four entire months of shelter. Four whole months of mercy.

I've just been given a golden opportunity at a time when I couldn't have needed it more.

I glance at Tasha, shaking my head in mute confusion. A small giggle erupts from my throat. Then another. It's too much to contain—the amazement, the hope...the incredulous relief.

I cover my mouth, but my joy spills over in a ridiculous snort of a laugh. "Did that really just happen?"

Tasha takes the envelope out of my slack grasp and peers inside. "Well, you've got fifty Benjamins in here saying it did." She grins at me. "Remember what I said about letting someone help you out once in a while? Yeah, you can thank me now."

4

Tasha insists on coming with me to check out Claire's apartment. I hadn't even been sure I intended to go tonight, but Tasha refuses to be swayed and I can hardly deny my curiosity either. Suddenly, the idea of waiting until tomorrow morning to see where I'll be living for the next four months requires a patience I don't have.

All night, the key to Claire's apartment has been burning a hole in my pocket—even more so than the money, which I'd reluctantly stowed in the bottom of my purse in the employee locker for the duration of my shift.

After we close at Vendange, Tasha calls home to let her family know what's going on, then the two of us set out for the Upper East Side address Claire gave me. Ordinarily, I'd think nothing of walking the handful of long blocks, even in the chill of a drizzly April night. But hoofing it a couple of miles after two in the morning with five grand in cash on me is a stupid risk I just can't take.

As we step out of the restaurant, I motion for Tasha to follow me to the curb. "Come on. We're splurging on a taxi. My treat."

Manhattan is impressive at any hour, but there is something magical about this part of the city so late at night. As the taxi rolls along the divided lanes of Park Avenue with its tree-lined median, my artist's eye greedily soaks in my surroundings. Street lamps and traffic lights spangle the wet pavement with shards of color. The mixture of pre- and post-war limestone and brick buildings on either side of the grand boulevard stand defiant beside soaring glass-and-steel residential towers and elegant five-star hotels. In front of all those buildings, the ribbon of concrete sidewalk ebbs and flows with a steady stream of pedestrians who are wearing everything from formal attire or club clothes to vagabond rags.

The colors, the shapes, the energy, the teeming life even at this late hour . . . all of it stirs the part of me that dreams in light and shadow, the part of me that can only speak with a paintbrush.

Tonight, after Margot's call, it hurts to hear that voice whispering to me, to see all of the pictures filling the fresh canvas in my mind. I close my eyes against the impulse, but I can't shut it off. It's been a part of me for too long. My art has been my escape, the only place I could go—the only place I could live—when everything else in my world was trying to destroy me.

Now I can't help but wonder how long that part of me will survive if it turns out Dominion's owner is right and my art doesn't deserve to be seen.

"Holy shit," Tasha gasps, dragging my attention back to the here and now. The taxi maneuvers toward the curb on my side and turns in to a U-shaped entrance in front of a monstrously tall high-rise. Tasha leans across me to gape. "Avery, is this the right building?"

I peer out my window as the driver slows to a stop under the sleek glass overhang and announces that we've arrived. Even so, I have to double check that the numbers etched in black on the gleaming silver plate mounted above the entrance of the tower match the address Claire gave me.

"This is it."

Tasha exits on her side while I pay the twelve dollar fare. She's already at my door as I climb out, a look of awe on her face. She hooks her arm through mine and leans in close as we step away from the taxi.

"Girl, do you have any idea where we are? This section of Park is prime real estate. We're talking billionaire row. I'll bet you can't even get a closet-sized studio for under a couple million in this building."

"Seriously?" My brows lift in surprise. "Apparently international commercials and Japanese game shows are lucrative business."

Tasha grunts a non-response as I crane my neck to follow the jutting column of glass before us. It's so high, I lose sight of it in the dark canopy of clouds blotting out the night sky. I've never even set foot inside a building of this caliber and as we approach the brightly lit lobby inside, I'm not sure if the sudden pounding of my heart is stemming from excitement or doubt.

I wasn't sure about any of this to begin with; now all I have are second thoughts. I feel conspicuous and nervous. This isn't my kind of neighborhood. It's not even in the same orbit I've inhabited for any of my twenty-five years.

What the hell was Claire Prentice thinking, drafting someone she's never even met before into house-sitting in a building like this?

Desperate, that's what she was. Desperate and without other options as she'd openly admitted. As desperate as I am to have a roof over my head until I can somehow get back on my feet.

But I sure as hell wasn't prepared for this.

Looking at the yards of polished marble and massive glittering crystal chandeliers that wait for me on the other side of the ultramodern lobby's glass facade—not to mention the fact that Claire is paying me to stay here besides—there's no question that I got the better end of our deal.

A middle-aged doorman in a dark coat and cap opens one of the chrome-trimmed glass doors and steps out to hold it open for us.

He greets Tasha and me each with a pleasant nod. "Good evening, ma'am. Ma'am." He's a big guy, slightly round beneath the long drape of his thick wool coat. But his hazel eyes seem genuinely kind and his smile is warm within the brackets of his gray-flecked goatee. "How can I help you ladies?"

I pause and smile back at him. "Hi. I'm Avery Ross, and this is my friend, Tasha. Claire Prentice sent me. I'm, ah . . . she's hired me to watch her apartment while she's out of town."

I start foraging anxiously in my purse for her business card as if that will be ample proof, but the doorman is already nodding his head even before I hold the card out to him. "Ms. Prentice called earlier this evening to let me know you were expected, Ms. Ross. Please, both of you, come in out of the cold."

Tasha and I step inside with the doorman following behind us. Silver-veined, gleaming marble spreads out beneath our feet, from the entrance to the towering banks of elevators across the lobby. Soaring walls of exotic dark woods and stone frame the polished steel elevator doors. Above our heads, immense, cascading crystal chandeliers glitter like waterfalls of twisting, sparkling ice.

"My name's Manny," the doorman says. He leads us to a reception desk across the wide expanse of the lobby. Grabbing a tablet PC from the desk, he taps on the screen a few times before handing it to me. "Please sign in where I've indicated, Ms. Ross. Will you be staying in Ms. Prentice's apartment starting tonight?"

The question takes me aback, if only because I'm still trying to wrap my brain around the fact that I'm actually standing here and not dreaming. I shake my head as I scrawl my finger across the tablet in a barely legible version of my signature. "I wasn't planning to stay, no. It's late and we just got off work. I only wanted to stop by to check things out."

"All right, then." Manny reaches around the counter of the reception desk and hands me a card. "That's the number for the lobby phone. If you need anything at all, you just let me know how I can help." He gestures toward the elevator banks. "Ms. Prentice's apartment is on the fifth floor, number 501. Take a left off the elevator."

"Thanks, Manny." I nod to him and pocket the card, grateful for his welcoming nature. Some of my anxiety has faded under the warmth of his smile. Maybe I won't feel quite so alone or out of place here, knowing there will be at least one friendly face in the building.

I give him a small wave, then Tasha and I head for the elevators. Neither of the two cars are parked on the ground level, so, as we wait for one to come down, I can't resist pivoting for another look at the opulence of the lobby.

A moment later, a soft chime sounds behind me as the elevator comes to a rest. I wheel back around and step toward the doors as soon as they slide open.

I don't even register that the wall I'm facing is human until I've almost crashed right into him.

I stop short and lift my head with a half-formed apology on my lips. The sound evaporates on my tongue as I glance up and my gaze collides with a pair of cerulean blue eyes. They skewer me from under the slash of inky black brows.

Brows that are furrowed into a deep scowl at the uncouth clod who nearly body-slammed her way onto the elevator.

"Um, sorry."

No reply from him. Not even a flicker of polite response in his handsome, sharply cut features. Under a crown of dark hair that's neatly trimmed, fit for a boardroom, but thick with rebellious waves that catch the light in a glossy, raven's wing sheen, his face is a blending of hard, chiseled angles. With his high cheekbones and square jaw, I'd be tempted to call his face brutal if not for the supple line of his mouth.

And he's tall and muscular too, dressed in a dark gray track jacket and pants that do little to disguise the physically fit body within. Despite his athletic appearance, I can tell immediately that he's not some meat-head gym rat who's more brawn than brain.

No, this man's eyes blast me with the kind of intelligence and seriousness—a powerful confidence—that I can't ignore.

A shocking and inexplicable heat pours through me as he holds my gaze. His stare is bold, unflinching, as if he's accustomed to taking his fill of anything in his sights. That air of assumption should offend me for many reasons, but as his brilliant blue eyes travel the length of me, all I feel is the rapid igniting of every cell in my body.

Tasha clears her throat when my muteness appears to be permanent. "Pardon us, please."

He barely acknowledges her comment, nor her huff of indignation that follows. No, those piercing eyes stay rooted on me alone. I feel stripped bare under that hard gaze, as if he can see right through me with a single glance and knows I don't belong here. Even worse, the barely imperceptible twist of his lips seems to say that he's very much aware of the effect he has on me.

He doesn't move, then I am mortified to realize it's because I'm standing in his way.

I wince inwardly and step aside, wishing I would just melt into the crack between the marble floor and the elevator shaft before I embarrass myself any more.

His path cleared, he steps into the lobby without a word.

I follow Tasha into the elevator, but all of my attention is on the dark-haired stranger now prowling across the marble with fluid, almost urgent strides.

I hear Manny greet him as the elevator doors slide shut, blocking my view.

"Evening, Mr. Baine. Enjoy your run, sir."

Once we're sealed inside the car, my breath leaks out of me on a groan.

Tasha arches a brow. "Hot as sin, but obviously a superior prick. Do yourself a favor and steer clear of that one, honey."

As if I need the warning.

Whoever he is, I doubt I'll be seeing much of *Mr. Baine*. In fact, I'm already promising myself I'll head in the opposite direction if I ever see him in the building again while I'm here. God knows, I don't need to relive tonight's awkward semi-introduction with the man anytime soon.

I push the button for the fifth floor, wishing it was as easy to push the memory of those searing blue eyes from my mind. The man radiated a palpable heat and power that I can still feel riding my skin—tripping all of my senses—as we ascend to Claire's apartment.

Oh, yes, I definitely intend to avoid the hot-as-sin, arrogant—disturbingly arousing—Mr. Baine at all costs.

5

Holy shit, will you look at this place?" Tasha sails ahead of me into Claire's empty apartment as I pause to close the door behind us. "Avery, you have to see this. It's incredible!"

She's right, it is. I'm barely able to contain my own amazement as I follow her inside. More gleaming marble covers the floors up here, from the foyer that's almost the size of my entire rental in Brooklyn, to the serenely elegant space that spreads out in all directions from the apartment's entrance.

In the living room, a dimmed crystal chandelier casts an inviting glow over creamy upholstered furniture and a pale gray patterned rug. Built-in bookcases line the entire span of the far wall, packed with enough reading material to keep someone busy for a couple of years. Delicate accent tables hold small collections of art objects and interesting trinkets that Claire has likely picked up from her travels. The entire room is a sophisticated, visual feast—all of it perfectly arranged before a pair of ten-foot square windows that look out at the sparkling nighttime city that surrounds us.

For what certainly isn't the first time, I find myself caught in disbelief that Claire Prentice's bad luck tonight has become my life-line.

And what a life-line it is.

I walk up to the immense panes of glass and can only stare out in awe at the incredible view. I've never longed for extravagance, and, God knows, I've never come close to having it, but I feel like a princess in her tower as I stand in the elegance of Claire's living room and look out at the city lights. The clusters of buildings overlap each other in my field of view, thousands of illuminated windows glittering like diamonds in the darkness. I can't wait to see the view from here in the daylight. With a few months ahead of me while Claire is away, maybe I'll even have the chance to paint it.

"Hey, check out this amazing kitchen!" Tasha calls from the adjacent area. "You sure you don't wanna come stay at my house and I'll water Claire's plants for the next four months? Hell, I'll even let you keep the money."

I laugh quietly and shake my head. I have no doubt I'd be far more comfortable in Tasha's cramped Queens duplex than here, but I know she's only kidding about trading places with me. At least, I think she's kidding.

We spend the next hour taking stock of Claire's gorgeous apartment. While Tasha ogles Claire's designer wardrobe and enviable shoe collection, I move through the place making a mental checklist of things I need to figure out or ask Manny or the building manager about when I come back.

Eventually, Tasha and I lock up, then head down to

the lobby to leave. We say our goodbyes outside the building, where I ignore her protests and spring for separate taxis home for both of us. After cursing me for being stubborn and wasting good money, she gives me a hug then follows Manny to the opened door of her cab, waving as she takes off.

I walk over to the other idling vehicle.

"Here you go, Ms. Ross," Manny says, holding the door for me. "Shall we look forward to seeing you tomorrow, then?"

"Ah, I guess so," I say as I climb into the backseat, though part of me is still processing the idea of trading my tiny apartment for this kind of opulence, even if only temporarily.

This isn't my world, and I'll do well to remember that. After four months, my time here will be up and I'll go back to the life I've made for myself in the real world. All of my problems will be waiting to reclaim me on the other side of this brief escape from reality . . . along with the secrets I carry that will never let me go.

With reminders of my past clinging to me, I pause to look up at the kind doorman before he closes my door. "Goodnight, Manny. And please, call me Avery."

"Very well, then. Goodnight, Miss Avery." He winks and inclines his head in a slight bow as he closes the door, then gives the roof of the taxi a light pat to send it on its way.

I tell the driver my address, then settle back for the forty-minute ride. As we cruise down Park Avenue, I study the neighborhood that's going to be mine for the next few months.

And when I spot the dark figure of a lone runner on the opposite sidewalk, heading back in the direction of the building, I can't help the jolt of recognition—of visceral awareness—that arrows through me.

Mr. Baine.

His strides are long, fluid. Aggressive. His muscular body slices through the darkness like a blade. Like a man who expects the world around him to make way for him, simply because he's there.

If I need reasons to stay away from a man like him—from any man, in fact—I have plenty. But that doesn't keep my pulse from speeding up as I watch his powerful body move. It doesn't keep my skin from heating and tightening at the memory of penetratingly sharp blue eyes piercing me—stripping me bare—earlier tonight.

He is not for me. I know this.

But once I see him, I can't stop looking.

Not until the distance stretches between us and he vanishes into the night behind me.

~ ~ ~

After a restless night on the pull-down bed in my one-room studio, reality wakes me in the form of my landlord pounding on my door just before eight in the morning. Dreams of glittering high-rises and glowering blue-eyed strangers dissolve under the relentless hammering.

"Avery, I know you're in there!" my landlord, Leo, shouts to me in his smoker's rasp through the dead bolted door. "We need to talk about the apartment."

Bam-bam-bam.

"Come on, open up, now. I know you got the eviction notice I left for you. How long you think you can avoid me? Avery?"

He pounds again. At the same time, my cell phone

starts ringing.

On a groan, I throw the blanket off me and drag my eyelids open to see who's calling.

Wonderful. It's my mother. The last thing I want is for her to hear my landlord threatening to break down my door and toss me out onto the street. She worries about me enough as it is. I'm not about to add any stress to her life.

"I'll come down to your office in an hour," I tell Leo as I get out of bed with my phone in hand. "I promise."

"That's what you told me last week," he reminds me.

When he starts banging again, I curse under my breath and pad out of the cramped living room-slash-dining room. I have to dodge the riverscape painting that sits half-completed on my easel as I make my way into the bathroom and close myself inside.

Seated on the cold lid of the toilet, I slump down with my elbows on my knees and accept my mother's call.

"I tried to call you yesterday," she says after we move past the usual preamble and hellos. "You didn't pick up, so I figured you must've had a busy day working."

"Yeah, I'm sorry I missed you, Mom. Things have been crazy here."

"You sound tired, honey. Is everything okay?"

"Everything's fine." I straighten up when I hear the concern in her reedy voice. Thankfully, Leo's decided to quit his pounding and shouting, so my attempt to reassure her stands at least half a chance of being believed. "Everything is going great with me, Mom."

"Oh, that's good, sweetheart." I picture her face on the other end of the line, her relieved smile, which I can hear in her voice. "Tell me about your new painting. Did your friend at the gallery like it?"

"Yeah, she did. Margot thinks it's going to do really well." The lie slides off my tongue without hesitation, but it leaves a bitter residue of guilt in my throat.

"Of course it will do well, honey. They all have. How many paintings have you sold now?"

I shake my head in silence, grateful that I don't have to look her in the eye every time I feed her this fairy tale of how I want her to imagine my life here in New York. She's given me so much, made sacrifices I can never hope to reconcile, all in the hopes of offering me a better life than she's had.

And while I know she loves me unconditionally, I feel a responsibility to make something of myself. I want to prove to her—and to myself—that I might actually be worth all of it one day.

"I'm not sure how many paintings I've sold, Mom. I guess I haven't kept close track."

"Well then, we'll have to make a list next time we talk," she suggests cheerfully.

"Okay, sure," I say. "Let's do that."

"I'm just so proud of you, Avery. I always have been. You know that, right?"

"Yeah, Mom. I know."

We talk for a little while about inconsequential things. The group of ladies she plays cards with on the weekends. The awful weather, which, she informs me, is making her arthritis act up. It soothes me, our conversation about everyday minutiae. I crave the normalcy of it, even though it also makes me ache sometimes that it's been so long since I've been to see her.

After a few minutes, she sighs. I try not to hear the

decades of weariness in that slow exhalation.

"Well, honey . . . they're telling me I have to wrap up now. My call time is almost over."

"All right," I murmur. "I know."

It's never easy to say goodbye to her. Our allotted fifteen minutes always go so fast.

For the past nine years, this has been our primary connection to each other—a handful of sentences shared over the airwaves, meted out in daily quarter-hour increments.

"I'll call you tomorrow, sweetheart."

"Okay, Momma. I love you."

She starts to tell me she loves me too, but the prison call timer runs out and our conversation is cut off before I can hear all of the words.

6

I made good on my promise to my landlord. Leo had practically choked when I showed up at his office that same day to inform him that I had vacated the apartment of my few belongings and then proceeded to pay my back rent—all twelve-hundred dollars and change—in cash.

My windfall from Claire is significantly lighter now, but so is my conscience.

And as I wake up on my second morning in Apartment 501 on Park Avenue, I am struck by a feeling of calm that I haven't known in a long time. Maybe never.

I am free.

For the next four months, at least, I am free. Released from the worry of shelter or money.

It's a start. And maybe a new start is all I need right now.

With that hopeful thought filling my sails, I take a

shower, then head out the door before noon. I'm determined to spend my day off from Vendange—my first truly free Sunday—exploring and enjoying the city.

After a coffee and a bagel at one of the delis that Manny recommends to me a few blocks down from the building, I aimlessly meander the Upper East Side on foot. It's brisk but sunny, and I relish the fact that I have nowhere I need to be and no pressure do anything at all. For the next few hours, I content myself with people-watching and browsing the upscale shops and designer boutiques on Fifth Avenue.

While I stroll the area, Claire calls from Tokyo to check in as promised and make sure I have everything I need at the apartment. I'm so upbeat and excited, I'm pretty sure I blather on for ten minutes straight about how incredible her building is and how much I would love to paint the view from her living room windows. She takes my gushing in stride, instructing me to make myself at home while she's gone.

"If you need anything at all, just ask Manny. He knows the building inside out, and he's a peach of a guy."

"Yes, he is," I agree. "He's already told me where to get the best coffee and breakfast, and he's been nothing but kind."

As I say that, my mind conjures a different face from the affable doorman's. One that I can't describe as kind. What fills my vision are piercing, bright blue eyes and razor-sharp cheekbones. A broad, sensual mouth that makes my pulse kick a little faster just recalling it now.

I don't ask Claire about him—Mr. Baine—no matter how much the question burns the tip of my tongue. After all, it doesn't matter who he is or what she might know about him. I'm staying at her place to do a job, not ogle her neighbors.

We end our call and I continue my casual tour of the Upper East Side and its intriguing shops and landmarks. I hadn't intended to visit the gallery when I set out earlier today, but as the afternoon winds down toward twilight, I realize I'm little more than a block from Dominion.

I've been meaning to call Margot for days just to say hi and let her know how I'm doing. It bothers me, the way I ended our call the other night when she was trying so hard to cushion the blow about my art's rejection. I was abrupt when we spoke. She needs to understand that I'll always be grateful for her trying to give me a shot at the gallery.

And despite her willingness to store my paintings for a while, my failure is not her burden to bear. God knows, there's certainly enough room for all of my unsold pieces in Claire's apartment. Hell, maybe I'll pack them into a taxi and take them back with me today.

I cross the wide avenue at the traffic light and head toward Dominion's understated storefront on the other side of the street. Soft light glows from within the deep space. I can see groups of people inside, browsing the collections and displays.

It looks busy for a Sunday evening, and it's not until I'm at the door that I see the gallery is hosting some kind of reception inside. Several dozen people fill the space—obviously more than to be expected on any normal day. Through the window, I spot Margot's petite form near the front of the gallery. She's chatting with a stylish older couple at one of the gallery's premier displays, all three of them engrossed in conversation and sipping from flutes of sparkling champagne.

Loath to intrude on a private event, I immediately

start to retreat.

I'm not even half a dozen steps away before I hear her call out from behind me.

"Avery?" Soft classical music and the drone of muffled conversation spills out of the gallery's open door as she comes outside. "Avery! I thought that was you."

And now she's walking after me, leaving me no choice but to abort my escape. I turn around and meet her confused look. She's dressed in classic New York black, from her chic long-sleeved blouse and ankle-length skirt, to her black stiletto-heeled boots. The look might be intimidating on anyone else, but with her petite Asian beauty, she's as delicate as a doll, even garbed in head-to-toe black.

"Where are you going?" Her brown eyes narrow as she stops in front of me on the sidewalk. She tilts her head, her sleek bob swishing against her chin. "I'm surprised to see you. What are you doing here?"

"It's my day off, and I happened to be in the area, so . . ." I shrug. "I thought it might be a good time to take my paintings off your hands."

She frowns. "I told you that wasn't necessary."

"I know, and I appreciate that." I wave my hand dismissively. "I'm sorry. I should've called first. I didn't realize there was something going on today. We can talk another time."

"Don't be ridiculous." She reaches out to take my hand. "It's an informal open house for some of the new artists and our best patrons before we open to the public. Very casual and low-key. And you're always going to be welcome at Dominion so long as I have anything to say about it."

I trudge behind her hesitantly. I can think of a hundred things I'd rather do than skulk around the gallery like a scorned lover who refuses to accept defeat. But Margot's tug on my hand is insistent, and I can't deny that I'm more than a little curious to get a look at the artist's work that replaced mine in the new displays.

Margot brings me inside and motions for her assistant. "Jen, will you take Avery's coat for her, please?"

The perky young brunette nods and holds out her hands with a polite smile. I don't move right away. In fact, I'm tempted to refuse to take my coat off if not for the fact that the combined body heat inside the gallery is several shades past balmy. No one else is wearing theirs, and if I'm hoping to be inconspicuous as an uninvited guest at this gathering, passing out from heat stroke in front of everyone surely isn't going to help my cause.

Reluctantly, I take my coat off and hand it over to Margot's assistant. Ordinarily, my day-off clothing choices don't need to take me anywhere more fashionable than the grocery store or an occasional meal out. Standing in the packed gallery now, I struggle not to feel awkward in my distressed skinny jeans and brown knee-high boots. My slouchy oatmeal-colored sweater and the yards of gauzy white scarf draped around my neck are far more comfortable than chic.

I sigh as Jen trots off to hang my coat in a closet near the entrance. No, there will be no blending in amid the sea of black-on-black in the room.

"Make yourself comfortable," Margot instructs me optimistically. "I need to go mingle for a little while, but I'll swing back around to find you. Have fun, okay? And have some champagne. We had cases of it brought in tonight."

She melts into the throng, and I'm left to my own devices on the peripheral of the crowd. My first stop is the bartender where I pick up a glass of champagne and knock it back in a couple of swallows. The liquid courage helps, so I take another flute and carry it with me as I begin a slow circuit of the room.

Dominion's reputation has been built on its eclectic offerings and a willingness to take risks when it comes to the artists they showcase. I see that on display in full force tonight. All of the new exhibits feature unconventional, avant garde paintings or unusual photographs. Some of the themes are violent and disturbing, scenes of pain and neglect and fear, all conjured or captured by an unflinching eye.

Other displays—like the one where my handful of meticulous, if tame, cityscapes had hung until a couple of days ago—hold collections of abstract works, formless images comprised of a confusion of bruising, clashing colors rendered in aggressive brush strokes and chaotic lines. I pause there long enough to finish my second glass of champagne before moving on to another area of the gallery.

Half a dozen people are clustered in front of another display where a single painting—one marked "Dominion Private Collection - Not For Sale"—dominates the wall. I stand behind the small crowd and look at the full-body portrait of a nude woman whose painted image is reflected on shards of broken, mirrored glass.

She's an odd choice for a model with her short, thinning hair and small, deflated breasts on a body that looks decades older than her haunted, but defiant, dark gaze. Her head is tipped back slightly, one hand raised and resting at the base of her throat. Her pale, cracked lips are parted on what looks to be a deep, anguished sigh.

More than a sigh, I realize almost instantly, my eyes following the line of her other arm, where her hand is buried between her naked thighs.

She's shattered into easily hundreds of jagged, glittering pieces on the canvas—both in the depiction of her orgasm and from the ravages of the disease that's destroying her. Yet she's standing, seizing pleasure. She's shining and defiant. Her spirit is unbroken.

Beauty, the unnamed artist has simply, tenderly—*perfectly*—titled this painting.

Emotion swamps me without warning, and I pull in a shallow, shaky breath. What the hell is wrong with me? I am not a crier. I haven't shed a tear since the day my mother was sent away for the remainder of her life to Muncy State Prison.

And even though my eyes are only prickling with the threat of tears now, the fact that I would feel such an unexpected reaction toward a painting—in public, no less—is unnerving. It's embarrassing.

Evidently, I've drunk too much champagne too fast with too little food. I blink and start to turn away from the other people gathered near me, deciding it'll be a good idea to cushion the alcohol with some of the finger sandwiches and other catered appetizers laid out on the other side of the gallery.

I no more pivot to leave when I crash into a wall of muscle and bone that I should not recognize but do.

Oh, God. I so do.

Like some mortifying replay of the other night in the

high-rise lobby, I lift my head and find myself immobilized by the searing, clear blue gaze that's been burned into my memory ever since.

Except, unlike a few nights ago, instead of catching myself before I collide into him, this time my reflexes are dulled by the drinks and there's no stopping my forward momentum.

My hands come up between us, one palm splayed against the heated solidity of his chest, my other hand wrapped around my empty champagne flute. There's not even an inch of space separating our torsos, and for an electrifying instant, my thighs brush intimately against his powerful legs.

My stomach flips, arousal igniting on contact with him. My nipples tighten where my breasts are crushed against the hard slabs of his chest. I register the warm outline of his hand on the small of my back, his strong fingers resting there as if to steady me even though neither of us are moving now.

Wet heat licks through every fiber of my being, and I know damn well I can't blame *that* on the alcohol.

I swallow and struggle to find my voice. When I finally do, his name tumbles out of my mouth on a breathless gasp. "Mr. Baine."

7

"Do you always charge forward without looking to see what's in front of you? Or am I just the lucky one?"

His voice is even deeper than I'd imagined it, smooth and polished, but dark. I sense a challenge in the rough-edged growl, one that vibrates through me like a caress on bare skin.

He doesn't smile as he says it. Not so much as a quirk in the sculpted line of his mouth. Nor does he do anything to make me feel at ease as I stare up at him in awkward, slightly tipsy, silence. Then again, all this man's presence has done is unsettle me since I first laid eyes on him.

"Um," I stammer belatedly. "Neither."

His eyes don't let me go. "Yet here we are. Déjà vu all over again, as they say."

It takes me a moment to realize that he hasn't removed his hand from my back. His touch lingers possessively and far too intimately for my liking, let alone for our surroundings.

And yet I *do* like it. I can't seem to ignore the scorching presence of his palm where it rests just above the waistband of my jeans. I can feel everything—the breadth of his large hand and the strong lines of his fingers splayed across my lower spine branding me through the thick layer of my sweater. Each second of contact with him makes my nerve endings come alive, tingling with the need for more of his touch . . . to feel it everywhere on me.

Shit. If he can incinerate my defenses with a hot stare and a casual touch in public, I'm afraid to think what this man can do to me if we were alone. Or, rather, I *should* be afraid.

The emotion that swamps me as the flood of erotic possibilities fills my head is anything but fearful. It's desire, plain and simple. As I stare up at him with that realization, the ache for more blooms even deeper inside me.

He's devastatingly handsome, no doubt about that. But it's the raw sexual energy radiating off every square inch of him that renders me stupidly silent in his presence.

With effort, I manage to mentally shake myself out of my daze. Heat rushes into my cheeks as his gaze continues to hold me captive. The intensity of his focus on me is blatantly sensual. It makes the crowded room seem too small and much too warm. As much as I'd like to think my sudden blush is purely from embarrassment, I know better.

Judging from the shrewd gleam in Mr. Baine's eyes, he knows better too.

I'm making a fool out of myself.

Again with this man.

I groan inwardly, cursing the champagne. The crystal flute clutched in my hand, I move aside, just far enough to break the contact. "No more charging forward without knowing what's in front of me. Or rather, *who*." I give him a little salute with the empty glass. "Sorry. I'll be sure I'm more careful in the future. You have my word."

I've given him the opportunity to move on, but he doesn't. I decide it will probably be wise for me to go instead, and I start to take the first step away.

"No need to apologize," he says. Without asking, he takes the champagne glass out of my grasp and hands it off to a passing caterer. It's an inexplicably intimate gesture, presuming he can look after me as if we are familiar with each other. His expression is equally intimate as his gaze bores into mine. "A little recklessness isn't a bad thing. As far as I'm concerned, it's a virtue."

"I'm not reckless." The denial blurts out of me on a frown.

Of all the foolish things I am or have ever been, reckless isn't one of them. I never would have survived my childhood if I had been.

I pause, using the opportunity to take full measure of him in his crisp, long-sleeved black button-down shirt and dark, tailored pants. I already know he's athletic, so I can only guess his body is as strictly disciplined as the rest of his flawless appearance. His chiseled face is clean-shaven, every inch of him impeccably groomed. Even those rebellious raven's-wing waves seem tamed tonight.

And the way his piercing stare refuses to release

me—just as his hand had lingered as if he had the right—I sense this man allows very little to escape his control.

Too late to keep the thought from turning carnal in my mind, I clear my throat and shrug as if he isn't making me wonder what he'd be like in bed. I tilt my head to better assess him. "You don't exactly strike me as the reckless type either, Mr. Baine."

Now, at last, that sensual mouth curves into a slow smile. "We've only just met. Give me time." He extends his right hand to me. "And call me Nick."

As much as I want to refuse to the temptation of touching him, I can't. "Avery." I say, slipping my hand into his firm clasp.

His eyes locked on me, he grunts in acknowledgment as our palms connect and his fingers engulf mine. That low, undeniably erotic rumble of his voice sends unbidden heat sizzling through my veins.

"Powerful, isn't it?"

For a second, I think he could be referring to the current of electricity that's crackling between us. But then he tilts his head in the direction of the painting on display behind me. I pivot to face the shattered beauty on the canvas and mutely nod.

"Incredibly powerful," I agree. "Is she yours?"

"Do you mean the painting, or the model?"

Both, I want to say. Fortunately, I'm able to keep my tongue in check as I glance back at him. "I mean, are you the artist?"

"No. I don't paint. Just an admirer." He regards the piece for barely a moment before the full weight of his intense blue eyes lands on me once more. "And you?"

I silently consider *Beauty* and the rest of the paintings

on display at Dominion tonight. I can't pretend I'm not painfully aware that my half dozen rejects are hidden in gallery storage somewhere, deemed unfit to share wall space with any of these better works of art.

I shake my head. "An admirer, same as you."

His stare holds mine, then he inclines his dark head in a nod. "What do you do, Avery, when you're not plowing into innocent bystanders in elevators and art galleries, that is?"

"Innocent?" I laugh, practically choking on the idea. "Has anyone actually ever applied that word to you?"

"Of course." He's smiling now too. "I believe I was around five or six at the time."

God, I like his smile.

His mouth is broad and lush-lipped, his teeth white and impossibly straight. Twin dimples frame his grin, giving the brooding, dark stranger I first saw in the lobby last week a fleeting trace of boyish charm now. But I'd be a fool to mistake anything about this man for innocence. I know that instinctively. Why the hell that understanding doesn't send me running for the nearest door, I have no idea.

"So, tell me," he prompts again. "How come I've never seen you in the building before the other night?"

The truth stalls out in my throat for reasons I can't explain. Maybe because I'm enjoying our conversation too much and I want it to continue. Against all better judgment, I'm enjoying *him.*

And some small part of me—the part of me that's so curious about this dangerously compelling man it can *only* be described as reckless—is too selfish to ruin it all by telling him I'm simply hired help. He's never seen me before because I don't inhabit the same orbit he and

Claire Prentice do. Even now, in the middle of Dominion's gallery party, I'm just an impostor pretending I belong here.

As we stand there, all but a few of the small crowd of patrons moves on from in front of the painting. I say nothing for a moment, using the slow shift of people around us to give me time to formulate my answer.

"I'm house-sitting for a friend while she's out of the country the next several months. My place is, um . . . being renovated, so the timing worked out well for both of us."

Just a small bending of the facts. Harmless enough, I rationalize, as he holds my gaze and makes a low sound of acknowledgment.

"Have you lived there long?" I ask, awkwardly trying to make small talk when my body is still humming with awareness of him and a bit too much champagne.

"Yes, I have," he says, and I can tell he's only humoring me. He's as much tuned in to whatever is arcing between us as I am. "I've kept an apartment in the building since it went up a few years ago. Is it *Beauty*'s pain or her pleasure that moves you the most?"

"What?" The abrupt change of subject catches me off guard. Especially when I know the handful of people standing near us can easily hear every word.

He doesn't seem to notice or care. "You were on the verge of tears when I came up to you," he reminds me. "I'm curious to know why."

"Oh. Was I?" I want to deny it, if only so I don't appear weak to him, but he's seen too much already. I shake my head vaguely, then shrug. "I don't know why it affected me like that."

"Yes, you do. Tell me."

I look away from him to the painting, glad for the excuse to free myself from his provocative stare. The impact of the piece hasn't lessened now that I'm familiar with the subject, but studying it now, with Nick Baine standing intimately close to me, the air feels charged and pulsing.

Everything has taken on newer, weightier context now that he's invaded my space. He's invading my senses, too, making my skin tight with awareness of him and my body's undeniable response.

"She's being consumed by pain and pleasure. It's shattering her," I murmur, my gaze fixed on the woman whose image is reflected in the countless shards of painted glass on the canvas. "She's alone, maybe she's frightened. But she's not bending to it. She's not afraid to feel the pain . . . or the pleasure. She's defiant. That's what makes her so beautiful. Her eyes tell you everything you need to know. Nothing's ever going to truly destroy her."

The words spill out of me, and I feel suddenly, irrevocably, exposed.

I haven't known disease, but I do know pain. I know corrosion—the kind that comes from within and from without. I've survived both. But as I look at *Beauty*, still whole and unbroken, despite the sharp fragments that comprise her, I'm reminded that deep down, I am a coward.

Inside the facade of my intact shell, I'm a thousand jagged pieces held together by fear and sheer will.

"You see more than most," Nick tells me, his praise and the low vibration of his voice wrapping around my senses. "Do you feel envy when you look at her?"

"No. It's not envy." I shake my head solemnly and

turn to face him. "It's hate." My honesty is raw and real. It's got the bite of acid on my tongue, even though my tone is quiet with shame. "I hate her for what she makes me acknowledge about myself."

His eyes hold mine unflinchingly, and for a moment, I wonder if he understands. Does he have sharp fragments of his own hidden behind those mesmerizing blue eyes and smolderingly intense good looks?

I can't take his silence. And I'm afraid of what else I might be tempted to reveal to him if I allow this strange meeting between us to continue. Until now, I haven't noticed that all but a couple of people have left the display where Nick and I stand. Leaving suddenly seems like a very good idea to me too.

I break his stare and awkwardly clear my throat. "I think I should go. I've had a little too much champagne tonight on an empty stomach. It's making me say and do things right now that I normally wouldn't. Things I'm probably going to regret."

"Is that so?" He doesn't smile at my attempt to deflect his study of me. Dark interest sizzles in the penetrating gaze that only homes in deeper now. "I don't think it's the champagne talking. I don't think you really believe that either."

When I don't answer, he reaches over to cup my jaw. The shock of his touch startles me. More than that, it inflames me. He bends toward me as if he might kiss me right in the middle of the gallery. But he smoothly bypasses my parted lips, bringing his mouth to the side of my face, maddeningly close to my ear.

"Art is meant to provoke emotions, Avery. Its sole purpose is to arouse our senses, even if it disturbs. Even if it's ugly. Even if it fucking scares the living shit out of you."

A gray-haired lady directly in front of me swivels an uncomfortable look at the both of us before shuffling away. It isn't long before the other remaining patron drifts away, too, and then it's only Nick and me in front of *Beauty*.

His voice is a velvet caress against my cheek. "Are your senses aroused now, Avery?"

I close my eyes in an attempt to deny what I feel. But I can't deny it. I can't deny *him*, even though everything cautious and rational inside me warns that I am venturing into dangerous territory with this man.

"Yes," I whisper, unable to stop the confession from slipping off my tongue.

"So are mine," he says. "I'm aroused by you. I have been since I saw you the other night." He shifts closer to me, until his lips brush the shell of my ear. "I wanted you even then. Does that scare you?"

I shake my head slightly, but that doesn't seem good enough for him. Drawing back from me with my face held in his hands, he looks at me with searching, turbulent eyes. "I want you in my bed, Avery. When I see something I want, I reach for it."

No man has ever been this bold with me before, not in all of my adult life. Then again, I've never met anyone like Nick Baine. Dark. Magnetic. Arrogant. Hotter than hell.

Hadn't I sensed this power about him that night at the elevator?

He had tripped all of my self-preservation instincts from the second I saw him. He'd terrified me, and I would have stayed away.

But now he's here, looking at me possessively, as if

no one else in the room exists. His intensity is a force I'm not prepared for, but I'm not terrified like I should be. I'm wildly, undeniably, turned on.

Desire is etched in his handsome face and the hard line of his rigid, square jaw. His eyes blaze into mine, searing all of the flimsy reservations crowding my thoughts.

"If you really want to leave—if you think this will be something you'll regret—then go now."

Yes. I should go.

I should pivot on my heel and get as far away from this unsettling man as I possibly can. I should damn well run.

But that's not what I want right now.

It's not what I do.

Without a care for the fact that we're not alone—never mind that we've only known each other for not even a full hour—I turn my face into the cradle of his hand. My lips touch the warm center of his palm and he utters a rough groan.

He doesn't speak. He doesn't need to. His eyes are dark with erotic promise.

I shudder with the ferocity of it. And I can't wait for him to make good on everything I see churning in his consuming gaze.

Without a word of coaxing or command, he leads me away.

8

I meant it when I told him I wasn't reckless. But those words feel like more lies added to the others I've told tonight, as I fetch my coat and leave the gallery party with a man I've only just met.

My pulse is racing with something far more potent than anxiety or doubt.

I'm excited. I'm so turned on, I can hardly breathe.

He leads me discreetly out the back of Dominion. Outside, a narrow alleyway runs between the tall buildings behind the gallery. We no sooner step out to the privacy of the darkness than he stops abruptly and turns to me. Without asking or warning, he pulls me into a kiss.

The instant our lips meet, all of the desire that had been kindling back inside the gallery erupts into something urgent and molten. His fingers slide into my hair as he draws me closer to him, his mouth firm and hot and possessive against mine. I'm unsteady on my feet, though less from the effects of the champagne now than the spiral of need that's twisting through me as I melt into the heat of his kiss.

I breathe him in greedily, reveling in the spicy, clean scent of him as he commands my lips with dizzying skill. I shudder under that force, my nipples tightening inside my bra, my clit pulsing with every frantic beat of my heart. There's no stopping the small moan that escapes me as his tongue sweeps across the seam of my lips, then pushes inside without hesitation.

Nick Baine is not a man who asks permission. He is not a man who needs to ask. I recognized this about him immediately. Now, I'm feeling the carnal truth of that understanding and it exhilarates me beyond all sense or reason.

I don't want him to ask. I don't need it. Not right now.

Not from him.

Seeing him that first night, talking to him inside the gallery . . . it's cracked something open inside me. He's seen through my fissures tonight the way I've never let anyone else before, and there's no taking it back. I don't want to take any of it back. Not when I'm kissing him out here in the darkness with the knowledge that this is only a prelude to where we're heading.

He rocks into me, our bodies melding together in perfect alignment. Part of me registers a jolt of shock at feeling the hard ridge of his erection pressing against my abdomen, but that part of me isn't the one in charge of my thinking now. I'm not thinking; only feeling. And what I feel is need—all of it centered on this man. It's wild and out of control, something very foreign to me.

It's reckless.

What I'm doing here is probably worse than foolish. Hell, I know it is. I also know I've never wanted anything more in my life.

A low, yearning ache thrums between my thighs. If I had any reservations about allowing myself to be pulled into his orbit, this kiss is the point of no return. The air is thick and heavy around us, charged with a current I can feel vibrating in him too.

I moan with the wave of arousal that floods me. As my lips open on that involuntary cry of need, Nick's tongue sweeps inside, claiming a deeper taste. Stoking my need.

His hands release me, but only so that one of them can begin a slow slide down the front of my body. My pulse speeds as his touch descends from my neck to my breasts, then down the side of my rib cage, leaving fire in its wake even through the layers of my clothing.

He doesn't stop there. With the same masculine confidence he's had from the first moment our eyes locked on each other, he reaches down to cup my sex.

He caresses me, kneads me ruthlessly. Pleasure arcs through me and I gasp with the force of it. I can't stop myself from rocking against the delicious pressure of his palm.

I clutch him as our kiss deepens and his hand continues to drive me mad with want. Sinking my fingers into his dark hair to anchor myself against the intense assault on my senses, I can't curb my sigh at the luxuriant softness. Especially when everything else about him is hard and powerful, from the broad curves of his shoulders to the muscled planes of his back.

As I run my hands over him, I feel the demanding jut of his cock surge even fuller against me. An erotic thrill chases through me as we grind together just steps from the crowd inside the gallery.

My blood is racing, my heartbeat throbbing in every pulse point, though none so demanding as the knot of nerve endings between my clenched thighs. He could unzip my jeans and take me right here in the alleyway and I wouldn't stop him. God, I'm so wet for him, I'm almost hoping he does.

He groans against my mouth, a strangled sound. When he pulls back to look at me, I see pure animal hunger in his hooded gaze. I see what looks almost like bewilderment—as if this fire erupting between us has caught him off guard too.

"Damn, you taste so fucking good," he says in little better than a growl. His breath skates across my sensitized lips on a low curse. He takes a step back from me as if he needs the space. "Let's get out of here."

I nod, not quite capable of speech yet. At the end of the alley is a private parking area I had no idea was back here. He pulls a key fob from his pants pocket and a sleek black BMW coupe chirps to life.

I follow him over to the M6, easily the most expensive vehicle in the lot. Nick opens the passenger side door.

"Get in," he instructs me, his voice a deep, velvet rasp.

But as I start to move in front of him to climb inside, he catches me once more and drags me into another fevered kiss. This one is swift, but carnal. Even more so than before. The heat of it licks through my nerve endings, straight to the wet ache pulsing between my thighs. I shudder, knowing if he touches me there again right now, I'll explode.

I pull away from his mouth on a jagged sigh. "Drive fast."

9

Nick operates a car with the same purpose and command I just witnessed in the alley with him. Aggressive, confident, smoothly in control. It seems like only seconds since we left the gallery before we're turning in to the Park Avenue building entrance.

To my still-thrumming body, it feels like hours.

Nick's hand stroking my inner thigh the whole time hasn't made it any easier. Although we haven't spoken since we got in the car, the electricity snapping between us hasn't lessened in the least. If anything, the short drive has only made me more impatient to pick up where we left off.

Driving up to the building, he bypasses the brightly lit main lobby where we'd have to pass Manny. I hadn't even considered that we might have to waltz past the sweet old door man together, and I exhale a soft sigh of relief to be avoiding that awkwardness.

Instead, Nick drives around to an underground

parking garage below the tower high-rise. He parks the BMW in an empty space closest to the secured glass doors leading into the building. The only one marked *Reserved.*

I dimly register that fact and what it likely signifies, but there's no room for logic or questions when Nick cuts the engine and pivots toward me. The soft gray leather rasps with his movement. He's so gorgeous, so intensely masculine yet beautiful at the same time, I have to remind myself to breathe when he looks at me. I am far out of my depth with this man. I sensed that from the instant I saw him. He's powerful, sophisticated. Obviously wealthy, based on the exclusiveness of his address and the price tag of his car. I have no doubt he could take his pick of any woman who lays eyes on him, and yet he's sitting here with me now. Touching me. Staring at me as if he wants to devour me.

I lick my lips, an involuntary movement that draws his gaze to my darting tongue. As he watches me, that sinfully sculpted mouth of his compresses into grim line.

"Last chance to change your mind." His deep voice is thick and rough in the silence of the car. As he speaks, his hand slides higher on my thigh, trailing fire in the wake of his touch. For a long moment, he doesn't say anything, just teases me with the sensual slide of his palm on my leg, his roving fingers coming closer and closer to my sex. "If you say the word, Avery, this goes no further. If you're not sure, it can end here and now."

No. I'm not having a single doubt, even if I have many reasons that I should. I don't do casual sex. Then again, I'm not very good at relationships either. What's happening here has no future—I recognize that. I accept it. Hell, I'm counting on the fact that it can't possibly last past tonight.

But I can't call this casual either. Nothing about what Nick Baine stirs inside me feels fleeting or insignificant.

His desire-drenched gaze is locked on me. His touch is possessive and bold, as if he understands exactly what my body needs and knows how to deliver.

Would he want me like this if he knew I was at the gallery party by coincidence rather than invitation? Would he treat me differently if I told him I was a failing artist and struggling bartender? That I had no money and nowhere to go before I'd suddenly gotten the chance to live in his fancy building for a little while?

What would he think if he knew all of my other secrets? The ugly ones. The dangerous ones. The ones I've never let see the light of day.

He doesn't know any of that. And he won't.

One night of this scorching desire—that's the only thing I'm sure of right now. It's enough for me, but I can't find my voice to answer his question. The words won't come. Not when he's caressing the tender inside of my thigh, turning the throbbing ache of my clit into an agonizing need for release.

"I can feel your heat," he says, his words inflaming me even more. "My fingers are on fire and I haven't even touched you the way I really want to. Christ, woman. You'll burn me up when I get inside you."

I let out a strangled moan, and he seems to take that for his cue to kiss me again. His free hand cups my nape as he draws me to him and our mouths come together. Twice already tonight he's given me a taste of his kiss—the first one explosive and consuming, the second swift and carnal.

But this kiss is something new. It's unrushed and

deep, a languorous melding of his lips over mine. This slow, masterful kiss seduces me even more than the ones that came before it. He's tasting, testing . . . and it nearly unravels me right where I sit.

On a low curse, he pulls back only far enough to separate our mouths. We're both breathing erratically now. I can feel the drum of his heartbeat beneath the hand I have pressed against his chest. He lowers his head to mine, resting our foreheads lightly together. His blue eyes are dark but smoldering as they hold my gaze. "Are you ready, Avery?"

I swallow and try to find my voice. "Yes."

God, yes. I'm on the verge of combusting.

He gets out of the car in fluid motion, then walks around to open my door before I have the chance to do it for myself. It's gentlemanly and proper, and I feel a blush creep into my cheeks in response. Which is ridiculous considering where this night began and where we both know it will end.

"Thanks," I murmur, accepting his hand as he helps me climb out.

We head inside the building, then into one of the elevator cars waiting at the garage level. Nick types a code on the numbered panel, then we begin our smooth ascent. I'm anxious now, conscious of his distance as he leans back against the wall of the elevator, facing me. Studying me.

I can see the hunger in his hooded gaze. Lower still, I can see the evidence of his desire in the immense bulge in his tailored pants. My entire body responds to that heat, my skin tightening, breasts tingling with my arousal. I want to kiss him again. I want his hands on me, right here in the elevator. I just want . . . him.

When I don't think I can take another second of the torturous waiting, a soft chime announces we've arrived. I see the letters *PH* on the digital display, but that doesn't prepare me for the jaw-dropping apartment that we step into as we exit the elevator.

Subdued lighting barely illuminates the mirrorlike marble floors of the foyer and the clean, masculine lines of his furnishings. The penthouse is open-concept and spacious, a mixture of gleaming metals, rich, exotic woods, and crisp white furniture. He's got the same massive windows that Claire has in her fifth-floor apartment, except there are more of them up here. With glass on three sides of the enormous living room, the view from the penthouse nothing short of spectacular.

"Come in." Nick's fingers brush mine in a gesture for me to follow him inside.

I trail along at his side, awestruck by everything in my line of sight—including the incredibly sexy man leading me into his domain. He takes my jacket and purse, setting both on one of the trio of sofas that outfit an elegant U-shaped conversation area that overlooks Central Park in one direction and, on the other, most of Manhattan and beyond.

I can't keep my gaze from straying to the constellation of city lights spread out before me as far as my eyes can see. Hundreds of tall buildings glitter and twinkle in the dark beside the iconic landmarks of New York's skyline and the pair of rivers running parallel on either side of the tower-spiked slice of land.

I stare out with delight at the illuminated Art Deco spire of the Chrysler Building, my favorite of them all. To the right, the tall needle of the Empire State Building is unmistakable. Both of the goliath skyscrapers seem dwarfed from this penthouse view.

I'm gaping in amazement and there's nothing I can do about it. "My God. What does someone have to do to get a view like this?"

He chuckles. "Write a really big check."

"I can imagine," I say. But truly, I can't imagine how much an apartment like this penthouse, in this exclusive building, with this incredible view, must cost. Many multiple millions. Probably close to a hundred of them if I had to guess.

I glance back to find him still standing near the sofa, his attention fixed on me. "What do you do for a living?" I ask. "Or did you inherit this seat at the top of the world?" I try to make a joke of it, but I'm genuinely curious. "Please tell me you're not one of those insufferable trust fund brats."

"No trust fund," he says, the seriousness of his expression at war with the lightness of his tone. "My business interests are varied. Investments and corporate finance, mainly. Real estate, on occasion. Art, when it suits me."

I nod as if I understand completely, then avert my gaze before he can guess just how far out of my depth I am right now.

"What about you, Avery?"

"Oh, I . . . I'm in public relations." It's somewhat true, considering my work behind the bar at Vendange is nothing but dealing with the public and keeping them happy.

Nick doesn't question me any further, even though I can feel his eyes on me, studying me.

A small twinge of guilt rides me as I stare out at the glittering lights. This would be the time to confess that virtually nothing I've told him about myself tonight is true. But I rationalize that my little lies have all been harmless enough. They're self-protective . . . and, yes, admittedly, they are selfish too.

If I thought for one second I would see Nick Baine again after tonight, aside from random passings through the lobby here and there these next four months, I might be tempted to take off my mask with him now. There's a part of me that wonders if he can see through it anyway.

Inexplicably, I want him to try—the way he'd done back at the gallery in front of *Beauty*.

Dangerous thinking, especially when I can't risk letting anyone get too close. I *won't* risk it.

Especially with a man like Nick.

I tilt my head for a better look at the city below, and to escape the weight of all my secrets. Between the champagne that's still swimming in my stomach and the vertigo-inducing height of the penthouse, I have to press my hand to my abdomen to ward off the feeling that I could fall. "What floor are we on?"

"Ninety-three," he replies, his breath sifting in my hair. "Welcome to the top of the world."

My words, served back to me in seductive invitation. He's directly behind me now, having moved there soundlessly. As awestruck as I am by the incredible view, the feel of his warmth at my back—the knowledge that he's close enough to touch me again—is a distraction to my senses that I can't deny.

"Do you like it?" he murmurs, his hands coming to rest on my shoulders.

"Oh, yes." I sigh the words as renewed heat chases through my veins.

He makes a low noise in the back of his throat as he frees the loose knot of my scarf and pulls the gauzy fabric away from my neck. My heated skin feels chilled, exposed. But only for a moment.

Skating one of his hands toward my neck, he gathers up my hair, sweeping it over my other shoulder to bare my nape to him. His mouth presses against that sensitive skin in a slow, sensual kiss. I moan with the pleasure of it, with the twisting anticipation of what's to come.

His tongue teases my skin, one hand stroking my hair, the other moving around to the front of me to caress my breast over my sweater. His touch, his kiss, the warm, hard press of his athletic frame at my back . . . it's all making me crazy with need. I suck in a ragged breath, my sex clenching with every heartbeat, my arousal turning molten all over again.

I can't take the torment. He's had me on the verge of coming since he touched me in the alley outside the gallery. Before then, if I'm being honest with myself. He's had me thinking about getting naked with him since that first hot clash in the lobby downstairs.

I want to touch him too. I want his bare skin on mine. I want to feel his hard flesh inside me where the ache is becoming anguish. Dammit, I *need* to.

With trembling fingers, I reach down for the button on my jeans, intending to speed this along before I completely lose my nerve. Or my mind.

I fumble for less than a second before his hand closes over mine, stilling me. "I'll do that." He draws my hand away, bringing it to my side. "When I'm ready."

I frown at the soft, but stern, correction. I'd expected him to pounce on me in frantic lust once we arrived in his place. I thought we'd fuck, fast and furious, no need for foreplay after the steam we're still carrying with us from the gallery.

I'd been prepared for that.

But not for this. He's taking his time.

No—he's not. He's taking control.

Part of me bristles at the idea. He can't know how deeply that unsettles me—the thought of surrendering my will to him or to any man—but right now it's impossible to disapprove of anything Nick's doing. My body is his, even if my thoughts flinch in rebellion.

Slowly, his body intimately close behind mine, he reaches for the hem of my sweater and slips his warm hands beneath it. The first skate of his palms on my skin makes me tremble. I pull air into my lungs, then release it on a shaky sigh as his touch moves higher, over my stomach, then up my rib cage to the filmy satin of my bra.

He cups my breasts, kneading both in his hands, his thumbs flicking over my erect nipples. I can't bite back my moan as he caresses me into a state of quivering, shameless desire. I want more. Need more.

My sweater is gone in an instant, peeled off me and discarded beside us on the floor. He removes my bra with sure, agile fingers. Then he slowly turns me around to face him.

"Beautiful," he utters in a thick rasp.

His face is all shadows and hard angles in the subdued light of the city behind us. But I see the flare of hunger in his eyes as they roam over me in slow, appraising study. He lifts one of my breasts in his palm, then bends his dark head and takes my nipple into his mouth. Pleasure arrows straight to my sex as he sucks and teases me with his tongue.

I bring my hands up to his hair and tunnel my fingers into the silky waves, holding on as he leaves one breast to torment the other. The ache between my thighs coils tighter with every flick of his tongue and each sharp, unexpected nip of his teeth. By the time he releases me, I'm panting swiftly, squirming where I stand and desperate to alleviate the yearning of my body for his.

Nick's breath is racing too. He exhales a curse that sounds like a growl as he catches my mouth in a scorching kiss. His hands slide down to the front waistband of my jeans. I feel the pop of the button, the hard yank of the zipper. Then the caress of his strong fingers as he shoves the denim over my hips, along with my panties.

I reach for him, but he sinks down in front of me to remove my leather boots and peel my jeans the rest of the way off my legs. I'm naked in front of him now, and although I can't ignore the sense of vulnerability that rushes over me, I feel no shyness whatsoever. How can I, when his gaze rakes my nude length with a hunger that I can feel in every electrified nerve ending in my body?

Kneeling in front of me, he skims his hands slowly up the outsides of my bare legs. "Christ, Avery. You're so lovely." His caress moves inward, his fingertips drifting over the patch of trimmed curls between my thighs. "So soft."

He plays there for a moment, making me crazy for more. When his fingers delve into my slick cleft, I whimper, helpless to bite it back.

He groans as he strokes my folds. His thumb grazes my clit, just enough to make me mad for more. Then I feel him enter me, his fingers sinking deep. I cry out as he fucks me slowly with his hand. "Your pussy is so wet and hot. I knew it would be." He strokes me some more, nearly to my breaking point, before withdrawing on a low groan. "Open for me, Avery. Before I fuck you, I need to know how sweet you taste. I want to make you come."

My head tips back as he guides my legs apart, then presses his mouth to my sex. His tongue slips wetly over my clit, swirling around the hard bundle of nerves in a rhythm that makes my vision blur with ecstasy. His lips drive me wild, mindless. And then his fingers join his mouth and I am lost.

"Oh, God," I gasp, as my orgasm crashes over me in a violent wave. I clutch Nick's hair in my fists as my hips buck against his mouth and my body shudders with release.

It's so good.

He is so good.

And he's relentless, wringing every last quiver and cry from me with the masterful play of his hands and lips and tongue against my sensitive flesh.

This night is going to spoil me for any other man. I think I knew that even before he put his skillful mouth on me.

If I'm not careful, Nick Baine is going to be my ruin.

But I don't want to be careful with him.

And as he rises up to take my hand and lead me out of the living room, I have to admit that right now, being careful is just about the last thing on my mind.

10

His hand engulfing mine, Nick brings me into his palatial bedroom. Crisp, modern furnishings and walls of windows define this space as well. Not that I have much chance to notice the details. As soon as we enter, he wheels me around to face him. His movements have an almost predatory grace and control as he catches me against the solid wall of his clothed body and his arms encircle my back, powerful and warm.

He takes my mouth in a consuming kiss. I can taste his need, his demand. I can taste myself too, in the lingering sweetness on his lips, on his tongue. I sink into his strength on a strangled cry, my nerve endings still vibrating from my orgasm a moment ago.

Still kissing me, Nick starts stepping me backward, toward the massive king-sized bed that I glimpsed from the door. With hands roaming, our kiss unbroken as we move, it's as if we're dancing, not walking. Legs entwined, arms wrapped around each other, our bodies refuse to part as he guides me through the darkened room.

I'm growing dizzy and hot all over again, my breath sawing out of my lungs in tempo with his as we reach the edge of a soft area rug near the bed. My bare feet sink into luxurious softness that feels as decadent as fleece beneath my soles. Another two paces and the backs of my thighs meet the side of the bed.

Nick has me caged in his arms, his hands burying in my loose hair as he greedily devours my mouth.

"Oh, fuck," I whisper harshly as the rush of another orgasm begins to boil inside me.

My cleft is soaking wet, both from the climax he gave me and from the unbearable need to have him inside me. I need it now. I want him so desperately, it staggers me.

Clutching him to hold myself upright, I tip my head back on a gasp as his kiss leaves my mouth and heads for my throat, his tongue dipping into the sensitive hollow above my sternum. His hands caress me with growing urgency now, descending my spine, curving around the swell of my naked ass. He squeezes my flesh, parting me, kneading me as his mouth trails fire onto my breasts.

He drags me closer, grinding our hips together. The huge ridge of his erection is a delicious pressure that speeds my pulse and leaves me shaking. He knows what he's doing to me, of course. He knows what I crave. Sliding his fingers between my thighs, he flicks my clit until I'm nearly frenzied with sensation.

I need to touch him too. I reach between us and feel him as strong as steel beneath the fine fabric of his pants. I squeeze and stroke his shaft over his clothing, reveling in the power that surges against my palm and fingers.

His answering groan only makes me hotter. Bolder. I unfasten the button closure and unzip enough so I can slide my hand inside. God, he's immense. Long and thick and pulsing. Slick moisture coats my fingers as I skim them over the head of his cock. His hips thrust and my sex clenches in response. I can't take the waiting for another second.

I squirm and shift in his arms, shocked at how easily this man can turn me molten.

"Nick." His name boils out of me on a low moan. "Nick, please . . . fuck me."

His reply is wordless, a tight snarl that gusts against my parted lips. He lowers his head and stares at me from under the slashes of his brows, his hooded gaze primal and ravenous. His face is taut with visible strain, his squared jaw rigid as his nostrils flare with every ragged breath.

His hands come up to rest on my shoulders. Although his touch is gentle, I can tell his control is at its limit when he gives me a little shove, pushing me down onto my back on the mattress.

I scoot toward the center, quaking with anticipation. My fingers have made his dark hair a wild crown of disheveled waves that gleam bluish-black under the twinkling city lights outside the large bedroom windows as he begins to strip out of his clothing. His hands move roughly over the buttons of his shirt as he steps out of his shoes. The shirt is tossed aside a second later, revealing broad shoulders and a muscled chest that tapers to a perfectly cut abdomen. His pants go next, followed by dark boxer briefs that barely contain his engorged cock. He finishes undressing and stands before me naked and mouth-wateringly erect.

He is handsome from head to toe. In fact, he's magnificent.

I realize I'm gaping, trying to decide what part of him I want to lick first.

I wait for him to climb onto the bed with me, but instead he seizes my ankles and drags me back to the edge of the mattress. His palms burn me where they settle on the tender insides of my thighs. He spreads me open. Then he lowers himself between my parted thighs and feasts on me with rough abandon.

"Oh God," I whimper, thrashing under the skill of his mouth. It's too much, and I'm too near the edge already. Pleasure ripples from my clit to my core. I'm breaking apart. About to shatter. "Oh, fuck. Nick, please . . . I'm going to come . . ."

"Yes," he murmurs against my wet, quivering flesh. "Many times before we're finished here tonight."

True to his word, he shows me no mercy now. As I splinter in ecstasy against the ruthless stroking of his tongue, I distantly register the quiet rustle of a condom being opened. Then he's at the soaking entrance of my body, the head of his cock pushing inside me.

He's big and I'm long out of practice. Even primed for him by a pair of pretty amazing orgasms, I arch off the mattress on a soft cry as he thrusts inside. He stretches my tender walls, filling me completely.

"Ah, Christ, you're tight," he hisses beside my ear as he begins to piston above me. "Feels so fucking good. So hot and wet."

His praise is like gasoline on the fire he's already set inside me. I hold on to his shoulders as he drives deep, impaling me with long, breath-robbing strokes. Our tempo is fierce, frenzied. There's no stopping the pleasure that rolls through me.

I don't want to stop it.

I just want to feel.

For tonight, I just want to be free. From my past, and from all of the old ghosts I buried there.

I slide my hands down and sink my fingers into the firm muscle of Nick's ass as he fucks me toward the crest of another ferocious orgasm.

I reach for it, and he gives it to me and then some.

Oh, yes. Nick Baine could very easily ruin me for anyone else.

Why that thought doesn't terrify me, I don't want to know.

11

A wet, distant hiss invades my senses, drawing me out of an unusually heavy sleep. I lay curled on my side in the dark in the middle of a large, rumpled bed. Nick's bed. I can smell him on the pillow beneath my cheek. His spicy, masculine scent lingers in my hair. On my skin.

I can feel the reminder of him in every dull, delicious ache of my spent body.

Memories of everything we did together flood in, and I can't curb the satisfied smile that spreads over my face. I can't deny that I'm hungry for him all over again, but when I stretch my arm out to search for his warmth, I find only cold, empty sheets. I'm alone in his bed and—

Wait. Is it . . . *morning?*

Startled by the thought, I lift my head, my eyelids snapping open. Yep, definitely morning. Quite early, from the look of it. Outside the windows, the muted glow of sunrise is barely a halo on the horizon behind the city skyline.

I stayed the night? I close my eyes on a groan. How the hell did I sleep so long?

Apparently, multiple orgasms and several hours of tireless sex in numerous creative positions will do that to a person. Not that I would know. Until last night, there was a lot I didn't know. Sex with Nick has been a revelation on many levels. Each one more pleasurable than the next.

But that was last night. Now it's the morning after, with all the discomfiture that comes with it. I never sleep over, especially with someone new. I hate the awkwardness that follows—the dread of seeing each other in broad daylight and pretending we're not reliving the night before in a haze of embarrassment or regret. I hate feeling the need for obligatory promises to call each other or get together again soon, while one or both of us act like we're not dying to bolt for the nearest door.

"Shit," I mutter under my breath as I swing my legs off the side of the mattress.

The urge to run is strong. How bad would it be if I just slipped out while he was in the shower? Will he even care? Maybe he'll be relieved. After all, neither one of us came here with any expectations beyond last night.

I glance around for my clothes, then remember in vivid detail that Nick stripped them off me in front of the windows in the other room. Just the thought of his hands on me—his mouth on every inch of my bare skin—ignites a wanton stirring inside me. I sigh with the all-too-pleasant memory. I have a feeling I'll be reliving last night in my mind, and in other body parts, for a damn long time.

Scooting out of the bed while the shower continues to run in the bathroom adjacent to the massive bedroom suite, I pad quickly into the living room to locate my clothing. Apparently, Nick's been up for a while or else he doesn't sleep much at all because it's obvious he's been out here while I slept. The aroma of freshly brewed coffee emanates from the kitchen. And instead of finding my jeans and sweater on the floor where they fell as he undressed me, they've been neatly folded and placed on a sleek white leather Barcelona chair. My lacy bra and panties rest on top.

I grab both and hastily put them on. By accident, I catch my reflection in the window glass and see the bed-tossed tangle of my pale blond hair. God, I don't even want to think about what my face looks like after sleeping in yesterday's makeup. To say nothing of my breath.

"There's coffee ready if you want some."

Nick's deep voice behind me halts me where I stand, half-dressed, my jeans pulled midway up my thighs. I wince, forcing a light tone into my voice as I look at him over my shoulder. "Oh . . . thanks. But, ah . . . I really need to go."

Arms folded over his chest, he's standing in the open doorway of the bedroom in nothing but a pair of black boxer briefs that cling sinfully to his narrow hips and sinewy thighs. The fitted shorts do little to disguise the outline of his cock, which is strikingly large even at rest.

His black hair is damp from the shower and inky-dark. Just looking at him, I can feel the thick, silky waves against my fingertips.

I can still feel how smooth his tan skin is, how powerful his muscles feel under my hands when he's moving above me . . . and inside me.

I clear my throat and go back to dressing. Anything to avoid his penetrating blue eyes that watch me from across the room. While I feel twitchy and self-conscious, Nick seems anything but. No, he's utterly in control and comfortable in his own skin, qualities he's demonstrated from the moment I first saw him.

With long-legged strides and a tight backside I can't help but admire, he strolls past me, unfazed, while I pull my sweater over my head and try to make some sense of my bedraggled hair.

"Cream or sugar?" he asks, heading into the spacious kitchen.

"Um, both. Thanks." As eager as I am to get away, I have to admit coffee sounds like heaven. And it won't be a total hardship that I can continue looking at him while I drink it.

I drift after him into the kitchen and take a seat on one of the low-backed modern barstools on the opposite side of the counter. Turns out it's the perfect vantage point for watching his back and shoulder muscles flex and contract as he pulls a pair of black mugs from a cabinet and starts filling them with coffee. I already knew he had an athletic, beautifully formed body. This morning, I have to correct that estimation. He is mouth-watering perfection.

I lick my lips, and not for the want of coffee. "Sorry I fell asleep. I didn't mean to stay all night."

"Don't worry about it." He pauses from adding cream and sugar to my cup, shooting me a heated look that makes my stomach flip. "In case you didn't notice, I wasn't in a rush to kick you out of bed."

No, he wasn't. He'd taken his time fucking me

senseless, making me come over and over again until I finally lost count. He'd been tireless, insatiable.

To be fair, I was insatiable with him too. And I still am. I try to ignore the fact that my skin feels too tight beneath my clothing, my nipples erect and straining for more of his attention. Between my legs, I feel the dull, lingering ache that his cock left behind and it's all I can do not to squirm and shift on the barstool.

"What I mean is," I murmur, attempting to regain my composure as well as some control over the conversation, "I don't want this to be awkward. Not for either one of us."

"Is it?" His sharp blue eyes pierce me and don't let me go.

It wasn't. Not really. And I'm not quite sure what to make of that.

When I don't respond, he walks over with the two cups of coffee and places mine in front of me on the counter. As he sets it down, my gaze snags on his right hand and wrist. More specifically, on a web of heavy scars that slash across the back of his hand and up his forearm.

I hadn't noticed them last night. I'd been too nervous at the gallery to focus that closely. Later, here at his penthouse, it had been too dark and I'd been too blinded by pleasure and desire. Now that I have seen them, I can hardly tear my eyes away from them.

Horror swamps me instantly . . . followed by sadness.

He must have suffered a terrible accident of some sort. A long time ago, by the look of it. The scars are so severe, I have to guess the injury had nearly severed his hand and fingers.

When I look up, he's staring at me in unreadable

silence. I'm sure my own gaze is not so hard to decipher. I feel my expression sag in shock, in sympathy and anguish for whatever happened to him. He doesn't invite my compassion, though. Certainly not my questions. His darkened, unblinking eyes seem to forbid it, in fact.

But he doesn't pull away. He lets me take my fill, even while his grim face refuses to let me in.

I glance down, sipping the sweetened coffee to give me an excuse to break the tension. I'm also thankful to have something to do with my hands while I weather the weight of his inscrutable stare.

Finally, he speaks. "Tell me if that's not how you like it."

I manage a faint shake of my head. "No, it's good. It's perfect."

He lifts his mug and his eyes hold me over the rim. "Creamy and sweet. My favorite combination as well."

It's a flirtatious statement since he's drinking his coffee black. Although his voice is casual and calm, I know there's something ugly behind his detached, unaffected exterior. Something much uglier than any physical scar I've just seen.

He's damaged. When I recognize that in him, I feel something shift and soften inside me. I want to know what other scars he's carrying, but I understand it's not my place to ask. He wouldn't tell me even if I did. I know this with the same certainty that I know I wouldn't tell him about any of mine.

Maybe in time he might trust me enough.

An odd, pointless, thought when I know nothing lasting can come of what happened between us last night. I'm no more part of his orbit today than I was yesterday or that first night I arrived at this building. For the next four months, I'm only borrowing this life, this world. After Claire returns, I'll go back to my own reality.

And back there, I can't ever be part of Nick's world—nor anyone else's. Not so long as I hide my own scars. My secrets are too many and they can't be shared.

Looking at him now, I wonder how many secrets he's hiding too.

Almost in challenge I feel, he holds my gaze as he leans his hip against the counter. "I have business later today in London. My driver will be picking me up within the hour. I'll be gone for two weeks."

"Oh, okay." His abrupt announcement seems to be ample cue for me to leave, so I place my mug on the counter and start to slide off the stool. "In that case, I definitely should go and let you do what you need to do."

What I really need to do is forget about Nick Baine and the amazing one-night stand we just shared, because that's all it's going to be. If I wasn't smart enough to realize before now that he would be trouble for me, seeing him in this new light this morning is more than enough to convince me. Having sex with him is one thing. Allowing myself to get close to him—to care—is a risk I can't afford. I *won't* risk that.

When I step away from the barstool to retrieve my purse from the nearby sofa, his quiet command halts me.

"Stop, Avery." He's frowning as he places his mug on the counter, but there's a trace of dark humor in his voice. He cocks his head, eyes narrowed on me. "Why is it that when you're not running into me, you're running away from me?"

"I'm not running away."

He grunts. "Aren't you?"

I go still as he rounds the counter and comes up close

to me. He reaches out with his left hand—his good hand—and smoothes some of my disarrayed hair off my face. His expression is grimly sober. Intense in a different way than I've seen him so far.

"I want to see you again."

I swallow. "Sure, okay. That would be great." The lie sounds almost convincing to me. "Why don't you let me know when you get back? We can try to make plans to get together for lunch sometime, or a drink maybe . . ."

He's shaking his head, those shrewd blue eyes far too cynical to believe a word I'm saying.

"I want to see you. I want you in my bed again."

I struggle to maintain my resolve. "What if that's not what I want?"

His brows rise as if he'd never considered I might refuse him. But then his fingers slide through my hair to the tender skin of my nape and I'm already melting. As much as I want to think I can walk away from this man and forget him after last night, my full body response to his touch clearly disputes that.

"I want you, Avery. I *will* see you again when I return."

Before I can manage another protest, he bends his head to mine and kisses me. His tongue breaches the seam of my lips, possessive and so hot I feel his demanding licks all the way to my core. I moan as I lean into him, fighting a losing battle.

When he draws back, his sensual, wicked mouth is curved in a pirate's smile. "Like I told you last night, when I see something I want, I reach for it."

Then, apparently to prove that point, his hand slips between my thighs to the furnace of wet heat already burning there. His breath leaks out of him on a ragged curse. We're standing close enough that I can feel the hard ridge of his erection. He's just as aroused as I am.

"Fuck it," he rasps thickly, his hands already working the zipper of my jeans loose. "My driver will have to wait."

12

I'm still floating when I begin my Monday night shift at Vendange. The satiated haze Nick left me in when I stepped out of his penthouse this morning has barely faded all these hours later. I'd like to blame that early morning assault on my senses for the fact that I not only agreed to see him when he gets back from London, but I even gave him my phone number—something I never do.

So much for playing it safe or sticking to my resolve that I wasn't going to let our one-night stand progress any further. But our one night and the morning after was beyond amazing, and I'm learning pretty quickly that Nick Baine is a difficult man to resist.

Make that impossible.

When I see something I want, I reach for it.

God, did he ever.

With his hands, his mouth, his wicked tongue . . . his insatiable cock. I didn't think I had anything left in me to give, yet he proved me wrong time and time again. I'd barely been able to walk steadily after we parted and I made my way back to the fifth floor apartment. Walk of shame? Not even close. I'd never felt so shameless. So alive.

I still do. A smile curves my lips and I don't even try to bite it back. Nor can I curb the twinge of arousal that ignites inside me just thinking about him.

"How's it going, Ave?" Tasha's voice snaps me back to reality. We've been so busy, she and I have hardly had a chance to say hello. But now she's standing next to me behind the bar, shaking a martini for a customer a few seats down. "You okay?"

"I'm fine. Why?"

"Why?" She arches a brow at me as she skewers two olives and dunks them in the martini. "You're pouring chardonnay in a pilsner glass, for starters."

I glance down at what I'm doing and wince to see she's right. "Oh, shit."

Tasha chuckles and leaves to serve her drink while I correct my error behind the bar. When she comes back, I brace myself for the inevitable interrogation. "So, what's going on with you?" She tilts her head at me. "Your recent change of scenery sure agrees with you. You look . . . different somehow."

"Do I?"

"Yeah." She studies me closer now. "You haven't stopped smiling since you clocked in tonight."

"I haven't?" I glance at her and my smile spreads over my face, derailing any attempt to play it cool. Then I laugh, and I'm totally busted before her shakedown has even begun.

"Oh. My. God." Her brown eyes go wide. "I know

that look. Granted, I've never seen it on you before. But, girl, that look says it all." Her voice drops to a private level. "You did it. You got laid, didn't you?"

Fire creeps into my face and I'm just thankful for the music and the din of conversation that lets me keep at least a little of my dignity intact.

"When?" Tasha asks. "And with who? You haven't even told me you're seeing someone."

"Because I'm not seeing anyone. Or I wasn't. I'm not. It's not like that." I shake my head, unsure how I would describe what happened between Nick and me. "It was sex, that's all."

"Oh, that's all," she prompts, clearly unsatisfied with my answer. "That's why you've been acting so giddy and distracted? Just some random sex, no big deal."

"Okay," I relent because she's not going to let it go anyway. "It was really great sex. And . . . not that random."

"Meaning, someone we know?" When I shrug coyly, her face compresses into a frown. "If you tell me that in a moment of weakness, you and Joel—"

"What? Hell no!"

I bark out a laugh at the ridiculousness of the idea, and, as if our thoughts have summoned the beast, I see Joel's brunette head swivel in our direction from the other side of the restaurant. He narrows a scowl on us from where he's standing at a four-top, playing the gregarious host alongside Kimmie, the one server who can tolerate his overbearing management style and lack of basic humanity.

Then again, Kimmie's not much better herself. The petite blonde has had her lips permanently affixed to our manager's ass since he hired her.

"Definitely not Joel," I assure Tasha as we both get busy filling drink orders while we continue to talk.

"But I've met this guy?"

I nod. "More or less."

She considers me for a moment, then shakes her head as if dismissing one guess for another. It only takes her a second longer before her expression lights up in disbelief. "No. No, you did *not.*" She drops her bar cloth in the small sink and rounds on me, both hands fisted on her hips. "That guy from the building? The one who almost ran us over at the elevator?"

"To be fair, I was the one who almost ran him over," I offer lamely.

Tasha gapes. "We're talking about that guy—tall, dark, totally arrogant. Acted like he owned the damn building or something. We're talking about the superior prick?"

Oh, God. She has no idea how superior. "That's him."

"Avery Ross, you little slut!" she gasps, grinning like a loon. "Tell me everything." I giggle and she smacks me lightly in the bicep. "I'm not kidding. You know how I spent most of last night? Watching TV in Antonio's ratty sweats with dried baby formula in my hair. I want details. I need details. Let me live vicariously, at least."

I laugh, then start telling her about meeting Nick at the art gallery, but I've hardly spoken three sentences before we hear Joel pointedly clear his throat behind us on our side of the bar. He crowds right in, obviously intending to break up our brief conversation.

"Tasha. Gimme four shots of whiskey for table nine." No *please.* No *thank you.* But that's Joel.

"Sure thing," she says, rolling her eyes at me as she

pivots out of his shadow to take care of his order. "You want top shelf for those?"

He huffs out an impatient breath. "Do I look like I give a shit?" I don't escape his glower, either. "Kimmie says you left her hanging fifteen minutes for a flight of tequila shots earlier tonight."

"What? That's not true."

In fact, it's a bald-faced lie. I glance past Joel's round shoulder to where his little pet is giving one of her tables a prolonged view of her cleavage in her low-cut black shirt. I'm not sure who is the one trying to jerk me around, but Joel is quick to make his point.

"You've been here a long time, Avery. Don't start messing that up now." He wags his finger between Tasha and me. "I see any more slacking off back here, I'll dock you both an hour. Don't think I won't do it."

I want to tell him to get screwed so bad, the words are jumping on the tip of my tongue. But I can't afford to lose the hour's pay, let alone this job.

Tasha sees my struggle for restraint and rescues me by drawing Joel's attention away. "Here you go. Four shots of Glenlivet, ready to roll."

Without so much as a word of acknowledgment, he snatches the tray of drinks and carries it out to the table.

13

It's nearly midnight by the time Joel sends me on break. Subtlety is not his forte, but he's not even attempting it when he finally comes over to the bar to announce it's my turn to grab a quick bite before we head toward closing time. The fact that he makes a point of checking his watch as he grants my fifteen minutes only sets my teeth further on edge.

Tasha gives me a dramatic eye-roll as he struts away from the bar. "I can't believe he made you wait until everyone else went first. What an asshole."

I shrug as I finish running a customer's card. "He's got issues, obviously."

Tasha snorts. "And a very small dick, I'm sure."

"Ew. Let's not even try to imagine, shall we?"

She laughs and grabs the tab from my fingers. "Go on. I got this for you."

"Thanks."

As I start to clock out on the bar console, Joel's fake

barrel laugh carries over the other restaurant noise. He's resumed his table rounds, pausing to greet customers like he's the damn mayor himself. Kimmie is right there in his shadow, fawning and flirting with him and every other male in the place.

Tasha groans at the same time I do. "Remind me again why we put up with this?"

I slant her a wry look. "Because on any given night, we make twice as much as we would anywhere else in the city without taking our clothes off for a living."

"Oh, yeah. There's that." Tasha nudges me with her elbow. "Go enjoy your break."

"Okay. I'll be back in fifteen."

She waves at me. "You know where I'll be."

I fill a glass with tap water from the soda gun behind the bar, then swing by the kitchen to grab a cup of the day's soup special and a hot roll for dinner. It's not much of a meal after eight hours of working, but it'll do. Lord knows, I've survived on much less for a lot longer than this.

How many times had a can of watered-down chicken noodle been the only thing standing between Mom and me and near-starvation when I was a little kid? Too many to count. I don't even want to try. Those lean years aren't something I like to remember. And hunger hadn't been the only trouble we'd endured together after my beloved daddy had died and left us alone.

No, she and I had gone through much worse.

Especially after she married my stepfather.

I close my mind against the ugly memories that are always too close to the surface, clinging to my conscience like poison. Memories of the terror, the pain, the shame. Memories of bloodshed and tears . . . of violence and death.

Shit. Will I ever be free of them?

I don't really need to ask. I know the answer. I'm no more free than my mother. The only difference is the steel bars and razor-wired walls that have kept her confined for nearly a decade. My bars and walls are self-constructed, but just as impenetrable. I've lived behind them for so long, I'm not sure I'd survive if I ever permit myself to step outside.

The air is too pure. The light is too bright, leaving me no place to hide. No chance to escape my past or the impact it's had on every facet of my life in the time since.

I am my own warden out of necessity. And yes, out of fear as well.

No one gets past my barriers.

At least, no one has until now.

Not until I allowed Nick Baine to screw me senseless, apparently.

"Reckless," I chide myself under my breath as I take my meal into the employee coat room to eat in privacy.

With the rest of Vendange's staff out on the floor, I grab my phone out of my locker then settle in on a rickety dining room chair reject, thinking I'll check my email and browse the Internet while I take my short break.

I see the text light blinking as I lay the phone down beside me and take my first bite of the hearty chicken stew. It's probably Margot messaging me after I slipped away from the gallery without explanation last night. I'm debating on how honest I need to be with her as I swipe the screen lock and tap the message icon.

Been thinking all day about how good you feel.

How fucking sweet you taste when you come.

Okay. Definitely *not* Margot.

My stomach flips and a big grin spreads over my face. Even though Nick had asked for my number this morning, I hadn't actually expected him to call or text me. My heart is racing as I read his sexy message again, erotic images of the two of us last night—and this morning—playing in my mind. Wet heat unfurls inside me, blooming into a deep arousal that makes me squirm and clamp my thighs together in response.

He's away on business, thousands of miles out of the country, yet he's thinking about me. Wanting me. I can't even pretend I'm not flattered. Although flattered is the least of what I feel. I'm turned on as intensely as if he were right here in the break room with me, growling his hot, dirty words in my ear.

I notice the time stamp on his text is about four hours old. Fuck. Did he think I was ignoring him?

Does he think I don't want to hear from him?

Granted, I shouldn't want to. I should hope he's taken my lack of response to mean I'm not interested and let the whole thing go right here and now. Before things between us get any further out of my control.

Right. As if we're not already heading that way faster than I can hope to stop it.

Even if my panties weren't damp from desire, I wouldn't be able to deny the thrill that's coursing through me at the thought of Nick sexting me from a continent away. As for him, based on what little I know so far, I don't believe for a second that one ignored text would be enough to dissuade Nick Baine from going after something he wants.

And what he seems to want right now is me.

Another delicious flutter of interest beats through

my veins. Several hours have passed since he sent his message. Given the five-hour time difference between New York and London, that means he sent it around one o'clock in the morning over there. Now it's barely five a.m. on his end. Much too early to send a reply.

Isn't it?

I set down my soup and lean back in the chair to read Nick's message again. My finger strokes the side of my phone as his seductive words lick across my senses. My body remembers everything about him too. I can feel him naked against me, our bodies slick with sweat and musky with the scent of sex as we move together in a driving rhythm. I can feel him inside me, his cock stretching me, filling me so completely it brings tears to my eyes.

And I can feel his mouth on me again too. Those skillful lips. That wicked, unrelenting tongue.

Oh, shit.

My breath is rushing out of me now in rapid pants. My heart is pounding hard, my limbs loose and heavy. My sex is soaking wet, my clit throbbing.

Impulse and sexual frustration get the best of me. Before I can convince myself it's a terrible idea, I type out a short reply: *Too bad you're not here to finish what you've started.*

I hit SEND, catching my lip between my teeth to stifle my grin as I picture Nick reading my text after he wakes up this morning. If I give him a case of blue balls with his coffee, it'll serve him right.

Not even a second passes before my phone buzzes with his incoming message.

So, you are there. Thought you might be playing hard to get.

I smirk and type out my answer. *After last night? Too*

late for that, don't you think?

His reply comes just as quickly. *Are you saying I've already got you where I want you, Ms. Ross?*

My brows rise. *Depends on where that might be, Mr. Baine.*

I don't have to wait long before his answer appears. His suggestions come at me one after another, each of them leaping to erotic life in my mind.

On your back.

On your knees.

On my face.

Anywhere and everywhere I command.

I swallow as I read that last text. Part of me flinches at the idea of giving up control to him or any man—an instinctual chafe against an old memory I buried a long time ago. It fades to nothing under the blaze of my arousal for Nick. How exactly would he command me? What other sensual games would he draw me into with him? I'm shocked at how intensely I want to know. How eagerly I am tempted to follow him wherever he may lead me.

I want you at my complete mercy, he adds. *Anywhere I can have you wrapped around my cock or squirming under my tongue.*

Oh, God. He's killing me. I lick my dry lips and text back my reply. *That certainly leaves things wide open.*

Yes, it does. What about you, Avery? Are you wide open for me right now?

I can almost see the darkly amused curve of his mouth as I read his response. Picturing him on the other end of the line as he sends me dirty texts makes my heart flutter against my rib cage. My clit throbs at a slower, deeper tempo, a dull ache I can't ignore.

Are you as wet for me as I am hard for you right now? he asks.

I am drenched with desire, but the idea that he's equally aroused is fuel to my fire. My breath races as I read his message. My sex is already pulsing and hot, but now it clenches in response to him. What I feel is primal and raw . . . irresistible.

Flushed with embarrassment and more need than I can handle, I glance toward the open door of the coat room. I should end this conversation before it goes any further. My fifteen-minute break is half over. I need to wrap this up soon and get my ass back out on the floor before Joel comes looking for me.

As for Nick, he doesn't know I'm at work bartending and I'm not about to tell him that I lied to him about my job last night. Among other things.

My phone vibrates in my hand with his incoming text. *Don't tell me I'm scaring you away so soon . . .*

I groan as the last shred of my good sense abandons me and I type my reply. *I don't scare that easily.*

His response is immediate. *Good. I'd be disappointed if you did.*

I grin and push up from the chair. I walk to the coat room door and peek out to the bustling restaurant and bar. My legs are shaky and loose from desire, my hands trembling as I reach for the door and pull it closed. I turn the lock—something Joel explicitly prohibits his employees to do—then I settle back in as my phone buzzes in my hand with Nick's incoming message.

You haven't answered my question. Are you wet for me now, Avery?

My finger hovers over the phone's touch screen, but only for a second. *Yes.*

Tell me.

I hesitate, uncertain at first. *I've never done this with*

anyone before.

Even better, he texts back. *Tell me how wet you are.*

My cheeks flush, but my reply is anything but meek. *My pussy's drenched for you. Just like last night. And this morning.*

It takes him a second to come back with a response. *Fuck. Do you know what that does to me?*

Tell me. Two can play this game. Reclining back in the chair, I let my legs relax and part, my hand drifting down between my thighs as I wait for his answer.

My cock is hard as hell. Has been since we started talking here. I'm stroking it now.

Oh my God. A jolt of heat arrows through me at the image he's conjured in my mind. I know what he looks like naked and aroused. I can easily picture his big hand moving up and down the thick shaft . . . palming the broad crown of his gorgeous cock.

My breath slips past my lips on a sigh. *I'm jealous of your hand.*

Then join me.

I catch my lip between my teeth at his instant reply. *Maybe I already am.*

As I send my message, I tell myself I'll only play along for a few minutes. I wasn't lying when I said I'd never done this before. The fact that I'm contemplating doing it at work, with my boss and coworkers and easily a hundred more people just on the other side of the coat room door makes me wonder if I'm losing my damn mind.

I must be, because even while I'm assuring myself I won't let this go too far, I'm popping the button on my black jeans and easing the zipper down to make room for my fingers to slip inside.

Tell me what you're doing. Nick's demand pulses onto my phone's display.

With my free hand, I tap out a brief reply. *Touching myself. Thinking of you.*

Fuck, yeah, he fires back. *I'm there, baby. You feel like silk. Wet. Hot.*

Yes, I confirm, trailing my fingertips into the liquid satin between my legs.

My cock wants inside you, he tells me, fanning my flames with a string of quick replies.

I know how good you feel.

How tight you are.

That sweet, greedy little pussy.

Can feel your slick walls gripping me all the way over here.

Oh, Christ. My breath rushes out of me as I read his provocative words. The teasing flicks of my fingers over my clit and into my heated cleft become more deliberate. I'm appalled at myself for this lack of control, but I can't stop what Nick has started. I shift on the chair, slouching lower and widening the V of my legs to give myself better access. My hips rise and fall in rhythm with my strokes, my body hungry for something more than I can give it alone.

I want him. If Nick was here right now, I'd fuck him without hesitation. Without a care in the world for the fact that my boss and a restaurant full of people are on the other side of the door.

Hell, as hot as I am for him, I'd fuck Nick in front of the whole damn place if it meant easing this unbearable need.

His incoming message pulses again. *So quiet now, Ms. Ross. Are you close? I think you must be.*

My eyes are glued to the phone's display as I rub and

stroke my pussy toward climax. Nick seems to know this. He seems to know instinctively what I need to push me over the edge.

Another string of texts come in and I read them through a bleary gaze as the first tremors of release begin to vibrate deep inside me.

I'm close too, baby.

So fucking hard.

I could drive nails with this cock.

Can you feel it?

Yes. Oh God, yes. My fingers stroke in and out, but it's a poor imitation of what I really want. What I need.

Tell me how you feel, baby.

Tell me how much you want me to fuck you.

So much. I want him here so badly, I whimper with the force of it.

I'm beyond control now. And I'm too lost to my need for release to even think about answering his wicked command. My fingers move faster, more fervently between my folds. Warm cream coats the pads as I rub my wet, swollen clit harder, stroking myself toward the climax that's just out of reach but swiftly roaring up on me.

My phone slides out of my other hand, onto the floor with a soft thud. I don't care. I can't focus on anything except the need Nick has stoked in me. I picture his fingers on me instead of mine. Spreading me open. Massaging my tight little bundle of nerves with ruthless, delicious friction. Penetrating me. Filling me. Hammering into me the way he did back at his penthouse. Making me scream for more.

My head drops back on a low moan. My body goes tense, my spine arched like a bow. As the first wave of orgasm breaks over me, I clench my teeth in a failed effort to hold my cry. Pleasure ripples through every fiber of my being, splitting me open. Shattering me.

"Fuck," I gasp, my fingers plunging deep, wringing every last shudder from the slick, wet channel of my body. My clit is swollen, hypersensitive to the swirling motion of my thumb.

I've never come like this—so fiercely, so shamelessly primal and raw—not even in my loneliest, neediest nights alone.

I'm lost to it . . . so much so, I hardly register the rattling of the doorknob across the room.

When the sound finally breaks through my daze—when the abrupt, powerful rapping of a fist on the locked door carries over the racket of the restaurant and music on the other side—I jerk to attention.

Joel's voice rumbles from outside. "Someone in there? Who locked this goddamn door?"

Shit! I scramble to pull myself together as he jiggles the doorknob again. Clothing straightened, jeans zipped, I adjust my black top and hastily smooth my ponytail back to order.

"Just a second," I call to him as I step around my cold cup of soup on the floor and reach to retrieve my phone from where it fell. "I'll be right out."

A glance at Nick's texts sends renewed heat into my cheeks. Especially the ones I missed while I was busy getting off. I hurriedly tap out a reply. *Sorry, gotta go now.*

You ok?

I giggle, beaming and out of breath. *Great now, thx. Was amazing.*

His answer hits my phone not even a second later. *Gonna make you come so hard next time I see you. Be ready. This was only the beginning.*

The dark promise spirals through me, arrowing right for my still-molten, quivering core. As if my orgasm a moment ago wasn't enough, every nerve ending in my body lights up all over again. I'm ready for whatever Nick has in mind. More than ready.

Damn. I'm in trouble with this man.

I can't contain my grin as I turn off the phone's display and quickly stow it in my employee locker. I head over to the coat room door and open it to find Joel's scowling, corpulent face glaring at me.

"What the hell are you doing in here? And why was this door locked?"

"Sorry," I say, sounding more than a little breathless. I clear my throat in an attempt to mask the small giggle that's bubbling up inside me. "I was, um . . . on a private call."

His beady eyes narrow on me. "Make calls on your own time. Your break ended five minutes ago."

"It did?" My tone sounds glib, but I'm genuinely surprised. And probably less contrite than I should be. "I guess I lost track of the time."

He grunts, disapproval in the flat line of his mouth. "That's all you got to say?"

I shrug. "Pretty much."

His frown deepens. "Well, it just cost you an hour's pay. Now, get back on the clock and get to work. This isn't your private lounge back here."

He pivots and stalks away, full of self-importance. I don't care about his overbearing attitude. Not tonight. I don't even care that I've just lost an hour's wages.

Because what happened in here with Nick?

Totally worth it.

Grinning shamelessly, my body still humming with pleasure, I dump my half-eaten cup of soup in the kitchen then head for the restroom to freshen up before I report back to the bar to finish my shift.

14

The rest of the week passes without any further communication with Nick. I have to admit I'm disappointed I haven't heard from him. After the way we'd left things, I had thought for sure he'd call or text again. And, yes, I've been looking forward to another round of long-distance sex with the man—craving it like the dirty girl I'm evidently becoming now. I want him, whether that's over the phone lines or in person.

Even worse, I miss him. Which is crazy, considering we hardly know each other. Not in real life, anyway.

I may be able to conjure his cerulean blue eyes and handsome, chiseled face without even trying, or reconstruct every strong, muscled inch of his incredible body in my mind, but outside of his bedroom—or the locked back room of my workplace—what I know about Nick Baine is very little.

I could go nosing around on the Internet to satisfy

some of my curiosity, but that's a line I refuse to cross. God knows, I wouldn't want anyone digging through my life, even if most of the records hadn't been sealed by the court years ago. I'd never be able to forgive a violation of my privacy, and I won't do it to Nick either.

I've already surmised the obvious basics about him, anyway. Intelligent. Successful. Wealthy. Far out of my league in more ways than I care to count. Besides, even if I was tempted to creep into his life online, the things I want to know aren't going to be listed on his Wikipedia page or in any article that might turn up on a search engine.

I want to know why a rich, devastatingly gorgeous man—who must be one of the city's most sought-after, eligible bachelors—chooses to live alone in his tower penthouse at the top of the world. I want to know why he wants me, of all the women he could have drooling at the chance to be with him. I want to know how he got the terrible scars on his right hand and arm.

Most of all, I want to know why I see flashes of hauntedness and pain in his eyes in those fleeting moments before he shutters his gaze to me. I want to know why I sense that this powerful man is hiding his own ugly secrets, that he might be just as damaged and afraid as I am.

I doubt I'll ever uncover all of Nick's truths. Maybe I shouldn't even hope that I can.

The fact that he hasn't tried to reach me all week only seems to confirm that just because we've been naked and sweaty together a few times, we're not suddenly going to be a couple.

It's a sanity check I apparently needed. Because whatever is going on between us—the dark, magnetic attraction that drew us together from the moment our eyes first met—it's temporary. It's not part of our daily lives and never can be. I know that. Hell, I'm determined that it won't be.

And yet, I find it takes all of my willpower to resist sending him a quick hello as I head out of our building to meet Margot at the gallery for lunch.

She's not on the main floor when I enter Dominion and greet her perky, brunette assistant.

"Margot's in a portfolio meeting with one of our artists," Jen informs me. "She's running a little late. They should be wrapping up in a few minutes."

I nod. "No problem. I'll just browse on my own until she's ready to go."

An attractive couple speaking to each other in a foreign language are the only other customers on the floor with me. I give them a brief smile as they pass by me on their way to another display. I'm shocked to feel a pang of envy as I watch them holding hands, their fingers laced together, eyes full of adoration as they quietly converse in front of the art.

It doesn't escape my notice when the man's hand drifts to the curve of his companion's backside. He whispers something in her ear and her reply is a low murmur, filled with desire. Will they go home soon and tear each other's clothes off the way Nick and I did? Or will they take their time making love, knowing they have forever in each other's arms? The pang in my chest sharpens, and I decide I really don't want to play this little game after all. Turning away from the couple, I divert my attention with a collection of abstract works on the other side of the gallery.

Although I intend to look at some of the displays I

missed at the party a few nights ago, it doesn't take long before my feet have carried me in front of *Beauty*. She is just as striking and starkly sexual today as she was the other night. Possibly more so, seeing how she was the catalyst for Nick and me leaving together.

Then again, considering the inevitability of our collision and everything that's followed, maybe Beauty was just an innocent bystander.

My lips curve at the thought of that night. My time in Nick's bed. The carnal need for him that's still simmering inside me, and only a single inappropriate thought away at any given moment.

"Dare I hope that smile means you like her?"

The deep male voice that sounds beside me is unfamiliar, but warm as whiskey. The faint traces of an easy, southern drawl only add to the smoky timbre.

I swivel my head and find a thirty-something man as tall and beefy as a linebacker standing next to me at the display. With his shoulder-length mane of luxurious sandy brown hair, his untucked, faded chambray shirt, black jeans and cowboy boots, he's gorgeous in a wind-tossed, rodeo rebel kind of way. A thick, neatly trimmed beard frames his ruggedly handsome, suntanned face and lopsided grin, while molasses-brown eyes hold me in a curious, interested stare.

The full power of which is trained on me.

I get the idea he knows his look works for him because he just stands there, waiting patiently for me to find my tongue.

I blink and clear my throat. "I do. Like it, I mean. It's an amazing piece. You have an incredible talent."

I don't have to ask if he's the unnamed artist who painted it. The look of quiet pride that lights his eyes at my praise is unmistakable. He glances at the canvas and nods thoughtfully. "It helps to have the right inspiration."

"Yes," I agree.

Before I can ask him about the woman in the painting, he pivots to me and extends his hand. "I'm Jared Rush."

"Avery Ross," I reply as he briefly clasps my hand. "Nice to meet you."

His grin is devastating. "You must be Margot's lunch date. Sorry for holding you up."

I shrug. "It's all right. I didn't mind waiting."

"Oh, there you are!" Margot exclaims from across the gallery. She glides over to us and pulls me into a quick hug. "When I didn't find you out front with Jen, I thought we might've missed each other again."

I shake my head. "Just browsing while I waited for you to wrap up with Jared."

Margot's gaze bounces between us in surprise and not a little intrigue. "You know each other?"

"Just met," he says, and I can feel the growing heat of his gaze on me while I pretend not to notice. "Avery was telling me how much she likes the painting."

"Isn't he brilliant?" Margot enthuses. "You should see his other work."

I smile at him. "I imagine it's all incredible."

"Avery's an artist too," Margot announces, much to my chagrin.

"Is that right?"

"Not really," I murmur. "I dabble a bit. I'm still an amateur, especially compared to you."

As I speak, Jared's intense gaze holds me even closer. "If you're interested, I'll bring you out to the Hamptons sometime to see my studio. We can talk process, share our techniques. I think you'd enjoy it."

I have no doubt I would. And I'm quite certain it's not only art techniques he wants to share. While his attention is flattering, the last thing I need to do is complicate my life any more than I already have. Besides, as gorgeous as Jared Rush is—as much as I'm impressed by his talent and dying to know more about his process—there's only one man who's been able to tempt me into his bed in more years than I care to admit, and he's currently a continent away.

Margot tilts her head as she looks between Jared and me. I can see her trying to gauge the situation, but I keep my face schooled to a neutral expression, the mask that's always ready whenever I need it. When my eyes tell her nothing, she looks at Jared. "Would you like to join us for lunch?"

To my relief, he shakes his head. "Can't today, unfortunately. I'm due back in Sagaponack to work. In fact, I'm late. Gotta make use of the daylight when I can."

He leans over and presses a light kiss to Margot's cheek. Then he pivots and holds out his hand to me. We shake again, and his eyes hold my gaze with a sensual promise that would make any woman melt on the spot. Even I'm not completely immune.

"Great to meet you, Avery. Let me know if you want that studio tour. Margot can put you in touch with me anytime."

"Okay." I nod, even though I doubt I'll be taking him up on the offer. "Nice to meet you, Jared."

"Pleasure's all mine." His charming drawl packs an added punch when he flashes me a broad, dimpled grin.

"Hope I see you around again."

As he steps away from us to leave the gallery, Margot gives me a sly smile. "An invitation to his studio? That's a first. I think he likes you."

I slant her a sardonic look. "I've got a feeling he likes a lot of women."

"True," she admits. "But let's face it, when a guy looks like that, who can fault him? Add in his creative talent and success—not to mention the fact that he's a genuinely good man in a city full of sharks—and it's no wonder he's got women practically trampling each other for his attention. If I wasn't happily married, I'd be right there with rest of them. Jared Rush is a bona fide catch."

"I'm sure he is, but I'm not casting my line to find out."

"Well, you could certainly do worse," she gently chides me. "You should seriously consider what he said, Avery. The invitation to visit his studio, if nothing else. He wouldn't have offered if he didn't mean it. Do you realize how many other artists would kill for a chance to study with him? And with Jared's connections in the art world, he might also be able to open doors for your work at other galleries too."

The reminder about my failure at Dominion stings, even though I know it isn't Margot's intent to make me feel bad. She's only trying to help.

"Speaking of potential new connections," she adds, "I'd been hoping to introduce you to some people who were at the gallery party last week, but when I came looking, you were already gone. You didn't even come say goodbye."

I wince inwardly, feeling guilty and awkward about the whole thing now. "I'm sorry. I should've let you or

Jen know that I wasn't staying. I kind of . . . left in a hurry."

She frowns, obviously confused. "Left in a hurry? Why? Did something happen?"

"Um, I guess you could say that." I'm hedging, but until this moment I wasn't even sure I wanted to broach the subject with Margot. She may be my friend, but I'm not sure she's going to appreciate the fact that I went home with one of her customers.

Anyway, I can see it's too late to dance away from the truth now. Margot's shrewd, almond-shaped eyes narrow on me.

"What's this about, Avery? Why did you go?"

"I met someone. At the party." I gesture to the area where we're standing now. "I bumped into him—literally—right here in front of this painting. Turns out, we'd met before. Well, not exactly met, but we'd seen each other a couple of nights earlier. Anyway, we started talking about art and . . . well, other things. Then we decided to leave together."

"Leave together." Margot's brows arch high on her forehead. She lowers her voice to a conspiratorial whisper, even though we're the only two people in this section of the gallery. "Are you telling me you went home with this man? As in, slept with him?"

My sheepish look is evidently enough of an answer.

"No wonder you have no interest in Jared!" Her face lights up with curiosity. "Do I know this mystery man? Tell me more about him. Like his name, for starters."

"Nick," I murmur, and it astonishes me that just the sound of his name on my tongue is enough to make me recall every delicious detail of our conversation that night at the gallery and the hours of skin-on-skin communication that followed at his place. "His name is Nick Baine."

Her smile falters, but it's so subtle I almost miss it. Almost.

"What's wrong?"

"Nothing. I'm sorry, it's just . . ." She lifts her shoulders in a faint shrug. "It's nothing. I mean, I don't think you're asking for my advice, right?"

That is so not what I want to hear. My stomach bottoms out at the cautious way she phrases her reply. The troubled flicker in her gaze doesn't help either.

"So, you're telling me you know Nick?"

"Of course, I know him." Her voice is tentative, trailing off quietly. I spot tenderness in her eyes—the hesitance of a friend who's reluctant to hurt me, yet who can't stand by and watch me stumble. "Avery, I work for Dominic Baine. He owns this gallery."

"Dominion belongs to him?" I hear the wooden quality of my voice. The confusion I'm unable to conceal.

Margot nods. "I'm guessing he didn't tell you that."

"No, he didn't."

I don't know why I should be so surprised. Nick's obviously incredibly wealthy, and well-versed in art. An admirer, so he told me himself. The fact that he would own a gallery shouldn't make my temples pound and my breath constrict in my chest.

And it wouldn't, if he owned any other gallery than this one.

If he wasn't the reason my own pieces were pulled from display to make room for other, more deserving artists. Was he aware of that when we talked in front of *Beauty*? When we fucked most of the night and then again the next morning? Was he only pretending he didn't know damn well who I was?

He's a shrewdly intelligent man. I don't imagine much of anything gets past him. Right now, I can hardly say the same for myself.

Humiliation burns my throat, but being played for a fool is only part of my disappointment. I'm angry too. For letting myself fall so easily into whatever game he thinks he's playing. For letting him draw me so effortlessly into his bed.

Most of all, I'm furious that he's lied to me—whether by omission or evasion. Can I trust anything he's said or done? Now, I'll never be sure.

And yes, I recognize the irony of my outrage. After all, I've given him little more than lies either.

I pull myself out of the dark spiral of my thoughts to glance at Margot. "If I did ask, what kind of advice would you give me about Nick?"

I've caught her off guard. She swallows, then licks her red-glossed lips and slowly shakes her head. "It's not my place," she murmurs. "I'm sorry. I probably shouldn't have said anything at all."

"Margot." I reach out, placing my hand on her shoulder. "What do I need to know about him?"

She holds my stare for a long moment, indecision clouding her deep brown eyes. Finally, she blows out a long sigh. "Just . . . be careful, Avery. That's all. Dominic Baine's not like other men you may know. He's not like Jared."

"In what way?" I need to know, but I'm not sure she'll give me the truth. I can practically feel her discomfort with this turn in the conversation. It's in the wariness of her expression, the hitch of her shallow breaths. "Margot, please. Tell me."

Her mouth compresses and gives a vague shake of her head. "He's damaged, Avery. Deeply. I don't know how or why. I don't think anyone can say they really know him. He doesn't allow it. Anyone I've seen try has been cut loose swiftly and banished from his life without a speck of remorse."

As she speaks, I'm astonished to detect the traces of an old wound in her normally calm and cool gaze. I want to press her about what else she knows about Nick—and how—but I'm not sure I really care to know the answer.

Then she blinks and the illusion of pain I thought I saw in her eyes vanishes. "I just don't want to see you get hurt."

I nod, uncertain what the appropriate response might be to her warning or her intimate insight into Nick, which I can only assume comes from personal experience. How had he hurt Margot? How many others has he cast aside, banished, when they tried to get too close? I feel certain there are many.

Just as I feel certain I will be next, unless I make every effort to steer clear of him.

15

"Hang on, Miss Avery. Let me help you with those."

Manny hurries outside to meet me at the taxi in front of the building. I'm just returning from lunch with Margot, bringing my paintings along with me in the backseat of the cab. The four pieces are crated and stacked against one another on the seat. As I work to pull the awkward cartons out by myself, he wheels a chrome-finished dolly out and moves close to assist.

"It's okay, Manny. I can handle it."

"I'm sure you can, Miss." He lightly taps my shoulder. "Please, allow me."

Although I'm more comfortable doing things for myself, he's such a kind man, refusing his help almost seems like an insult, so I step aside.

"All right, then. But please be careful with them."

"Of course," he assures me.

Although he's not young, he's stronger than he

looks. I pay the driver, then watch Manny gently lift each bulky package out of the vehicle with smooth, steady arms. As he sets the last carton on the dolly, I notice him glancing at the Dominion Gallery logo on the crates Margot gave me for transporting my pieces.

"Been doing a little shopping, have ya?"

I practically laugh at the idea that I could afford to buy art, especially from a gallery as exclusive as Dominion. *Nick's gallery,* I silently amend. The reminder of my conversation with Margot puts a bitter taste in my mouth. "No shopping today. I'm just bringing a few things home that belong to me."

"No kidding?" The doorman's eyes brighten with genuine delight. "You're a professional artist, Miss Avery?"

Maybe because it's Manny—because I feel safe with him, secure, in a way I rarely do with men in general—I don't try to deny the one thing that's always given me such joy. I don't feel the need to justify myself to him, not even when he's wheeling my rejected work ahead of me into the building.

"I paint a bit. It's something I've loved doing since I was a kid."

"Well, that's just terrific," he enthuses as we cross the lobby together, heading for the elevators. "What kind of things do you paint?"

"Landscapes and cityscapes, mostly. A still life, here and there. I've done some portraiture, but I had to give it up." I shrug. "No matter how hard I try, I can never get faces to look real enough."

Manny chuckles. "Tell that to Picasso."

I smile as he gestures for me to step into the open elevator ahead of him. He follows me inside with the dolly and presses the button for the fifth floor. As the car begins to ascend, he indicates the cartons holding my art.

"So, what kinds of paintings are these?"

"Oh, just a few scenes from around the city." I dismiss his interest with a small smile. "Nothing special."

"Special enough to be in Mr. Baine's gallery. I'd say that's far better than most."

I wince internally. The doorman knows Nick owns the gallery? Oh, God. Does he also know I spent the night in Nick's penthouse last week?

I glance up to the small security camera mounted in the corner of the elevator car and can hardly suppress my groan of mortification. Although the one Nick and I took from the garage was a private car, it's too much to hope that it isn't equipped with the same kind of security equipment as this one.

Wonderful. As if my day hasn't been humiliating and awkward enough. My only saving grace is the fact that Nick isn't here to witness me schlepping my crates through the building right now too. I consider everything Margot said about him—and the fact that he played me that night, letting me believe he was only at the gallery as a customer. Seducing me with all of his talk about passion and pain and the pleasure of being reckless.

I imagine him in London these past several days, chuckling at my idiocy—at how easily my legs fell open for him—and it makes my blood boil with outrage. I burn with disappointment, too, but that's harder for me to acknowledge. I don't want to feel hurt where Nick Baine is concerned. I don't want to admit, even to myself, that he has the power to wound me. That would really make me his fool.

"A friend of mine manages the gallery," I tell Manny, dismissing his well-meaning, but grossly misplaced praise. "The only reason I was there was because she helped me get in. Unfortunately, Mr. Baine has decided to award my space to some better artists."

"Oh." Manny's bushy brows furrow with his frown. Obviously embarrassed for me, he averts his gaze and shifts on his polished shoes as we wait for the elevator to climb. "Well, I'm sure you'll do just fine somewhere else," he says. "After all, plenty of other galleries in the city, right?"

I force a smile. "Sure."

"That's right." He nods his head as if hoping to convince me. "You know, a lot of people pass my way every day. Thousands of 'em. I see good folks, and the not so good. After a while, you learn to spot who's who pretty quick. Like you, for instance."

I stare at him, half in curiosity, half terrified of what he might say.

"I've had you pegged right off the bat."

"You have?"

"Yes, ma'am, I have. You're one of the good ones. Got a feeling maybe no one's told you that often enough, but if you don't mind me saying, I think you need to hear it today." His mouth curves warmly, and he reaches out to lightly pat my shoulder. "You're a good person, Avery. You need to remember that, no matter what life hands you."

I'm silent, taken aback. I don't know what to say. Words clog my throat along with my breath, but it's not because of the weight of his kindness.

It's because he's wrong.

I'm not one of the good ones.

If he knew anything about me—about my past, about where I've come from—he wouldn't think so either.

It takes some effort to find my voice. When I finally do, it comes out quiet, a thready whisper. "Thank you for saying that, Manny."

Before his tender gaze can see through me, I glance away from him. I stare straight ahead as we ride the rest of the way to the fifth floor. In the hammered steel of the elevator doors, my reflection stares back at me, a blurred and distorted mask.

~ ~ ~

I'm getting dressed for my evening shift at Vendange when my cell phone rings. Cursing, stumbling out of the massive walk-in closet in just my half-buttoned black work shirt and underwear, I dash for the living room where I dropped my purse on my way in earlier this afternoon.

Although I'm not anticipating that Nick might call—more accurately, I'm convinced that he won't—I still race for my phone as if I'm running a marathon. My mind swirls with a dozen cutting things to say to him, all of the icy responses I've been rehearsing since my lunch meeting with Margot.

But it's not Nick calling.

Of course, it's not. The bastard probably deleted my number by now.

Some of my anger fizzles out as I register the Pennsylvania area code on the display. I've already spoken with my mother this morning. It's rare that she's allowed to call more than once a day. Practically unheard of. Something must be wrong.

Alarm jolts through me as I swipe to answer. "Mom?" The automated collect call message talks past my rushed greeting. Anxiety spiking, I wait for it to finish. "Yes, I accept. Mom? Hello, are you there?"

"I'm here honey." Her voice sounds thin, a little weary, but that's nothing unusual the past couple of years. "Am I calling at a bad time?"

"No, you're not." I wedge the phone between my ear and shoulder as I fasten the rest of the buttons on my shirt. "What's going on? Is everything all right?"

"Oh, yes. Everything's fine, sweetheart."

"What's up, then? Why are you calling again today?"

"Mr. Stadler came to see me a little while ago."

I frown at the mention of the public defender handling her case. "What did he want? Has there been any progress on your appeal?"

"Nothing yet on that, sweetheart. But he's working on it."

I refrain from pointing out that Stadler's been working on her appeals ever since the state sent her away. All we've seen is one roadblock after another. Honestly, I don't know where my mother gets her patience. Maybe she's eternally optimistic. Or maybe, in order to survive where she is for the past nine years, she's had to give up any hope that she might ever see her conviction overturned or her sentence reduced.

I hate that I can't do anything to help. I hate that she's in a cage two-hundred miles away from me and I can't see her face. I haven't hugged her in more than a year.

I hate that the woman I love more than anyone else

on this planet has been labeled a monster by the judicial system. A killer who shot her husband—my drunk of a stepfather—dead in cold blood.

It's not like she denied it. My sweet, loving mother had shocked everyone in the court, including me, when she pleaded guilty to first-degree murder.

"We don't have word on the appeal, Avery, but Mr. Stadler did have some other news."

Her soft voice breaks into my thoughts. I hear something odd in her tone now. Something light. Is it . . . excitement?

"What kind of news? What's going on?"

"We got the parole board interview."

Elation soars through me. "Momma, that's wonderful! When?"

"Mr. Stadler says it could be as early as next week. Probably sooner."

"I want to be there."

I hear her soft inhale. "Honey, I don't think that's a good idea—"

"I want to be with you, Momma. I need to be."

Even as I say it, I know what her answer will be. I can sense it coming in her tender sigh on the other end of the line.

"Avery, I don't want you to come." Her denial is heavy in her prolonged silence, and I know her heart is breaking as much as mine. "I don't want you here for any of this. You know how I feel about that."

I say nothing, all of my arguments dying on the tip of my tongue. From day one, she's insisted on fighting this battle alone. As a sixteen year old girl, I was too terrified and weak to stand by her. Now, I'm a twenty-five year old woman who can't do a damn thing to save her.

"Avery, honey. Tell me you understand."

I shake my head mutely, wishing things were different.

Missing her like the scared, uncertain girl I was back then.

"Yes, Momma," I finally agree. "I understand."

16

Hello, beautiful.

The text message hits my phone as I disembark from a Sunday morning subway at the Flushing station in Queens. I'm heading out today for the 10:30 A.M. baptism of Tasha's baby girl, followed by a small gathering at their house.

I was in a cheerful, upbeat mood when I left the apartment an hour ago—happy to be outside on the gloriously warm, early May morning and to have an excuse to wear something other than bartending clothes or the oversized T-shirts and sweatpants I tend to live in when I'm off work.

As I begin walking the couple of blocks to the church in my pale gray dress and heels, I glance down at Nick's unexpected message and feel my joy leech away. In its place is a spike of disbelief and a slow-simmering annoyance.

Is he for real?

Does he actually think I've been sitting around all this time, waiting for him to get in touch? Or is he trying to line up his stateside conquests now that his two weeks in London have passed?

The arrogant prick.

I roll my eyes and toss the phone back in my handbag, determined to ignore him.

The chime of another incoming text sounds only a minute or two later.

Don't look. Don't even think of looking, I command myself. And yet in spite of my own dignity and better judgment, I retrieve the phone again and swipe the screen lock open.

You there? Got you on my mind in a bad way.

"Oh, please." I stop in my tracks on the sidewalk and glare at my phone. Because I'm thoroughly pissed off and can't help myself, I tap out a scathing reply.

Why? Have you already run through all the available women in London?

I hit SEND and resume my walk, hoping my digital fury will be enough to shut him down and end this farce right here and now.

My phone starts ringing immediately.

Dammit.

I know I should just let it go to voicemail. I should pretend Dominic Baine no longer exists and carry on with my life, such as it is.

Instead, my feet slow to a halt. I curse under my breath and angrily swipe to answer.

"I really don't have time for this, *Mr. Baine.*" I lean heavily on his name, not even trying to sound cordial.

He's silent for a second and I know I've caught him off guard. "You're upset. Tell me why."

No greeting, only a demand. Clipped and direct with concern.

God, I've forgotten how velvety dark his voice sounds. It caresses my ear, strokes my senses. If I wasn't so stung and infuriated, I might not be able to repress the quickening response of my body to his deep, masculine growl. But I bite it back, clamping my molars together in sullen silence as he tries to understand my change of attitude.

"Avery, what the hell is going on?"

"You tell me."

"You're angry with me."

"How brilliant of you to notice."

"Because I haven't been in touch until now." Not a question, but a self-assured statement of fact.

I practically snort in reply. "I'm sure you'd like to think so."

It's amazing how convincing that sounds, even to my own ears. Until I'd spoken to Margot, I actually *had* been upset that he hadn't called or texted. Now that he's on the other end of the line, I can't wait to end this conversation with him and erase the night we spent together from my mind.

"If you think you need to explain or make excuses, Nick, trust me—you don't."

"I don't do anything because I think I have to," he says, somewhat sternly. "That's not how I operate."

I can't say I'm surprised to hear him admit that. "What *do* you want, Nick?"

"I'd have thought my text made that clear enough. You've been on my mind, Ms. Ross. Ever since our very stimulating conversation the other day. In fact, I've thought of little else since."

Just the mention of what we did together via text makes my body quicken in vivid remembrance. I close my eyes and release a pent-up sigh. "You know what? I can't do this with you. Not right now." Not ever again, I vow, and I'm almost desperate enough to believe I actually mean it. "I'm busy, Nick. I have somewhere I need to be and—"

"So early? And on a Sunday besides?" He asks it almost conversationally, but I can hear the seriousness in his tone. "Where are you going?"

"I don't see how that's any interest of yours."

"And yet it is," he says, unfazed. "Everything about you interests me, Avery."

God help me, but the way he says my name in that deep voice of his is working its dark magic on me all over again. I should be incensed at his arrogance and offended that he evidently thinks I'm idiot enough to buy what I'm certain is nothing more than a line. Instead, I stand mutely on the sidewalk, all of my anger clogged up in my throat.

When my silence stretches out for a long moment, Nick fills the quiet. "It wasn't my intent not to contact you these past couple of weeks. Unfortunately, things got in the way. It couldn't be helped."

I tell myself that whatever game he's playing, I'm not going to be party to it. Real or not, I don't need his attempts to soothe my anger. I don't need his consideration. But there is a sober quality to his voice that makes me keep my claws sheathed. At least, for now.

"The day I texted you, I had to leave for Dubai to finalize an acquisition," he says. "In fact, I only got back to London less than an hour ago."

"Oh." I try not to acknowledge the idea that he's reaching out to me so soon after his return. For all I know, he's probably lying. He could be, except I hear a sincerity in his words. There's a faint heaviness in his slow exhalation and in his voice I hear what sounds like genuine weariness. Possibly something deeper.

"The deal dragged out longer than anticipated. It was complicated . . . unpleasant. They tend to be, when one side has its back against the wall."

I don't need to ask if he's talking about his own back. I'm sure Nick conducts his business the same way he does his pleasure, and I can't imagine he ever finds himself in a position of weakness, no matter what he does. Or with whom.

I realize I'm stopped in the middle of the sidewalk as I listen to him. Moving to the side of the concrete walkway, I let a group of people step by me and wait for Nick to tell me more. As much as I want to deny that I care what he has to say, I'm curious.

And yes, there's a part of me that's concerned for what he went through while he's been gone. If that makes me an even bigger fool now, so be it.

"What happened in Dubai?"

"I'd been negotiating to purchase a property I've had my eye on for several years. A landmark hotel in a prime location. The family who owned it for three generations fell on hard times and was eager to sell. Most of them, that is. We had the signoff from four of the shareholders, but the last one—their grandfather—had been stalling the deal from day one. Since he held controlling interest at fifty-one percent, nothing was going through until we moved the old man to our side."

Luxury hotels. Jetting off to conduct real estate

business deals in London and Dubai. Nick mentions these things as if they're all par for the course for him on any given day. I've never been outside the States, let alone somewhere as far-flung and foreign as the Middle East. As for the kind of money Nick's talking about, I can't even begin to imagine. If I'd been trying to guess at the level of his wealth before, now I'm all but certain it has to start with a "b."

"I take it the deal didn't go as you hoped."

"No. Not quite." I hear the rasp of his hand scrubbing over his jaw. "The old fool had too much pride for his own good. He couldn't admit to his family's mismanagement of their fortune. Because of his blinders, the hotel was suffering too. It was headed for bankruptcy long before I set my sights on acquiring it, but he couldn't be convinced it was time to let go."

As he speaks, my anger toward him slips a bit from my grasp. I distantly note how the city continues to pulse around me—cars and taxis and buses roaring by on the street, groups of chattering people strolling past on the sidewalk—yet all of my focus is trained on Nick and the darkening tone of his voice. He is all I hear. He's all I can feel as I wait for him to tell me the rest.

"I suppose it should've been a clue when he abruptly phoned my team in London to say he was ready to be done with the whole ordeal. Hell, in retrospect, maybe I did know where things were heading." He blows out a short exhalation, a vague laugh devoid of humor. "The old man insisted that we meet at the hotel in Dubai, in his penthouse suite. When my team and I arrived, he was outside on the terrace that overlooks the gulf. He'd been drinking. He demanded that he and I talk privately out there, away from his traitorous grandchildren and the two teams of lawyers."

I don't say a word. I'm not sure I'm capable at the moment. My breath is trapped in my lungs, my heart pounding in dread for what's coming next.

Nick goes on, his voice level, inscrutable. "I knew immediately that he hadn't called us there to wrap up the deal. He had a different agenda. What he wanted was to tell me to my face to go to hell. So, he did. He said he'd rather die than sell a piece of his soul to someone like me. Then he lunged for the terrace railing and leapt off the building."

"Oh, my God." My hand flies to my slack mouth in horror. "Nick, how awful."

"His family was inconsolable, naturally. Everyone was in shock over what he'd done."

"I'm sorry," I murmur. "I'm sorry you had to be there to witness something like that. I'm sorry for the terrible things he said to you."

He grunts in acknowledgment. "It wasn't the way I'd have preferred to close the deal, but sometimes things don't go the way you plan."

"Wait. What?" My brow pinches as I register what he's telling me. "You still went ahead with the deal to buy the hotel?"

"Yes," he says matter-of-factly. "After an appropriate delay for the family to mourn and organize his legal affairs. We finalized the sale last night."

I gasp at the level of his apparent detachment, although I'm not sure why I should feel so shocked. "Nick, that man killed himself. In front of you, no less."

"Yes, he did. It's not as though I pushed him." He goes silent and I wonder if I've struck a nerve. After a long moment, he clears his throat. "It's just business,

Avery."

"Right. Just business," I say quietly, as something Nick said to me that first night at the gallery skates across my memory. "And when you see something you want, you reach for it."

My crisp reminder of his own admission doesn't escape him. "Does that bother you?"

"What bothers me is being made to feel like a fool. Why didn't you tell me you own the gallery?"

He doesn't miss a beat. "You've been talking with Margot."

"She's my friend, Nick. Do you know how stupid I felt when I told her I'd met someone that night—that I'd slept with you—only to find out you'd already been with her too?"

"She told you that?" He sounds displeased, his deep voice lowering to somewhere near a growl.

"Not in so many words, but then, I don't hear you denying it." He goes silent and my head fills with steam again. "She told me you were damaged. That you hurt anyone who gets too close to you, that you cut them loose. She warned me to stay away from you."

He chuckles, but there's little humor in it. "I met Margot Chan four years ago, before she came to the gallery and before she married David Levine. We had a brief affair, nothing more. I realized it was a mistake, and it ended as abruptly as it began."

"Why?" I demand. "How come you ended things with her?"

"I decided I'd rather have her managing my gallery than warming my bed."

I want to believe him. Since Margot still manages to work with him, he can't be all bad. Still, her caution that he isn't like other men I might know—the implication that he is somehow dangerous—keeps my protective walls in place. I've been wounded before. I've been damaged in ways I can never speak of, least of all to this man.

"Why didn't you tell me Dominion is your gallery?"

"Why does it matter to you that I own the place?"

I suck in a sharp breath. "You had my art removed only a few days before that. You told Margot my work wasn't good enough to be in your gallery, yet that didn't stop you from fucking me the first chance you got."

"Your art *isn't* good enough, Avery. Maybe one day it will be," he replies evenly. "But none of that has anything to do with what's going on between us now."

"Like hell it doesn't!" A pair of elderly women dressed in their Sunday best turn sharp looks on me as they pass, and I realize my voice is climbing with my outrage. I dial it back, glancing at them apologetically before unleashing my anger on Nick in a tight whisper. "You lied to me. You could've told me the truth, but you didn't. What else will you lie to me about?"

"And when I asked if you were an artist, you could've told me you had paintings in the gallery at one time. What else are you hiding from me?"

A flood of secrets and lies crowd my conscience in the seconds I remain mute. I shake my head and release a long breath. "This is a bad idea. I thought it was from the beginning, but now I know for sure. I can't do this, Nick. Please, don't call me again."

He grinds out a low curse. "I'll be back in New York in a few days. We can talk about this some more when I see you."

"No," I murmur. "I don't want to talk."

"Then we won't talk. I can think of far better things we could be doing together."

"Nick, I'm serious—"

"So am I, Avery. I've upset you, and I'm sorry." His voice is solemn, a deep rumble that caresses my senses. "As for that night, your art and my gallery had nothing to do with what happened between us. We fucked because we both wanted it. We'll do it again because that's what we both want."

I wish I could deny it. Every fiber of my being tells me this is my chance to halt what can only turn out to be a massive mistake. I don't have room in my life for Dominic Baine or the complicated twist of emotions that he stirs in me.

And the desire.

I shouldn't give that room in my life either.

But it's there, just as he says.

I want him, even now.

"I have to go," I murmur. "My friend's daughter is being baptized this morning. I only have a few minutes to walk the rest of the way to St. Michael's for the mass."

"St. Michael's on 99th?"

"No, in Queens." I glance at the time on my phone and wince. "I really have to go now."

"Okay," he relents, but I can hear his reluctance to release me. "And Avery?"

"Yes?"

"I'll see you when I get back to the city."

I don't reply. There's no need to say the words. I end our call, then close my eyes on a soft curse, too well aware of my own need for this man to even think I'll be able to deny him.

17

Tasha's home is small and cramped, her family large and boisterous. The chattering, happy crowd of thirty-plus aunts, uncles, and cousins of varying ages fills the first-floor kitchen and living room of the little duplex. In the hour or so following Zoe's baptism, the women have served up a potluck buffet big enough to feed an entire neighborhood, and the men are clustered around, balancing paper plates in one hand, beers in the other, while they talk sports and argue over rival teams.

It's a comfortable warmth—a palpable sense of love and security—that I can't help but envy a little.

As I weave through the guests and return to the food-laden buffet table, I smile at a shy little girl with big doe eyes and dark brown pigtails who peeks at me from behind her mama's legs. I put my finger against my lips and wink conspiratorially before helping myself to a second piece of chocolate sheet cake. She's enjoyed some recently, too, as evidenced by the rainbow ring of frosting still clinging to the corners of her cherub mouth.

"Are you having a good time?" Tasha appears from behind me, looking radiant in her cream-colored dress from church and her mane of spiral curls swept off her face in a pretty updo.

"Are you kidding? I'm having a great time." I hold up my plate. "This cake is amazing."

"I know, right? My mother-in-law is friends with one of the ladies who bakes at Martha's in Forest Hills." As Tasha talks to me, she waves at some more guests who've just arrived. "Sorry to abandon you to my family after we got back from the church. Zoe needed some mommy time after all of that activity this morning. Hopefully, she'll sleep for a while, so I can get something to eat now."

She reaches for a plate and begins filling it with slices of spiral-cut ham, green beans, and several dollops of the assorted noodle and potato salads.

"I didn't mind hanging out with your family," I tell her, forking a big bite of cake into my mouth. "Everyone is so nice. I've been having a lot of fun chatting with your cousins and especially your aunts, Mary and Rosa. I also met your uncle, Jerry."

Tasha slants me a glance. "Tell me he didn't bore you with his dissertation on homemade wine-making."

"Yeah, he did mention it, actually." I smile, having endured a full thirty minutes of the old man's apparent devotion to the art and craft of kitchen-table fermenting. "From what he tells me, he makes a mean cabernet."

She laughs. "Oh, it's mean, all right. Trust me. Wine-making has become Uncle Jerry's obsession since he retired a few years ago. The bad thing is, he's even got

Antonio experimenting with home-brewing. Except Tony's been playing around with beer, not wine. For the record, I don't recommend either one."

"Hey, I heard that!" Antonio calls out from within a group of young men standing on the other side of the crowded kitchen. Tasha's linebacker-sized husband is holding a dark brown bottle in his hand. He raises it in mock salute to us, then points at the homemade label. "Don't knock it 'til you try it. You want me to grab you a cold one, Avery?"

Tasha shakes her head at me. "Believe me, you don't."

"Maybe later," I tell him, laughing as he gives me a thumbs-up then goes back to talking with his companions.

"Hey, Tasha." Another of her relatives—one of her many cousins—comes into the kitchen from the back door. He's holding a massive floral arrangement in his arms. An explosion of white and pink roses, freesia, and half a dozen other types of fragrant white and blush flowers and glossy greenery overflow the big vase. "You got somewhere you want me to put this for ya?"

"Oh, that's right. The bouquet from the church. Thanks for bringing it home for me, Robbie." When he nods, she sets down her plate and walks over to an antique sideboard in the open concept dining room, clearing a place for the arrangement. "Put it here, please. I want to be able to enjoy it from wherever I look."

I follow her over to admire the enormous bouquet as her cousin departs. "It's stunning." My nose fills with the incredible scent of the blooms. "And it smells like heaven."

"Doesn't it? God, it must've cost a fortune," she

murmurs, lifting one of the roses toward her face and inhaling deeply. "I wonder who sent them."

"Wasn't there a card with it?"

"Nope. No card. No envelope. Nothing." My instincts prickle at that. She lets go of the flower and gently straightens some of the greenery. "When I saw it at the church, I assumed they provided it for the mass, but Father William told me it had arrived just before we began. A mystery gift, apparently."

No way. I feel my head slowly shaking as I recall Nick pressing me for where I was going. Had he actually sent such a generous, thoughtful gift to my friend? Someone he'd never even met? I'm surprised to think so. More than that, I'm touched.

Tasha glances over at me and frowns. "What's that little smile about, Avery? You didn't send these, did you?"

"No." I shake my head more vigorously. "I wish I could say it was me, but no. I could never afford something this extravagant. Now I know why he asked me which church."

Her eyes widen. "You mean, *he* sent them? Dominic-the prick-Baine?"

She's taken to calling Nick that from the moment I told her about my talk with Margot. At the time, I'd agreed. Now, I feel obligated to defend him—at least, a little. "You have to admit, it was a nice thing for him to do. God, I can't believe he was able to get flowers delivered so quickly after we talked."

Then again, nothing is impossible if you have enough money. Or if you're Dominic Baine.

"Okay, hold on one damn second." Tasha fists her hands on her hips. "Back up, girl. Yes, the flowers are amazing, even considering the source. *I suppose.* But does this mean you're actually on speaking terms with him? As in, you spoke with him as recently as this morning?"

"He texted me from London while I was on my way to the baptism. I sent him a pissy response, and the next thing I knew, he was calling me. I wasn't going to pick up, but I knew he wouldn't quit until he reached me. So we just . . . started talking."

She arches a brow at me. "What the hell happened to 'he's a player and a liar and I never want to see him again'?"

I sigh in the face of my defeat. "It's a long story."

"Are you back together with him?"

Am I? I'm not even sure we were ever together. Not in any meaningful sense of the word—unless great sex counts for something.

The way my body quickens at the thought of him, it's hard to argue that it doesn't count. And, to be fair, the sex I had with Nick far surpassed *great.*

"I don't know what's going on with us," I admit. "I told him I didn't want to see him again. I let him know I was pissed as hell that he didn't tell me he owns Dominion. I even told him I knew he'd slept with Margot before."

"So, what did he have to say for himself?"

"He said none of it had anything to do with us."

We fucked because we both wanted it.

We'll do it again because that's what we both want.

His words chase through me like a lick of fire through my veins. I press my lips together and meet Tasha's expectant gaze. "He said he wants to see me again when he gets back to New York."

"Mm-hm. I'll bet he does. And what about you? Do

you want to see him again?"

"I don't know. Yeah, maybe I do." I hedge, shrugging my shoulders. "I really shouldn't . . ."

"No, you shouldn't. But how often does any woman do the things she should when it comes to a man she can't resist?"

At that precise moment, Antonio swaggers up to us. "Talkin' about me again, I see." He flashes his wife a devilish grin and pulls her under the wing of his beefy arm. "Got this one right where I want her," he tells me. "She never could resist me. But I mean, really. Who could—am I right?"

"You're such an ass," she says, laughing as she smacks his broad chest lightheartedly.

Their affection for each other is unmistakable. They don't try to hide it. Antonio bends his head to give her a sweet kiss. I watch a private look flicker through their locked eyes, and some of the envy I felt for Tasha's big, loving family morphs into another shade of longing.

Will I ever have this with someone? Not with Nick—I'm not naive enough to think we're heading for anything long term. Still, I can't quell the pang of yearning I feel as I watch Tasha and her husband.

"Hey, Avery," Antonio says after a moment, dragging his gaze away from his wife. "Check it out. You ready to sample one of my best brews?"

He raises the hand that's not wrapped around Tasha and I see he's holding an unopened bottle of homemade beer.

Tasha frowns. "Oh, for God's sake, Tony. Don't make her drink that—"

"Whatta ya mean? I've been perfecting this recipe for a month now. It's damn good," he says. "Go on, Avery, you be the judge. Give it a try."

Undaunted, he thrusts the dark brown bottle out to me, then pulls an opener out of the back pocket of his jeans. Before I can decide one way or the other if I want it, he pops the cap off the bottle and nods for me to take a drink.

"I'm sure it's not that bad," I offer optimistically, lifting the bottle to my lips and tip it back.

And no, it's not bad. It's completely awful. The bitter tang courses sharply over my taste buds like a hop-flavored mouthful of turpentine. The second it hits my tongue, I start coughing. My throat muscles contract, but I force myself to swallow the sip of so-called beer.

"See?" Tasha says while I wheeze and cough. "She hates it, Tony."

He looks crushed. "You don't like it?"

My eyes are watering. My esophagus feels like scorched pavement. "It's um . . . a bit strong."

"Look at the poor girl. She's about to keel over." Tasha grabs the bottle out of my slack grasp and pushes it back into her husband's hand. "Avery and I were talking about very important things before you rudely attempted to poison her. Go on, let us chat. And take this swill with you."

Antonio lifts his bulky shoulders. "Okay, more beer for me." He takes a big swig of the bottle. Evidently, he's built up a tolerance because he doesn't even wince as he swallows the awful stuff, then heads back over to his friends across the room.

Tasha shakes her head at me apologetically as another cough seizes my throat. "I tried to warn you. Are you all right?"

"Yeah," I croak. "Fine."

Now that we're alone in our little corner of the gathering—and now that I can breathe somewhat normally again—Tasha crosses her arms over her breasts and gives me a sly look. "So, I believe you were about to tell me how a certain flower-gifting, truth-omitting, probably no-good-player managed to convince you to see him again. Aside from obvious reasons, that is—and I will concede there are many."

"Yes, there are." I bite my lip, but it doesn't suppress my smile as I start listing Nick's numerous attributes. "Gorgeous. Smart. Intriguing. Powerful. Absolutely amazing in bed."

"You forgot rich as a Rockefeller," Tasha adds drolly. "I mean, even I have to admit a guy like Dominic Baine is attractive enough without all of his money. What does someone do with a net worth of two-point-four billion, anyway?"

Two-point-four? I feel my throat close up again, but it has nothing to do with Antonio's terrible beer. Could Nick actually be so wealthy? And the fact that Tasha names such a specific figure makes me tilt my head in question. "How do you know what he's worth?"

"It was in a Forbes article I found on him."

"You looked Nick up on the Internet?" I'm mortified. "Tasha! You didn't."

"Of course, I did. What kind of friend would I be if I didn't give this guy a thorough Googling?"

I gape at her. "That's just . . . wrong. It's invasive."

She pushes out a dramatic sigh. "Well, it's not like I found much, anyway."

Although I don't want to condone her snooping, it's nearly impossible to keep my curiosity in line with my principles now. "What do you mean, you didn't find much?"

"I mean, aside from estimates of his net worth over the past ten years and a handful of high profile acquisitions that Baine International has on public record, Dominic Xavier Baine appears to be a closed book."

His full name is a prize on its own—a morsel of information I'm only learning for the first time now. Nick's full name is elegant and dark and mysterious, like the man himself. The syllables slide through my senses and I savor them as I would any stolen sweet.

"They say he hates publicity of any kind," Tasha continues. "One magazine interviewer even called him the 'shadow mogul' because of how elusive he is with the media. He keeps his business dealings far under the radar and no one seems to know much about him personally either, aside from the official bio stuff on record with his firm's website. That's practically a miracle by itself in this day and age. While the majority of his fellow bazillionaires never met a camera or headline they didn't love, the most anyone can say about your Mr. Baine is that the man is an enigma."

I absorb this new insight in silence. I sensed from the beginning that Nick was intensely private, even secretive. Now that feeling settles over me with more weight than I care to examine.

I didn't want to get nosy about him or his personal life. The fact that he's taken steps to keep himself out of the spotlight—despite his significant success and wealth—shouldn't bother me.

It shouldn't matter that he is damaged and solitary, as Margot has warned me. Or that he is elusive and protective of his secrets—whatever they may be—as

Tasha's revelations seem to imply. But yet, it does.

All of these things trouble me deeply.

Because I have enough secrets for both of us.

18

I step back from my easel, frowning as I tilt my head to assess my work in the soft peach light of sunrise. I'm set up in the living room of Claire's apartment, a rumpled sea of paint-stained, thrift-store sheets spread out over the floor beneath my bare feet and the unfinished cityscape I just can't seem to get right no matter how hard I try.

Clipped to the top of my easel is the photograph I've been struggling to bring to life on the canvas. My scowl deepens as I stare at the sallow light and lifeless lines of my painting. Maybe Nick is right. My art isn't good enough. Not for his gallery, or anyone else's.

As if in evidence of that fact, I spot an errant shadow on one of the brownstones I've meticulously painted today. I move back to the painting to correct it, but my fiddling only makes the problem worse.

"Dammit."

I've spent weeks trying to perfect this piece. Now

I'm tempted to trash the whole thing. Before I let myself give in to that urge, I toss my brush down in frustration and head into the kitchen to forage for breakfast.

It's barely eight in the morning, although I've been awake for hours. After spending yesterday at Tasha's house, last night I went to bed restless, my mind crowded with a thousand distracting thoughts. Many of them having to do with Nick.

I can't pretend that Tasha's Internet digging into his life doesn't bother me. Not only because she did it without asking, but also because the information she uncovered—sparse as it was—has spawned an unwanted, but nagging curiosity in me.

Curiosity and caution, both in equal measure.

I want to know more about him. If I'm being honest with myself, I want to know everything about Dominic Xavier Baine.

The fact that he shared what he went through in Dubai carries new weight today, now that I'm aware of his reputation for privacy in both his business and personal lives. I feel special that he confided in me, that he trusted me. He didn't have to do it. He didn't have to explain himself to me at all, and yet he did.

I don't do anything because I think I have to, he'd said.

And no, I don't suppose he does.

But there is more to Nick than simple elusiveness or strict discretion. I sense it the same way all wounded things are able to recognize the scars carried by others. He's enigmatic for a reason. He's forbidding because there is safety in isolation. It doesn't take billions of dollars or a penthouse mansion to learn those lessons in life.

Whatever is in Nick's past—whatever walls he's built

around himself now to protect him in the present—it is his own to contend with. I don't belong there. No more than he belongs in mine.

I drop a slice of multigrain bread in the toaster, then pour myself the last of the tepid coffee I brewed several hours ago. After stirring in some cream and sugar, I lean my elbows on the white marble countertop and flip open my tablet to check the weather for my commute to Vendange later today. I groan. Cloudy with heavy rain in the evening. Wonderful. Bad weather usually means a slower night for tips.

My toast pops and I pivot to retrieve it. Munching on a corner of the dry bread, I return to my tablet and start to close down the browser.

I mean to close it. But all of my thinking about Nick and the scars we both carry rakes open an old wound inside me too. My finger hovers over the search bar.

Don't do it.

My hand trembles, and, for an instant, I almost lose my nerve.

Don't do it. Don't open that door again. After all, there's no need to look. I already know what I'll find at the end of that long, dark hallway.

"Don't . . ."

The sound of my own voice startles me. But not even the warning spoken out loud dissuades me now. With the toast caught between my teeth, I use both hands to slowly type a name into the search engine.

Martin Edward Coyle.

The page fills with search results—most of them dated after my mother's arrest. I see her name listed in nearly every record. And in all of those mentions of my beautiful, kind, and loving mother, she is described primarily by her crime. As if her conviction has become an appendage of her entire identity.

Brenda Leigh Coyle, charged with the shooting death of her husband in their home on the afternoon of August 21 . . .

Brenda Leigh Coyle, who confessed to the brutal killing of her husband, Martin . . .

Brenda Leigh Coyle, now serving a life sentence after pleading guilty to premeditated murder . . .

More than a few of the articles depict my stepfather as an innocent victim. Online obituaries written by his relatives and well-meaning church members praise him for his strong work ethic and his commitment to the community. Those are the ones that nauseate me the most. None of them tell the real story of who he was. None of them shine a light on the kind of monster he was behind closed doors.

The fact that I didn't turn a spotlight on his true nature myself when I had the chance is a regret I'll carry with me forever.

It might have saved my mother, if she had only let me testify.

If she had only let the case go before a jury instead of pleading guilty to avoid a trial, I might have been able to spare both of us the pain of these past nine years.

A knock on the apartment door jolts me from my drift down the darkest corridors of my past. I jump, dropping my half-eaten toast onto the counter.

"Just a second," I call out as I shut down the tablet and stow it in a kitchen drawer.

I'm not excited about seeing anyone dressed as I am, but I assume it's only Manny or one of the maintenance men since no one gets in or out of the building besides them, unless they live here. Making a hasty attempt to straighten my extra-large T-shirt over my baggy sweats, I pad my way into the foyer to answer the door.

I put my eye to the peephole and suck in a sharp breath.

Oh, God.

My stomach starts fluttering—half in surprise, half in mortification. Reluctantly, I pull open the door.

"Nick."

"Good morning." His sexy smile scatters every unpleasant thought to the furthest corners of my mind. He's standing there in dark jeans and a black blazer. His starched white button-down is unfastened at his throat, but even dressed in business-casual, he looks like a cool million bucks.

More precisely, two-point-four billion, my subconscious corrects.

"Um, hi. When did you . . . what are you doing here?" I try to sound unaffected, but my stammered greeting betrays me. I'm dying a little inside and trying not to gape at him, well aware that I must look like a sleep-deprived bag lady in my paint-speckled, baggy clothes and messy ponytail. "I thought you weren't due back for a couple more days."

"I told my London team to handle things for me and I flew home early. I just got in from JFK a few minutes ago." Despite my bedraggled disarray, his eyes drink me in slowly, appreciatively. "I'm hungry. Thought you might be too."

"Hungry," I murmur. He watches my mouth as I say it, and I don't think I'm imagining the flicker of interest that seems to light in his gaze. My pulse responds to him instantly, kicking into a faster tempo even while reason cautions me to keep my head. "You mean, go out for breakfast? I'm not exactly dressed for that."

"Then we'll stay in." His sensual lips curve in a wicked smile. "Actually, I prefer that idea even more. And we can decide about breakfast afterward."

I laugh, but I'm still not ready to let him in. "It's Monday, Nick. Some of us have to work for a living."

"Call in sick."

I hold his stare, wondering if he has any idea how tempted I am. "I can't do that."

"Okay." He inclines his head in acknowledgment, but clearly not in surrender. Reaching into the pocket of his blazer, he pulls out his cell phone. "Tell me where you work. I'll make the call for you."

"You will not!"

He doesn't know that my self-described "public relations" job is performed behind a bar six nights a week, but that doesn't stop me from gasping when he acts as if he really means to make the call. I lunge for him, repeatedly grabbing for his hand, which he holds just high enough to be comfortably out of my reach. I'm tall at five-foot-six, but he's easily six inches taller, and my effort to stop him only draws our bodies flush against each other.

"Are you going to call in, or am I?"

He's playing with me, and there's a part of me that's all too eager to go along with him. It doesn't escape my notice that he's somehow managed to move inside the foyer with me, when I had good intentions of keeping him on the other side of the threshold. Now, we're standing together on the marble tiles, less than a hand's breadth between us.

The air feels electrified, crackling with energy. With mutual awareness.

With his eyes locked on mine, Nick reaches out and quietly closes the door behind us.

I groan, sensing my imminent defeat. "I can't miss a day of work just because you want me to, Nick. My boss would probably fire me for it."

"Then quit." The quirk of his mouth suggests he's joking, but the dark glint in his gaze tells me that he's absolutely serious. His fingers cup the side of my face, the pad of his thumb gently stroking my lower lip. "I want to spend the day with you. And the night."

I stare at him, unspeaking, captivated by the pleasure of his touch and the power of those compelling blue eyes. My breath leaks out of me on a sigh. "Is this what life is like all the time for you? Issuing commands and expecting the whole world to follow them simply because it's what you want?"

"You say that like it's a bad thing."

I smirk in spite of myself. "I guess if you're Dominic Baine it probably isn't."

"Is that a yes, Avery?"

I tilt my head at him. "To breakfast, or something else?"

"To everything I want to do with you right now." He smiles as he says it, but it's not humor I see blazing in his eyes. His large hand is still curved against my cheek, his fingers still coaxing me into submission.

It doesn't take much for all of my arguments to wither under his touch. Then he bends his head and kisses me, and every last bit of my control abandons me.

I want him, and all of my reasons for why it's a mistake to let him in—to crave this man the way I do—scatter away as his tongue sweeps past my lips to tangle with mine.

19

In the two weeks since he's been away in London, I've almost managed to convince myself that my memory of sex with Nick has somehow expanded and evolved into a bigger than life fantasy—one that can't possibly resemble reality. As Nick kisses me, I realize just how wrong I've been to think that. If what we've already had together was intense, the spark has only grown hotter in the time we've been apart.

My body ignites on contact, as if my nerve endings are already trained to recognize their master and awaken in eager response. His mouth dominates mine in a deep, possessive kiss that leaves my heart racing, my limbs boneless. I'm already melting into a desperate state of arousal, but each stroke of his tongue past my parted lips makes my sex pulse in answer, already wet and yearning with the need to be filled.

I recall how he was the one who set our pace that first time. I remember how he controlled our progress—

how he almost demanded I give him the reins to my pleasure. But he's stirred something greedy in me and I have no patience to wait for his cues right now. I reach down and press my palm against the massive ridge of his erection. He groans coarsely, almost a growl. But he doesn't stop me. Not even when I grab for the buckle of his belt and tug it loose.

He's as consumed as I am.

I see it in his heavy-lidded eyes, in the sharp flare of his nostrils as he draws back from our fevered kiss to hold my gaze while I unzip his pants just enough to take his hard flesh in my hand. I wrap my fingers around his thick shaft and stroke the length of him, watching the azure blue of his irises turn stormy and dark, filled with so much desire it staggers me.

When he comes back at me for another kiss, this time his mouth is savage. The sheer force of his sensual assault knocks me back on my heels. Only the wall of the foyer behind me holds me steady as Nick's body crashes up against mine.

His tongue invades my mouth as his hands slide under my T-shirt and close around my naked breasts in a firm, almost bruising grasp. I moan, trapped between pleasure and pain as he kneads the mounds and rolls the aching peaks of my nipples between his fingers. I feel his cock wedged at my hip, the rigid line of it grinding against my pelvis as he rolls his spine in a hard thrust while he kisses me breathless.

I'm beyond wet for him already, and the rhythmic friction of our bodies is nearly enough to make me come despite the fact that we're both fully clothed. Shameless, I straddle his strong thigh, clamping around him as he moves against me and continues to kiss and caress me into a state of frenzied need.

He pulls away from me on a harsh curse, his gaze locked on mine. "Fuck, Avery. What have you done to me? I've been wanting you like this since the day I left New York."

"I know." My words are little more than a gasp. "Me too."

The instant I confirm it, he reaches down and tugs my sweatpants off my hips. The loose fabric sags around my ankles, leaving me bare from the waist down. Nick's fingers slip between my thighs, into the warm slickness that's gathered there. I drop my head back on a moan as he strokes my swollen clit with his thumb. His fingers delve deeper into the wet heat of my cleft, making me cry out as his touch penetrates and teases.

"This pussy is going to be my obsession," he utters thickly, groaning as my sheath constricts around his pistoning fingers. "Christ, it already is."

He increases his tempo, and his kiss becomes something even wilder. The torment is relentless, maddeningly good. But it's not enough. He's not giving me what I really want. What I need.

My hands find his cock again. Unzipping his pants the rest of the way, I reach into his boxer briefs and pull his erection free. He breaks our kiss and exhales a low moan as I take hold of him. Curses tightly against my jaw line as I squeeze him and run my fingers along the veined underside of his shaft.

I haven't forgotten how powerful his cock felt in my hand that first time, but right now the silken, steely length feels immense, formidable. I stroke him appreciatively, hungrily, reveling in the sharp flex of his hips as his body pumps in time with my movements, his cock swelling even larger within my grasp.

Still, I need more.

Shifting on my feet, I push him backward a step. I see the flicker of surprise in his darkened gaze—the hesitance to give me this much control. My hands still wrapped around him, stroking every delicious inch of him from broad tip to balls and back again, I meet his challenging stare with my own. "When I see something I want, I reach for it too."

His faint smirk doesn't escape my notice as I sink down onto my knees before him. My discarded sweatpants offer a thin cushion, but if the marble floor is hard and cold beneath me, I don't notice. Leaning forward, I lick my way around the crown of his cock, lapping at the salty drop of wetness I find at its tip.

Nick's hand tangles in my loose hair as I begin to explore the rest of him, my tongue memorizing his intoxicating taste and texture. His strong legs are spread to allow me access, one hand braced on the wall behind me as if he needs something solid to ground him. "Fuck, that feels good. Ah, Christ, baby."

I close my lips around him and draw him deep into my mouth, savoring the heat and power of this man who's turning me into something wanton. Someone fearless and bold. Someone I barely recognize.

Someone I've never allowed myself to be with anyone else.

With Nick, all I know is need. It's pure, untainted. Primal and raw.

Although I could feast on him for hours, he drags me off him all too soon, hoisting me roughly to my feet. He grips my shoulders in his strong hands, his eyes searing me with the ferocity of his gaze. On a curse, he hauls me to him and claims my mouth in a ravenous kiss. "I'm done playing now. I need to fuck you."

"Yes," I agree, my voice thready.

I only notice just now that he's still wearing his blazer. As he shrugs out of it, he reaches into an inside pocket and withdraws a condom packet. I can't help arching a brow at him.

"Awfully sure of yourself, aren't you, Mr. Baine?"

"Always." The corner of his mouth twitches with a wicked smile. "But I also believe in leaving nothing to chance. And I need to be inside you, Ms. Ross. Now."

He kisses me hard and long and deep, and I feel him maneuvering to put on the condom. Before I know what he's doing, his hands cup my bottom and he's lifting me onto my toes, spreading me open as his cock finds its position between my legs. He teases me with a few wet slides of our bodies against each other before he guides himself to my entrance and slams home, beginning the driving rhythm we both crave.

Holding me aloft in his hands, he commands every thrust, every impaling plunge. I cry out with the impossible fullness of him inside me as he lifts me to the crown of his cock, then settles me all the way to his root. His tempo isn't gentle, but then, gentle isn't what I want from him. From the wild look in his eyes and the savage grimace that twists his mouth as he fucks me so thoroughly up against the foyer wall, I don't think gentle is what either one of us needs right now.

Our need is carnal, urgent. And it feels so good, so achingly right. My orgasm is building, rising swiftly, powerfully. I close my eyes to the immense force of the pleasure that's spiraling through me. I'm overcome by how desperately I need this.

Need him.

Nick's hot breath skims my cheek. "Open for me, Avery. Let me see you come."

My lids lift. I have no choice but to do what he says, because I'm there at the edge now. I'm panting his name, whimpering as my orgasm takes hold of me. I break apart on a strangled scream, staring into his eyes as my release jolts through me.

Nick doesn't let up his rhythm for a second. He doesn't show me an ounce of mercy. And I love it. Clutching his broad shoulders, I writhe on him as he continues to drive into me, supporting all of my weight on his palms and forearms. I thrash and buck, my entire body shuddering as my core convulses with wave after wave of violent, shattering bliss.

It's not until I start to sag against him, my head dropping onto his shoulder, that I feel Nick's hold on me shift. He's still hard inside me, our bodies still intimately joined, though he hasn't yet come.

"Wrap your arms around my neck, baby. Hang on to me."

I do, and then we're moving. Away from the foyer, into the living room.

Nick carries me as if I weigh nothing, an added turn-on that also strikes me as ridiculously romantic. But that's where his softness ends. When we reach the sofa, he sets me down onto my feet. I groan in protest as our bodies separate. Without a word, he strips off my T-shirt, then makes quick work of the buttons on his white dress shirt and throws the clothing aside. His cock is still as erect as when we started—in fact, more so. Even if it wasn't, his scorching gaze leaves no room to wonder if he's finished with me.

"Turn around."

I stagger on boneless legs, hurrying to obey his rough command. When I'm facing away from him, he folds me over the arm of the sofa. My ass is in the air, my sex and backside totally exposed to him. I hear dark approval in the low growl that escapes him. I feel power and demand in the hot skate of his palm as it trails fire along the length of my spine.

His hand travels farther down, between the cheeks of my ass, his fingers stroking me indecently, exploring every inch of my nudity. I feel him part me wide open, then to my shock—to my unspeakable pleasure—he kneels down and buries his face between my legs. I clutch at the sofa cushions as his mouth and tongue flick hotly, wetly, along the entire seam of my body. He works his way down to my clit and sucks the swollen pearl into his mouth. As he does this, he pushes one finger into my vagina and eases another into the tight rosebud of my anus, which he's made slick with his tongue and my own juices.

"Oh, God." It's only a brief tease of his fingertip inside me, but I gasp and feel myself go still, rocked with sensations I've never felt before.

As good as it feels, I'm also bewildered and more than a little afraid. Not because he scares me, but because of how badly I want him. I am alive with need, and terrified of how carnal he makes me feel.

"Have you ever?" His murmured question gusts against my bare ass, sending a shiver of anxious anticipation over my body.

"No. Never."

"Good. Then it'll be all mine. But not this time." I hear him moving. I register that he's standing up again, positioned directly behind me, his thighs warm between my own. He leans over me, putting his mouth beside my ear. "I want you too much to take things slowly right now. Do you understand?"

I nod, and before I can tell him that I don't need him to go slowly, he enters me with a long, hard thrust I feel all the way to my throat.

And Nick doesn't go slowly now.

He fucks me with unleashed abandon, as if he can't get enough. As if he truly has been wanting this—wanting me—all this time we've been apart.

As I brace myself for each furious stroke, tilting my hips up to receive him as he pounds relentlessly toward climax, I realize that I've been wanting this too. I've been wanting him.

And if I've been worried that I'm letting myself get in too deep with Dominic Baine, today I realize the futility of that thinking.

Because I'm already there.

I'm in too deep, and what's even worse is I can no longer pretend I'm not exactly where I want to be.

20

A couple more orgasms later, I'm newly showered and wrapped in a towel, sitting on the edge of my bed in Claire's guest room while I deliver what is probably the worst performance of a sick call I've ever given in my life. Fortunately, it's early enough in the morning that Vendange isn't open, so I mumble my excuses about being wiped out with a bad stomach bug into Joel's voicemail at the restaurant.

He won't be happy. He'll most certainly punish me for leaving him short-staffed today, either with shitty schedule changes or docked pay. Hell, I wouldn't put it past him to threaten to fire me the next time he sees me. At the moment, I really can't give a damn. My body is deliciously spent, and I know there's more pleasure waiting for me at Nick's apartment, where he's gone to clean up and make breakfast for us.

I hit END on the call to the restaurant, and I'm already grinning as I dial Tasha to fill her in. No sense making her worry about me, which she will, when she shows up at work and sees I'm not there.

"Hey, girl." She picks up after several rings. "Hold on for a sec. I've got a baby vomit situation to deal with over here."

She doesn't wait for me to reply before dropping the phone to tend to her child. In the background, I hear the muffled racket of general family chaos—water running in the sink, Antonio asking Tasha where he left his keys, a television chattering somewhere in the other room, and Tasha soothing little Zoe, whose hiccupping cries quiet down almost immediately under her mother's tender care.

"Sorry about that," she says as she comes back on the line. "What's up?"

"I'm not going in today. I called in sick, left a message for Joel saying I think I have food poisoning or something."

"Oh, no! Honey, are you okay?"

"Yeah, I'm fine. It's just—"

"It was Tony's beer, wasn't it?" She interrupts me before I can finish talking. "Didn't I tell you not to drink that shit?"

I can't bite back my giggle. "The beer was nasty, but I'm not sick. That's what I'm trying to tell you. I'm not going in because I'm spending the day with Nick."

"Get out. You, who hasn't missed a single shift since you started working there, are actually playing hooky?" She lowers her voice. "Are you with him right now?"

"No. I'm at the apartment. He left a little while ago."

She snickers. "No wonder you sound all chill and relaxed. Go ahead, tell me. The sex was amazing, right?"

"It always is with Nick," I admit. I toy with a loose

thread on my towel, my body aching in all the right places when I think about how we spent the past couple of hours. "He showed up at my door this morning. He'd just got in from London and said he couldn't wait to see me . . . to be with me. Now he's back at his place, making us breakfast."

"Do you have any idea how much you suck right now?" She says it sardonically, but I can practically see the smile on her face. "I'm standing here with a puddle of baby puke on my shoulder and a cup of lukewarm coffee in my hand, and you're basically telling me you just spent your morning having amazing monkey sex with a gorgeous billionaire and are on your way to his penthouse to enjoy a delicious breakfast with him. A delicious breakfast, which I can only imagine he'll be preparing for you while looking sinfully hot doing it. I seriously hate you, woman."

I laugh. "I would probably have to hate me too. Anyway, I just wanted you to know I'm okay. But Joel's going to be pissed."

"Fuck him," she says sharply. "The way you work? You deserve a night off and a little fun. You deserve to be happy, Avery."

"I am," I say, and it astonishes me how genuinely I mean it. My smile has hardly dimmed since Nick left the apartment.

To be honest, it's barely dimmed since I met him.

"I have to run now, okay? He's waiting for me upstairs."

"Yeah, yeah, rub it in," she says, exhaling a quiet laugh. "Go on. Enjoy yourself. I'll expect a full report tomorrow."

~ ~ ~

Tasha was right. Nick does look sinfully hot making breakfast. She'd be even more jealous to know that not only is he amazing in bed, but he's also incredible in the kitchen.

Seated on one of the tall barstools behind the island counter, I take a sip of my bubbly mimosa and stare in awe as he delivers two plates of perfectly prepared eggs Benedict that look like something out of a gourmet magazine. Fluffy poached eggs float atop a lightly browned English muffin stacked with a folded slice of Canadian bacon and a thin bed of dark green spinach. Creamy yellow Hollandaise sauce is artfully drizzled over the whole thing, with finely chopped green onions sprinkled on top. He's finished off each plate with a colorful serving of cut fruit and juicy, ripe berries.

"When you said you were making breakfast, I pictured scrambled eggs and bacon. Maybe a slice of toast on the side. This meal is insane."

His mouth curves. "I don't believe in doing anything halfway."

"So I'm noticing." I smile up at him. "Lucky me."

His gaze is locked on me, and the look he gives me makes my stomach flutter with something deeper than basic hunger. After a moment, he indicates for me to start eating. "Bon appetit."

I slice into the egg and can't hold back my moan as I savor the first decadent bite. Nick watches me the whole time, seeming in no hurry to dig in to his own meal. As I chew and swallow and sigh at the explosion of delicious flavors filling my mouth, his blue eyes glint with a spark of interest that's nothing short of carnal.

Seeing desire that hot in his intense gaze makes my thoughts heat up too. It doesn't help that he's standing there shirtless and barefoot, wearing just a pair of faded jeans that hang low on his lean hips. For what certainly isn't the first time, my eyes roam the muscled planes and ridges of his chest and arms and rippled abdomen.

He's beautiful; there is no other word for him. Not even the tangle of angry scars that slash his right forearm and hand can diminish the masculine perfection of Nick's body. His face is equally devastating—especially when he's looking at me as if he's about to leap over the counter and devour me.

"It's good?" he asks.

"So good." I lick my lips, uncertain what I find more appealing—him or the fantastic breakfast he prepared for me. "You cook better than a lot of chefs I know."

"Is that right?" He seems surprised, flattered. He shrugs, but I can see the pride in his expression. And something else, which I'm tempted to call regret. "Cooking started out as therapy for me. A hobby I picked up many years ago when I needed to work to regain the use of my hand."

He says this as if we both know what happened to him. I want to ask, but I don't want to dampen this moment the way I sense forcing him to explain his scars to me would.

Leaning his hip against the counter, he crosses his muscled arms over his chest. "I cook now mainly because I enjoy it. It still helps me focus and recalibrate the way nothing else can. Almost nothing, that is."

I smile as I stab a ripe, red strawberry on the end of my fork. "Well, I think you should know I'm feeling very spoiled right now."

"Good. We're only getting started."

His smirk is dark with erotic promise, and I feel a mix of disappointment and relief when he finally breaks eye contact to pick up his fork and begin eating his breakfast over the counter. We eat in companionable silence for a few moments before he reaches for the bottle of champagne and refreshes my mimosa.

"No problems getting away from work, I hope?"

"No. No problems." I give him a nonchalant shrug, hating the acid taste of my lie.

I should have told him before now what I do for a living. If he'd think less of me because I earn my paycheck serving drinks, then I'd be better off without him. I'd be smarter to find out now, while I can still break away from him with my heart and my sanity intact. That's what I tell myself, but the fact that I've let the fib exist for this long only makes the truth seem all the further out of my reach.

"What about you?" I ask, trying to soothe my parched throat with a sip of champagne-spiked orange juice. "You've been gone for two weeks. I'm sure you have important business things you should be doing right now."

He smiles as he chews a bite of his Benedict. "I can't think of a single thing I need to be doing, business or otherwise. Except you, Ms. Ross. Which I mean to take care of just as soon as we finish here. You're going to need sustenance for all the things I have in mind."

I feel my cheeks flood with warmth, but I can't resist teasing him. "Oh, now I see what's going on here. This amazing meal isn't so much about impressing me with your culinary skills as it is fueling me up for a marathon in your bed."

He chuckles, his eyes riveted on me. "Marathon, yes. Without a doubt. The bed is optional."

I laugh with him, though inside my nerve endings thrum with anticipation. He leans forward to cup the side of my face in his palm, dragging me toward him for a long, slow kiss. Like always with Nick, just the barest touch, the briefest brush of his lips over mine, sends a rush of adrenaline through my veins. I can't curb my response to him and there's a part of me that doesn't even want to try. I melt, I ache, I want . . . always for this man.

"God, you taste good," he murmurs against my mouth as he deepens his claim. "I could eat you up right here and now."

Yes. Yes, please, Nick. I start to say it, ready to give in to him—but at that same instant a cell phone trills with an incoming call. Nick's phone is on the countertop where it's been since I arrived. It rings again, vibrating against the black granite.

On a low growl, he slowly pulls away from me to glance at the device. I can't help looking too—just a reflexive flick of my gaze to the name and photo illuminated on the display.

Lily Fontana.

She's pretty. Jet black hair and milky white skin. A heart-shaped face that I put around my own age. Her smile is confident, her exuberant expression just as lovely as her name.

"I have to take this," Nick says, holding the phone toward his chest. "Will you excuse me for a minute?"

I nod, because what else can I do? He walks away, into the living room to speak while I try not to feel awkward and out of place in his kitchen.

"Hello, Lily. Word travels fast, I see." His voice is low, but it carries through the penthouse. "Yes, I got in this morning, actually."

Although his tone with her is authoritative and firm, there is also a familiarity to their conversation—an intimacy—that kindles an unpleasant jealousy in my gut. I force myself to keep nibbling at my breakfast, even though my mouth feels parched and my stomach feels full for the weight of my disappointment.

"No, you're right," he tells Lily. "I should've called to let you know my plans had changed." He listens for another moment, then exhales a short sigh. "Ah, damn. That's tonight? No, I can't make it. There are other things that I've already committed to do."

As he says this, he walks back into the kitchen where I'm idly pushing my eggs around my plate. Our gazes connect, but I can't hold his intense stare. Not while he's got another woman on the other end of the line, pressing him to be somewhere else instead of with me. A very pretty woman whose face is now seared into my mind.

"I understand, but Mayor Holbrook's gala is the least of my concerns. Tell him I'm still in London. Hell, tell him to make an appointment with me during business hours like everyone else." Nick stares at me as he speaks to Lily, and there is no mistaking the sensual heat that's still present in his eyes—all of it focused on me. "I'm sure there will be other opportunities for him to pick my pocket about the upcoming campaign. Well, what's he going to do, tie up the permits on the rec center? If he does, I'll just work around any roadblocks as they come."

Nick pauses to listen some more, then gives Lily instructions to convey his regrets to the mayor and to shuffle a couple of meetings on his calendar for the week ahead. He ends the call and sets the phone back down on the counter.

"My assistant," he informs me. "Lily likes to run a tight ship. She's good at keeping me on track, but I don't always make it easy on her. Needless to say, she isn't happy that I cut London short without telling her I was back in the States."

"Oh." His assistant. I nod, astonished at the depth of my relief. But I can't pretend I'm not also aware that he has business obligations waiting for him. Ones that evidently involve rubbing elbows with the city's elite. I finish off the last swallow of my mimosa, feeling the gap between our two worlds more clearly than ever.

"What is it, Avery?"

I glance up at him, unnerved as always by those penetrating oceanic blue eyes that seem so adept at seeing through me. Seeing past the mask I've been able to hold up around everyone else. Nick's sharp gaze sees too clearly. Still, I attempt to deflect him. "What do you mean?"

"Something's changed in you just now. Was it the call from Lily?" His piercing eyes narrow on me. "You thought she was another woman—someone other than a colleague? Did it make you jealous?"

I shrug, but it's a weak denial. "She's very pretty. I didn't mean to look at your phone when she called, but it was right there on the counter."

"Lily is attractive," he admits. "But she's my employee. I don't fuck my employees. And anyway, when it comes to beauty, she's got nothing on you."

He approaches me where I sit on the counter stool, his fingers threading into my loose hair, then trailing around to cup my nape. His touch enthralls me. My senses fill with the intoxicating scent of him—his warm, bare skin and clean, shower-damp hair. I look up into his bright blue eyes and I'm captivated, holding my breath for the moment I'll feel his lips brush against mine.

He doesn't disappoint. Bending toward me, he takes my mouth in a deep, bone-melting kiss. His large hands frame my face, holding me to him as his tongue sweeps past my teeth to stroke, and taste, and tease. I moan with the force of my desire for him. As our kiss turns molten, I wrap my arms around his neck, reveling in the feel of his muscled chest pressed against me, his erection a rigid demand at my hip.

But as good as he feels—as right as we feel together, like this—I am now reminded of the impossibility of us becoming anything more than what exists between us right now. He can touch me and kiss me, pleasure my body in ways no man ever has before, but that's where Nick and I end. I can't expect him to invite me into the other parts of his life when I damn well can't invite him into mine.

I draw back, slowly shaking my head. When I pull in a breath, my lungs constrict as if they're caught in a vise. "Nick, I'm sorry. I think maybe I should go."

I watch his gaze narrow on me, his brow furrowing with a scowl. He isn't pleased with this sudden change in my mood. He may even be suspicious. "Go? You're mine for the day and the night, remember? You ditched work for me today. I mean to make it worth your while."

I know all too well how worthwhile he can make it, and I have to work hard to ignore the eager pulse of my body in the wake of his erotic promise. "Nick, if you have somewhere you need to be tonight instead . . . If the mayor—"

"Fuck the mayor." He draws me closer to him, stroking his hand along my cheek. I tremble with arousal as his fingers skate down onto the swell of my breast. "I am where I need to be," he insists, his voice thick and rough with need. "Right here, with you."

"What about the rec center?"

He pulls back and now I see some of the disregard fade from his demeanor. "What about it?"

"It sounds like it's important to you."

He nods. "It is. I've had the plans for a children's recreation center on the drawing board for nearly two years. I'm funding the entire project. Building it from the ground up, which isn't my usual mode of operation. But I want this done right. I want it to be perfect."

His candor surprises me. More than that, so does his vulnerability. I can hear his commitment to the project in every word. I can see his determination—his passion for it—in the steady, unblinking gaze that he holds me in now.

"I heard what you said to Lily about potential roadblocks if you don't have the mayor's support, Nick. If the event tonight is something you should attend, then I don't want to be the one standing in the way of your being there."

He frowns, studying me closer. "You really mean that, don't you?"

"Yes." I reach up to stroke the dark stubble on his jaw. "I want you to go."

He considers for a long moment, then finally nods. "All right. If that's really how you feel."

"It is."

He kisses me, then reaches down to pick up his cell

phone. "Lily's extremely efficient. I'd better tell her about the change in plans before she sends my regrets to Mayor Holbrook's people."

He hits a number on the phone, all the while stroking my thigh with his free hand. As much as I want to spend the rest of the day—and the night—with him, I know he's a busy man with significant obligations. And if the rec center means as much to him as he's conveyed to me just now, then he should do everything in his power to make it happen.

"Lily," he says when she picks up a moment later. "I've reconsidered tonight's event. I will be attending after all. And I'm bringing a date. Please have Patrick pick us up at seven-thirty."

21

We spend the bulk of the day naked together in Nick's penthouse. True to his word, he makes it his mission to keep me well-pleasured and multi-orgasmic both in—and out—of his bed.

After the hours of creative, vigorous exertion, I'm not sure how I have the strength to stand upright as we ride the elevator down to the lobby to meet the limousine waiting to take us to the gala. I can't deny that I'm anxious about tonight as well. The closest I've ever gotten to an elegant black-tie gathering is the handful of weddings I've worked as a part-time bartender on those rare occasions when the opportunity arose and my schedule at Vendange allowed. Now, here I am, attending possibly *the* social event of the year as Dominic Baine's date.

Standing next to me in a black tuxedo, starched white shirt, and black silk tie, Nick is the epitome of confidence and class. He's attractive no matter what he wears—and even more so when he wears nothing at all—but seeing him dressed in formal attire is a revelation. Like this, the wealth and influence he commands is unmistakable. Although his stance is relaxed beside me, his long legs slightly apart, power vibrates off every inch of his tall, athletic form.

I notice how his hands are folded loosely in front of him, the unmarked one resting lightly atop his scarred one. It's a stance I've seen in him before, and I realize only now that this is part of his mask. He looks so handsome and commanding, there's little chance that anyone would notice his flaw. But he hides it anyway, as if the damage shames him.

It doesn't diminish him at all in my eyes. I see a survivor. I see a man with secrets and hauntedness of his own, and I want to understand him. I want him to know that there is nothing about him that I find displeasing. In fact, he's so magnificent, he takes my breath away.

He's so damn sexy, he makes me hunger for him all over again, even though I've certainly enjoyed my fair share of him already today.

"Keep looking at me like that, Ms. Ross, and we won't make it into the car, much less to the party." When I glance up, I find a spark of humor in his eyes, and in the smirk that tugs sensually at the corner of his mouth. "On second thought, keep looking. I'll call Patrick and tell him he can return the car to the fleet garage."

I laugh and give his biceps a light smack. "You will not."

"No, but I should." He reaches over to smooth the backs of his knuckles gently along the side of my face. The look he gives me is as solemn as it is heated. "You look beautiful, Avery."

"Thank you."

I want to look good for him. I've spent the past forty-five minutes getting showered and ready back at Claire's apartment, both excited and apprehensive about the prospect of arriving anywhere on Dominic Baine's arm. Although I would give anything to be wearing something as elegant as the designer cocktail dresses and couture gowns that fill Claire's walk-in closet, my budget runs more toward department store discount racks.

I'm anxious as I stand beside Nick in the little black dress I bought on clearance with Tasha last year and the strappy black Jimmy Choo sandals I got for a steal at a second-hand store in Park Slope not long after I settled in Brooklyn. Will everyone sense the imposter in their midst tonight? For that matter, will Nick?

Whether he senses my nerves or not, as the elevator chimes with our arrival on the street level of the building, Nick takes my hand in his and leads me out to the lobby. Manny is there at the main door as we stroll across the gleaming marble toward the sleek black limousine waiting just outside. I detect the faintest lift of the doorman's brows as we approach, but it's there and gone in an instant.

A consummate professional, Manny merely smiles, then smoothly opens the door for us. "Good evening, Ms. Ross. Mr. Baine."

"Evening, Manny." Nick nods in greeting, placing his hand at the small of my back to allow me to exit ahead of him.

As I pass through, I offer Manny a smile that feels a little awkward, considering our conversation the other day and the fact that the doorman is probably aware of the time I've been spending in Nick's apartment. His face shows no judgment. If anything, I can't help thinking there is a small note of approval in his kind eyes.

"Have a pleasant evening, Miss. Sir," he says, escorting us to the standing limo where Nick's driver waits with the back door open.

We climb in and are quickly on our way. It doesn't take more than a few minutes to make the drive down Park Avenue to the five-star hotel that's hosting the gala. If my nerves were jangling before, they spike with new apprehension as the limousine pulls in behind a parade of similar glossy black vehicles at the hotel's entrance.

Clumps of reporters and media personnel are gathered behind crowd control barriers, the cacophony of their shouts and chatter audible even through the glass and steel of the limo. Cameras, cell phones, and tablets flash like strobe lights as the press attempts to get their shots of the arriving guests. No sooner does Patrick roll forward, closer to the fray, than another limo rolls right up behind us.

"Apologies, sir," he says from up front. "We're not going anywhere fast, unfortunately."

"Not your fault," Nick replies, but I can see the displeasure in his face. I can feel it in the tension of his body beside me.

At that moment, one of the men with cameras jumps the line and snaps a photo through the windshield of our car. I see Nick drop his head to avoid the shot, but the flash of the camera is faster.

"Shit," he hisses, as his name goes up in a holler among the crowd.

Like a cloud of locusts, a number of reporters now break away to converge on the limousine. The barrage of flashes outside the windows is blinding. The voices rising to a chaos of indistinguishable shouts.

"Oh, my God."

I swallow, both astonished and repulsed by the feeding frenzy that awaits on the other side of the limousine doors. If this is what it's like to travel in Nick's circle—to have his wealth and social standing—no wonder he holds his privacy so close to his vest. I suddenly regret pushing him into attending this party. Not only for Nick's sake, but my own, as well.

Old, rusty memories of another time slash through my mind, uninvited. Camera flashes snapping and exploding in my face. Relentless, demanding shouts from reporters—interrogations, accusations—their terrifying voices ringing in my ears. And I remember my own cries too. The wracking sobs that felt as though they would split me in half.

I close my eyes, trying to keep the ordeal banished to my past, but the memories are too strong. Too raw, even after all these years.

Mama, no! Mama, please, don't go! Don't leave me!

Nick growls from beside me, startling me back to reality. "Fuck this." He glowers at the clamoring madness outside the vehicle. "We're getting out here, Patrick."

"Very well, sir."

When I glance uncertainly at Nick, his determined gaze locks on me. It grounds me, even though he can't possibly know how desperately I need it right now. "You give me your hand as we get out of the car. Just keep your head down, hold on tight, and follow me. All right?"

I nod. He opens the door on his side and helps me across the seat to exit with him. His strong hand is wrapped around mine, just as he promised. He doesn't let go, not for a second.

I hurry alongside him as he weaves us through the logjam of vehicles and the gauntlet of yammering press and media. We head for the pair of doormen who have their hands full admitting arriving guests and dignitaries while a small security detail barks for the media to stay on the other side of the barriers.

As soon as we approach, one of the doormen greets Nick by name and lets us inside. We enter the hotel, leaving the bedlam behind us, and my relief is instant and profound. Soothing classical music plays softly in the background as we step into the opulent lobby. Some other couples in formal wear walk ahead of us, clearly heading for the same event we are.

As we approach the check-in stand outside the Grand Ballroom, I can't help noticing that the hem of my dress is shorter than most, the cut of it skimming my curves a bit more snugly. With one hand still caught in Nick's grasp, I use my other to smooth the skirt down and subtly tug at the hem.

"Relax," Nick murmurs. He leans toward me with a smile that sends heat arrowing through my veins. "If anyone here had your legs, they'd be showing them off too."

"Good evening, Mr. Baine," says one of the tuxedoed hosts as we approach the front of the line. "Mayor Holbrook wants you to know that he's honored you were able to make time to be here tonight."

"Of course." Nick's tone is level, his smile perfunctory, as we step away from the stand and walk through the soaring double-door entrance to the ballroom.

I don't miss the fact that more than a dozen heads turn as we enter—or, rather, as Dominic Xavier Baine enters the room.

Men and women pause in midsentence or look away from their companions as he strides into their midst with the unapologetic confidence of a king. Or a god. It's mesmerizing to watch the effect he has on the mere mortals who surround him.

Men stand a little straighter, their chests puffed out as if subconsciously compelled to at least attempt to measure up to him—no matter how futile. Women lower their chins and gaze coquettishly at him from under their lashes, fingers reaching idly up to touch their mouths or toy with the ends of their hair. A few even lick their lips, desire sketched across their faces no matter their marital status or age.

Nick's presence is magnetic, his orbit all-consuming, attracting everyone and everything in his path, drawing all of those lesser objects into the heat of his sun. I'm no more exempt than anyone else. He has a hold on me I can't even begin to deny anymore. Each time we're together, I feel that hold tighten, drawing me closer, pulling me onto a path that I've been warned may destroy me.

I know I should be wary of those warnings.

I should resist this pull I feel with him. I should fight it with everything I have before I drift too close and end up burned to ashes.

Instead of resisting or fighting, I let go of a small sigh when Nick releases my hand and turns to face a big man in a dark gray suit who's approaching us from across the ballroom. If the man's size and demeanor didn't give him away as security, his headset and wireless microphone do.

"Good evening, Mr. Baine. Mayor Holbrook would be pleased if you'd join him for a moment. He'd like to thank you personally for coming out to support his campaign tonight."

Nick grunts. "Let me guess. He'd like to thank me in front of the cameras over there?"

Although the big man doesn't confirm nor deny, I glance past him to where a cluster of reporters are interviewing the ambitious young mayor who's currently running for his second term in office. I have no doubt that having Nick's endorsement—implied or absolute—is worth more than most of the contributions that will be pouring in during tonight's gathering.

Nick turns to face me. "Will you be all right for a few minutes without me?"

"Sure. Of course."

From the look he gives me, I know he's tempted to touch me. Maybe even kiss me. But his demeanor has grown more cautious since we arrived. Whether that's to protect me from the glare of the spotlight he has to endure or to protect himself, I can't be sure. Right now, though, it doesn't matter. We're here to help the rec center. My insecurities and desires are insignificant compared to that goal.

"Go on," I tell him. "I'll be fine."

He nods. "I'll be right back."

I watch him walk away, savoring the cut of his suit on his fine form and the loose, animal prowl of his limbs as he crosses the ballroom and is greeted by the beaming politician. Mayor Holbrook pumps Nick's hand enthusiastically as the small crowd of reporters close in on them.

I stand there for a moment, then decide to busy myself with a glass of wine. I drift through the elegantly dressed crowd, wending my way toward one of the bartenders positioned near the ballroom's dance floor.

I can't say that I'm completely comfortable among this elite crowd, but the music being played by the small orchestra at the front of the ballroom is relaxing and the sea of beautiful gowns and tuxedoes provides plenty of distraction for me as I request a glass of Pinot noir and settle in to people-watch until Nick returns.

With wine in hand, I begin weaving back through the gathering. The ballroom is packed and bustling, both with the mayor's invited guests and the army of hotel catering personnel who stroll the room offering fancy hors d'oeuvres to the clusters of conversing partygoers.

As I meander back toward the other side of the room, one of those catering servers accidentally pivots into my path, nearly crashing into me with her silver tray of crudités. In reflex, I hold my wineglass up and out of the way as the short blonde comes to an abrupt halt, facing me. For a stunned moment, neither one of us speaks.

"Avery." Kimmie's pinched expression goes from shock to confusion as she looks me up and down. "What the hell are you doing here?"

22

I *am so busted.*

Dread washes over me as I stare at my least favorite coworker from Vendange. Kimmie is the last person I expect or want to see here tonight. She could screw me in any number of ways right now, and the thin sneer that spreads over her face only drives that point home even harder.

I tell myself to ignore her attempt at confrontation. After all, considering the situation, my best defense is likely an offense. "I'm surprised to see you here, too, Kimmie. I didn't realize you work for the hotel."

She's still scowling, but my question seems to catch her off guard. "I don't, usually. My cousin is the catering manager. I fill in when they have large events and need the extra staff."

"Oh. Well, enjoy the party then. Don't work too hard." I force a light smile and start to step past her.

"Does Joel know you're here?"

Her acid tone freezes my feet in place. I should've guessed she wouldn't let me skate by so easily. But the note of accusation in her voice pisses me off. I swivel a cold look on her. "What does that matter to you?"

"It doesn't. But I think it'll matter plenty to him." Her lips purse, and I can already see the glimmer of satisfaction in her face. "When he called me to see if I could take your shift today, he said you called in sick. Funny, you don't look sick to me."

"How nice of you to say so," I reply with equal venom.

"So, what are you doing here? You can't possibly be on the guest list for something this swank, so how'd you get in?" She glances around me, her gaze searching now. "You here on a hot date or something?"

She titters as she says it, as if she finds the idea preposterous. But her question hits its mark with laser accuracy—even more than her implied threat about ratting me out to Joel. And as she scans the crowd, obviously looking for clues as to who I could be with, genuine panic blooms in my stomach.

If she sees me with Dominic Baine, I have no idea what she'll do.

If she decides to confront me again, when I'm standing near him, I'll not only be humiliated, but sick for the embarrassment it could cause him. Especially in such a public place.

The thought settles on me with a weight I can hardly bear. If Nick were to find out I've been lying to him, pretending to be someone I'm not, he'll be furious.

If it should happen in front of his peers or the mayor—or, dear God, in front of the press—he'll have every right to despise me.

Kimmie studies me with open amusement. "What's wrong, Avery? I swear, you look like you just swallowed a bug."

It feels like I swallowed an entire hornet's nest, but I'm not going to dignify her needling me by giving her any kind of response.

I down my wine and set the empty glass on her tray without comment. I hear her outraged scoff as I brush past her, but I don't turn around to enjoy the moment. I don't hesitate for a second as I step through the crowds at a brisk clip, desperate to get away from her. With any luck, I can find a ladies' room to hide in somewhere until I'm able to calm my jittery nerves enough to return to the party and wait for Nick.

I'm so preoccupied with that mission, I hardly register the presence of a tall, handsome man emerging from out of a cluster of tuxedoes up ahead. Warm brown eyes dance with friendly greeting as Jared Rush flashes his megawatt smile at me.

"This party just got vastly more interesting," he drawls as I slow to a pause in front of him. "Good to see you, Avery."

"Jared, hi." Summoning my composure, I return his welcoming smile. "Nice to see you here too."

As rattled as I am, his laid-back charm helps calm my nerves. It also doesn't hurt that he's incredibly easy on the eyes. Tonight, his long brown waves are contained in a loose ponytail at his nape. The look is considerably tamer than the first time I saw him, but even dressed in an impeccably tailored tuxedo with his wild mane swept back off his face, Jared still exudes a swaggering, rebel vibe that he wears without a trace of apology.

I like that about him and am genuinely glad to think

I have at least one ally here tonight.

Making his excuses to the other men he'd been talking with, he turns his full attention on me. "Where were you heading so fast? Don't tell me you're about to leave."

"No, um . . ." I shake my head in vague denial. "I was just thinking about getting some air."

"Can't say I blame you. Anytime you have this many politicians in one room, all that hot air makes it damn hard to breathe." Jared nods toward the open French doors of the ballroom. "I'd be happy to escort you outside if you'd like. If you'd like something better to eat than the frou-frou appetizers they're passing off as food tonight, I'd be happy to buy you dinner as well."

"Oh, I—" My gaze drifts away from him, searching out Nick on the other side of the gathering. He's still talking with the mayor, and, since I last looked, there is a growing crowd of other men and women all vying for his time now too. "I'm actually here with someone, Jared."

"Ah." He inclines his head in acknowledgment. "I should've known I wouldn't be so lucky to find you here unattached."

"I'm sorry."

"Don't be." The grin he gives me is boyish. And a little wicked. "Although, I have to wonder what kind of fool would leave a woman as lovely as you all alone for even a minute in a room full of wolves like me."

"She's not alone."

Nick's deep voice slashes through the din of the room, low and level. I turn and find him standing directly behind me, as if he crossed the length of the room in an instant. He must have broken away just as I'd searched him out a moment ago. Even the mayor and his companions seem befuddled to have lost him so abruptly, their stares rooted on him from across the ballroom.

Nick seems utterly unconcerned with anything other than me.

From the thunderous look on his face, I half-expect Jared to stammer an apology and retreat as fast as he can. But he doesn't. Instead, he exhales a sardonic chuckle and slowly shakes his head.

"Well, I'll be damned. I guess if I've got to lose out to someone, it might as well be you, Baine."

"Glad you feel that way, Rush. As for wolves looking to encroach on my date, you'd be wise to keep your paws to yourself. Be a shame to lose them."

Nick says it with wry humor, but to me, his eyes tell a different story. There's a warning in his eyes as he jokes with Jared, who's clearly a friend. And I'm sure I'm not imagining the flare of possessiveness I see in Nick's face when he turns his sharp blue gaze on me.

"Didn't expect to see you here tonight, Jared," he says as he reaches out to give his offered hand a firm shake. "Don't tell me you're suddenly taking an interest in politics?"

"Me? Hell no. I'm just here as part of Kathryn's entourage. You know she lives for this crap."

At the mention of another woman—one Jared is evidently attending tonight's event with—I can't help but look at him in question, especially considering he'd been putting a fairly strong move on me.

"Kathryn is an old friend of mine and Nick's. She's practically family."

"Oh." I smile, curious to know more. But as I glance

in Nick's direction, I swear I catch the slightest hint of a shadow skate over his schooled expression.

Jared seems to sober a bit now too. "You should say hello to her, Nick. It's been too long. She'll never say it, but she misses you."

Nick remains silent for a long moment. "I've already endured one command performance. That's enough for one night."

I don't know what to make of the tension that's suddenly descended on the conversation. I can see Jared's pensiveness, his silent frustration. In Nick, I see the same, but there is anger there too. I see the wall go up around him. Jared seems to recognize it too.

Nick looks at me, his expression shuttered, impenetrable. "Are you ready to get out of here?"

"Okay, sure." I nod, unsettled by his darkening mood. I'm also well aware that I have my own reasons for leaving—namely Kimmie. Somewhere in the ballroom, she's floating around, no doubt waiting for another chance to pounce.

Nick turns to Jared and holds out his hand. "Give Kathryn my regrets."

"You're an asshole. You know that, right?" There is no anger in Jared's voice as he shakes Nick's hand, only sadness. "How long are you going to shut her out, man?"

Nick doesn't answer, merely tips his head in a nod and mutters, "Goodnight, Jared."

23

Nick doesn't take me out the front of the hotel. Instead, he guides me down a luxurious mirrored corridor, texting Patrick along the way.

I hurry alongside him, past soaring marble columns and massive floor urns filled with luscious greenery on either side of us. Nick's pace is clipped, and I struggle to keep up in my delicate high heels.

Although he projects an air of cool, collected purpose to anyone looking at him now, I know him too well to be fooled by his outward demeanor. He's brooding, practically vibrating with agitation. He hadn't been overly enthused about attending the gala to begin with, but after running into Jared, he's all but dragging me out of the place.

"This way," he says, catching my hand in his.

We turn down another glittering passageway, one that carries us farther away from the hubbub of the party. Up ahead is a discreet side door for the hotel. Through the brass-trimmed glass, I see a glossy black limousine roll to a stop just outside.

Patrick gets out and meets us on the other side of the car as we exit the hotel. He opens the back door and Nick gestures for me to slide in ahead of him.

"Back to the apartment, sir?" Patrick asks.

"No. Just drive," Nick tells him. "I'll let you know when I want to stop."

He gets in and as Patrick shuts the door behind him, Nick presses a button on his armrest and the privacy panel closes. The opaque glass descends silently, sealing us in together in the backseat of the long sedan.

"Would you like something to drink?"

He's already reaching for a cut-crystal tumbler on the center console between the two rear-facing seats in front of us. When I shake my head, he lifts a decanter of dark amber whisky and pours a two-finger measure into his glass.

"Do you want to tell me what that was about back there?" I ask hesitantly.

"No."

Without looking at me, he throws back the liquor in one swallow. A curse erupts out of him as he sets the tumbler down on the console. When he sits back against the leather squabs of the bench seat we share, his gaze is turbulent, haunted.

The car pulls away, easing out into the evening traffic. For a long while, the only sound is that of the soft jazz coming from the limo's sound system and the heavy drum of my own heartbeat.

"I'm sorry," Nick murmurs. He reaches over to me, idly stroking my thigh. The hem of my dress has risen well above my knees from sliding into the limousine, and Nick's thumb traces a slow, sensual pattern along my bare skin. Yet despite his tender touch, his gaze is hard on me, his tone edged with ice. "You looked like you were having a good time talking with Jared before I came over. I didn't mean to cut your night short. If you would rather have stayed—"

"I don't care about the party." I'm pissed that he would even suggest it. I place my hand on his, squeezing my fingers around his larger ones. "As for Jared Rush, he's interesting, but I don't care about him either."

Nick grunts. "You'd flay his ego if he heard you say that. I don't think he's ever met a woman who's immune to his charms."

"Yeah, I kind of gathered that when I met him at the gallery last week."

"Last week?" When I nod, his eyes flare darkly. "You never mentioned that to me."

"I just did."

Nick studies me intently now. "Jared Rush loves beautiful women. I'm sure I don't have to guess whether he made a pass at you."

"He didn't. Not really." I shrug. "He was nice. Friendly."

"I'll bet."

I hear the sullen note in his voice, but I'm not quite ready to call it jealousy. Resentment, perhaps. Suspicion, most definitely. "We talked a bit about art. When he found out I paint, he invited me out to his studio to see some of his work."

Nick chuckles, but there's little humor in it. "That's a new approach, at least." His gaze bores into me as his fingers continue to dance lightly on my inner thigh. His jaw, however, is clenched tight enough to make a tendon tick in his cheek. "What did you tell him?"

"I didn't tell him anything. I have no interest in Jared Rush."

I'm astonished to realize how true that statement really is. I can't deny that Nick's friend is attractive. Jared's attention is flattering. Any woman would think so. But in a ballroom full of handsome men, I was aware of just one. The one I've been unable to resist from the start.

Lifting my hand to touch Nick's face, I draw in a fortifying breath. "The only man I'm interested in is sitting next to me right now."

"Is that so?" His tone is level, but that just tells me how on edge he truly is.

"Yes. Only you, Nick."

That furious pulse in his cheek throbs against my fingertips as I softly caress his jaw. His eyes search mine in the darkness of the limousine. Outside, the city flashes by in strobes of bright light and color and a frenzy of street noise.

The moment feels tentative, charged with electricity, yet fragile. I want to ask him about the woman Jared mentioned. Kathryn. I want to know who she is and what she means to Nick. Or, rather, *meant* to him. Jared said she was an old friend. Practically family to both of them, he'd said. Obviously, that was no longer true for Nick.

Why? I want to know. It's clear that she has no place in Nick's life now, yet I feel a pang of jealousy kindle inside me. I feel a twinge of wariness too, because I've just witnessed Nick's forbidding side firsthand. Margot's warning about him slicing people out of his life when they get too close to him chases through my mind.

Is that what happened to Kathryn? Will I be next?

There's a part of me that wants to know—*needs to know*—before I let myself tumble any deeper into a fantasy that won't last . . . cannot last.

I'm on the verge of asking him, but Nick's fingers are working their magic on me. He slides his hand beneath my knee and gently guides my legs apart. Then he turns toward me on the seat, his heated gaze holding me captive as he skates his palm under my skirt and up my inner thigh.

"Come here," he murmurs thickly, reaching out to grasp my nape with his free hand. He drags me against him, taking me in a fierce, consuming kiss while his other hand cups my sex.

His lips are greedy, his tongue demanding as it sweeps inside my mouth. He tastes of whisky and thinly held aggression and so much desire it staggers me. His touch intensifies between my legs, and I can't hold back my moan when his fingers push aside my panties to touch my bare flesh. I'm drenched already, trembling with arousal and aching for him.

"Christ, your pussy is soft," he rasps against my lips. "So fucking sweet, Avery."

I feel a tug, followed by the sharp pop of rending lace and satin. He doesn't ask for permission or forgiveness, just rips away my panties, then shoves my dress up above my hips to expose me to his hungry gaze.

I'm boneless now, utterly his to command. He pivots me on the long bench seat and stretches me out before him. In some distant part of my conscience, I'm aware of the driver just on the other side of the glass and of the city bustling on either side of the moving limousine. I'm aware of all the reasons I shouldn't be with Dominic Baine. All the reasons I shouldn't want this reckless passion we share.

But none of those things matter right now. Not in this space. Not in this moment, when he's looking at me as if no other woman exists. As if I belong to him, body and soul, and he can't wait to take what's his.

"Damn, you are beautiful."

His palms are hot on my naked inner thighs. They are firm and strong. He parts me wide, lifting my knee so that one leg is resting against the backrest of the bench seat, my other leg draped over the edge. His fingers trace my skin, from the arch of my foot strapped into my delicate black sandal to the apex of my thighs.

"I want you to come for me, Avery."

I moan because I'm practically there already. Just the anticipation of his touch, of his mouth, of his cock buried inside me is enough to fire my nerve endings into a heated frenzy. He rubs the pad of his thumb over my clit and I arch at the contact as if touched by a live wire. Each erotic caress makes me quivery and I squirm, desperate for more. I gasp when he drives two fingers deep inside me, tiny spasms of sensation pulsing in my core as my body clenches around him, trying to hold him tight. Hungry for more.

He watches me writhe, looking devilish in his tuxedo and tie while his hand plays my sex with sinful skill. His face is taut, his mouth curved with satisfaction as he drives me toward the brink of madness.

He fucks me with his fingers, long strokes that plunge deep, stretching my walls. His thumb swirls over the taut pebble of my clit, slicking me with my own juices. I don't even try to hold back my climax. It slams into me, splintering me on a sharp cry that I'm sure can't be masked by the soft jazz playing in the car or the privacy glass.

"Oh, God . . . Nick!"

I curl up off the seat, reaching for him as the waves continue to pour over me. He catches me in his arms, kissing me fiercely. His strength never ceases to amaze me. In one smooth movement, he hoists me onto his lap and sits back against the seat, leaving me to straddle his thighs. I feel decadent and wild, my dress bunched around my waist, my nakedness spread across his fine trousers. My knees are bent on either side of him, my ass resting lightly on the lengths of my sandals' heels.

Together, we attack his zipper and free his cock. I register Nick reaching into his pocket for a condom, but I'm too caught up in the feel of him in my hands to even pretend I have the capacity to think about protection. I stroke his length, swirling my hand around the thick stalk of his shaft with one hand, while my other gently lifts his balls out of his pants.

"Ah, fuck, baby." He throws his head back on a curse, his neck tendons straining. He throbs in my grasp, his erection jerking under my fevered caress. Hot, silky fluid weeps from the tip of his cock, slicking my fingers as I intensify my rhythm.

Nick's answering snarl is animalistic, the hottest sound I've ever heard. He shackles both my hands in his fist, then swiftly rolls the condom onto his erection with one hand. Gripping me by the hips, he adjusts our position, then guides his cock to me. On a harsh grunt, he thrusts inside, at the same time pulling me down to take the full measure of him.

I gasp at the enormity of him inside me at this angle.

Nick is big, but sitting atop him like this, I feel stretched to my limits. Full to the point of pain. And then . . . he begins to move.

There is nothing gentle or cautious in the tempo he sets for us now. Our bodies crash together urgently, feverishly. It's primal and raw, so incredibly arousing.

He fucks me like he can't get enough—like he's as desperate for me as I am for him.

I wrap my arms around his shoulders as he levers me up and down on his cock. "Feels so good . . . Oh, God . . ."

His answering growl vibrates against my breasts, and his hips pump more vigorously. I ride him with complete abandon, the entire world winnowing down to just this moment. Just this pleasure. Just this man.

"It's so good . . . yes . . . harder . . . don't stop," I whisper brokenly, tears prickling the backs of my eyes from the intensity of what he's doing to me. I'm wanton, wrecked, out of my mind with sensation and the spiraling need to come again. "Oh, God, Nick . . . don't stop."

He doesn't stop. Hammering into me, he draws back to watch my face as my orgasm rips through me. I shudder and break on a scream I can't contain. I want to look away from him, embarrassed by the ferocity of my response, but when I try to lower my gaze, Nick's fingers are at my chin, refusing to let me hide.

He drives into me again and again and again. His strokes are coming harder, ramming deeper, prolonging my release while he chases his own. I see the tension grip him now. His muscles turn to granite under my fingertips as I cling to him. Inside me, his cock feels even more immense, pulsing, and hot as fire.

Our gazes lock and hold even as his big body arcs beneath me with one final, bone-jarring thrust. I feel his cock jolt as he comes. I see the ferocity on his face as he buries himself deep and his climax explodes out of him.

And still, he keeps pounding. Branding me with the heat of him, making every cell in my body submit to his will, to the power his body has over mine.

"Yes," I gasp, as if answering the command. "Nick, yes . . ."

I clutch his shoulders as he sends me toward another peak. When I tumble over the edge a moment later, the tears I've been holding back spill over with me. I tell myself the reaction is merely physical. I tell myself that the hot constriction in my chest is nothing more than my body's response to desire and pleasure I never dreamed I'd know.

And as I cling to Nick in the back of his limousine, cocooned from the city and the rest of reality waiting outside, I tell myself the biggest lie of all . . . that I'm not falling for this man who will never be mine.

24

If I'd been harboring any delusions about Kimmie not throwing me under the bus at work, they evaporate no sooner than I walk in the door for my shift the next afternoon. Joel is standing in back of the restaurant signing for a delivery when I walk past the hostess stand at the front of the house. His dark head lifts and swivels in my direction. Seeing him with an unpleasant expression on his face is nothing out of the ordinary, but today, his scowl is thunderous.

Tasha zooms out from where she's folding silverware setups to intercept me, her eyes wide with warning. *He's pissed*, she mouths to me.

Yeah. As if I can't see that for myself.

"Hey, Avery!" she calls out with exaggerated volume. "Are you feeling any better today?"

"Don't bother," I tell her, as she walks with me back to the coat room.

I quickly fill her in on my evening out with Nick and

my unexpected, ultimately unpleasant run-in with Kimmie at the hotel.

"That back-stabbing little bitch. I guess that explains why she's walking around like the cat who ate the canary today." Scowling, Tasha folds her arms over her chest. "I hope you make her choke on the feathers."

I give her a wry look in acknowledgment. "I honestly don't give a shit about Kimmie. And I don't regret a single second of yesterday." I slant Tasha a grin. "Or last night."

She exhales a dramatic sigh. "Okay, go ahead and tell me how awesome it was parading around in front of the *Who's Who* of Manhattan on Dominic Baine's arm."

I let go of a small laugh. "Well, I wouldn't call it parading, but, yeah, being with him is always pretty awesome."

I shrug my purse off my shoulder and sit on the chair to switch out of my flats into my work heels. The same chair where Nick made me come with just the power of his words. Heat creeps into my cheeks and I slowly shake my head.

"I like him, Tasha. It's scary how much."

"You like him, he obviously likes you. You're both unattached, gorgeous, and sickeningly hot for each other. Oh—and his personal net worth could support the entire population of a small country. Remind me how any of this is scary?"

Maybe it wouldn't be for someone else. Anyone else. But I have a hundred reasons to be afraid of what I'm feeling for Nick, each more terrifying than the next. If I were to begin listing them for Tasha now, I wouldn't even know where to start.

I do, however, know where they all end. My truth.

My lies. And the dark place where I've buried all of my ugliest, most damning secrets.

"When are you going to tell him?"

My head snaps up at Tasha's question. For a moment, I'm startled. Did I speak my fears out loud?

"Sooner or later, he's going to find out you work here, Avery. If he's got a problem with that, then he damn well doesn't deserve you."

I nod because I know she's right. I should tell him. I dodged a bullet last night with Kimmie, but just because she didn't have the opportunity to out me to Nick in public doesn't mean I should try to prolong my lie.

There is a chance he would forgive me for this small untruth I've told him. As for the rest of them—

"Avery." Joel's grating voice shakes me from my thoughts. He's just arrived in the open doorway, his eyes cold on me, his thin lips compressed in a flat line. "My office. Now." His glare lands on Tasha next. "Get out on the floor. I don't pay you to stand around and shoot the shit with this one."

She gives me an apologetic look before scurrying out of the coat room. I glance up at Joel, hating the way he seems to delight in making everyone cower.

Even though I should hustle to obey my boss's orders, too, I remain seated on the chair. It's strange, but just feeling the cushions surrounding me, supporting me, gives me a fortitude I can't explain. Just a few weeks ago, I did things in this chair I never would've considered doing before I'd met Nick. And now, I feel a different kind of boldness building in me—one that can't be bowed by an overbearing, abusive bastard like the one fuming across from me in the doorway.

I take my time putting my flats away in my bag, then

I get up and carefully stow my things in my locker. I'm being spiteful and defiant, but at the moment I'm finding it hard to care.

Joel's rising agitation is nearly palpable. He huffs out a sharp breath. "Maybe you didn't hear me. I said, my office. Right fucking now."

I shut the locker door with more force than necessary, then pivot to face him. "I heard you. But guess what? You don't pay me to jump at your command. Unlike Kimmie, I'm not here to kiss your ass. I'm here to work. And I have been—six days a week without fail for the past year and a half."

I've taken him aback, I can tell. But Joel's a natural bully and he recovers quickly. "Maybe you should've considered that before you bailed on your job yesterday and left me in a lurch behind the bar. What am I supposed to do about that?"

"I haven't missed a day since I started working here, Joel."

He ignores me, his face going red. "And leave Kimmie out of this. At least she's reliable."

I snort, unable to hold it back. "Oh, she's reliable, all right. How long did it take her before she told you we ran into each other last night? Did she wait until she got in today, or did she call you right from the hotel?"

Judging from his constipated expression, I'm guessing it was the latter.

"People who work for me only get one strike. After all this time, I'd have thought you knew that." His mouth purses as he judges me now. "So, as of today, you're off the night schedule."

"What?"

I see the smile tugging at the corner of his lips, as if

he's taking great joy in doling out my punishment. "Since you obviously have better things to do, I'm putting you on days. You can begin with three shifts a week, just like anyone else starting fresh on the job."

The bastard. "That's going to cut my income in half, Joel. This is bullshit, and you know it."

"You wanna lose this job?" He steps forward, his barrel chest puffed out as if he thinks he can intimidate me. "Frankly, you've always had a bit of an attitude, Avery. I gotta tell you, it's pissing me off."

Of course, it would. I know about men like him, men who equate control with oppression. Men who don't think twice about grinding their heel on someone's head to make them obey. Men who bully or beat or abuse the people around them.

I've known men far worse than Joel—my stepfather being one of them. But just because Joel is less of a monster doesn't make him right. It doesn't mean my hackles don't rise in reaction as he moves in even closer to me, crowding me in the small room with no one else around.

His voice softens now, but I feel it as the threat it truly is. "In case I'm not being clear, let me help you understand something right here and now. You need to show me the respect I'm due. I'm a reasonable man, Avery, but I won't tolerate insubordination."

"How do you feel about complete and utter loathing?"

I can't help it—the words fly out of my mouth before I can stop them. And once they're out, I don't even want to try to take them back.

With anger fueling me, I turn away from him. Steeling myself to the weight of his glower, I go back to my locker and calmly collect my things. I can feel his eyes on me as I sling my purse over my shoulder. When I swivel around, I find him gaping, his jowly face corpulent with color, his upper lip beading with sweat.

I pause in front of him. "In case I'm not being clear, let me help *you* understanding something. I fucking quit."

I step past him and stalk through the restaurant, telling Tasha I'll call her later and ignoring Kimmie's slack-jawed stare from across the room as I go.

~ ~ ~

I'm nearly to the subway station when the reality of what I've just done finally sinks in.

Fuck. I have no job.

Worse than that, I've torched the bridge at Vendange beyond repair. Not that I'd ever want to go back now—not if it means working for that imperious asshole, Joel. For what certainly isn't the first time, I reflect on how fortunate I am to have Claire Prentice's house-sitting money to cushion my fall. I've managed to save most of it, minus the back rent I paid my former landlord. Still, my remaining thirty-five-hundred will only take me so far.

This is the first time I've been unemployed since I was legally old enough to work, and some of my bravado falters as I hoof my way up Madison Avenue in my work heels with no place really to go.

"Shit, shit, shit." I slow at a corner for a traffic light, thankful that I'm in New York, where a woman muttering expletives to herself in the midst of a pedestrian crowd doesn't draw as much as a wink of attention.

Have I lost my freaking mind? I think maybe I have, because as terrifying as my not-so-distant future is, right now, I also feel a conflicting yet undeniable sense of liberation.

I'm unshackled, but I'm also well aware that it's only a temporary freedom.

Throwing away my job and paycheck is one thing. There is a harsher reality awaiting me just a few short months from now. When Claire returns from Japan, I'll not only be jobless, but homeless too.

And then there's Nick.

I meant it when I told Tasha I'm afraid of how much I like him. Each time we're together, I feel myself falling deeper under his spell, against my better judgment. Against all of my self-imposed rules about not letting anyone get too close to me.

Yet, in spite of all that, as I step away from the curb with the rest of the crowd to cross the street, it's his face I want to see the most. It's his voice I need to hear.

I retrieve my phone from my purse and bring up our text conversation—the one I've revisited more times than I care to count. Nick's number is just a finger-tap away. When we parted last night, I told him I wouldn't be able to see him for a couple of days because of work. He hadn't seemed pleased about that, but he'd allowed that he also had business that needed to be attended.

While I don't want to bother him if he's working, right now, there's a part of me that simply needs to feel connected to something solid and real. As hard as it is for me to admit it—even to myself—Nick is becoming the steadiest, most secure harbor I know.

Before I can lose my nerve, I tap his number and send the call.

He answers before the first ring has died out. "Avery."

"Hi."

"This is an unexpected pleasure." His voice curls around me, warm and dark and velvet-soft. I hear him quietly dismiss someone in the background, his tone all business. That terse edge is gone when he comes back to me a moment later. "How are you today, beautiful?"

I smile, savoring his tender endearment. "I'm fine. Still thinking about yesterday. And last night."

He makes a low sound in the back of his throat, something sensual that makes my insides melt a little. "I've been thinking about nothing else but you all morning. More specifically, I've been thinking about how gorgeous you were, riding me in the back of my limo, and about all the ways I want to make you come again."

Oh, God. Since I can hardly manage to walk a straight line when he's saying such delicious things to me, I ease out of the flow of foot traffic and take up a position near a men's clothing store.

"Nick, I'm sorry to call you at work."

"Don't be." He hesitates. "Is that traffic noise? Avery, where the hell are you?"

I glance up at the sign on the corner. "I'm on Madison, at the corner of Forty-sixth." I inhale, then push my breath out on a sigh. "I quit my job today."

Nick is quiet for a short moment, steady as always in his calm. "You sound rattled. Are you all right?"

"Yeah, I think so. I guess . . . I guess I just wanted to hear your voice."

"Don't go anywhere," he orders me. "I'll be there in less than ten minutes."

"Nick, that's really not necess—"

"There's a hotel right where you are. Wait for me in the lobby. I'm on my way now."

He ends the call without giving me a chance to refuse or say anything more.

And, true to his word, before ten minutes have passed, I watch his glossy black BMW slide up to the curb. One of the hotel valets steps out to greet him, but Nick waves off the assistance. Hurrying under the marquis entrance of the stately hotel, he pushes through one of the revolving doors and finds me inside.

"Avery."

As it always does, my stomach flips at the sight of him. He's dressed in a graphite gray suit, the jacket open over his white shirt. No tie today, but even with the top two buttons of his collar unfastened in an office-casual way, he still looks every inch a world-class business titan.

I sense more than see, the attention Nick draws simply by entering the building. As if he brings a live electrical charge inside with him, a jolt of awareness travels the high-ceilinged, sumptuous lobby. And it's no wonder, really.

Dominic Baine is as gorgeous as he is rich and powerful. And within his carved, devastatingly handsome face, his breathtaking bright blue eyes are locked unwaveringly on me.

I know he must be aware of the attention he's stirring, but for all of his discretion and reputed secrecy regarding his personal life, Nick seems not to care in the least. As I rise from my seat on one of the lobby's sofas, he is right there, collecting me into his arms. I am enfolded in a strong, protective embrace that makes me feel safer than I have at any other moment in my life.

After a few seconds, he pulls back to look at me. His frown deepens, solemn with concern. "Do you want to talk about it?"

"No." I give a small shake of my head, hoping he'll understand that I'm not ready to talk. Just as he has, I too have my own walls. Steep walls no one can climb. And as much as my heart wavers now, especially when Nick is holding me in his arms, I'm not yet ready to let him in.

What's more, deep down, I know I won't ever be able to let him in. Not without seeing his concern turn to pity and disgust—or something even worse.

He studies me, and while I'm sure his keen gaze can see all of the cracks in me as no one else ever has, he seems to understand that pressing will only make me break.

"I don't want to talk, Nick. I don't want to think about anything for a little while, okay?"

"Okay." He strokes the side of my face, his touch gentle as he continues silently assessing my wellbeing. "I know just the place for that."

25

As soon as we get into the car, Nick calls Lily and instructs her to clear his schedule for the rest of the day. I don't know what he has in mind for us, nor does it matter. Seated beside him in the BMW, his fingers curved over the top of my thigh as he smoothly navigates the afternoon traffic, I already have everything I need.

After we've been driving through the city for a little while, he slants me a look. "I hope you like seafood?"

"I love it."

"Excellent. I want to take you to one of my favorite spots."

I can't even begin to guess where that might be, especially now that he's heading toward the tunnel that will take us to Queens. "Are you going to tell me the name of it?"

"Nope."

"Not even a hint?"

Now he arches a dark brow in my direction. "What's the matter, you don't like surprises?"

"Not particularly."

In fact, I hate surprises. I've had too many in my life, beginning at the age of seven, on the day I learned that my father had died of a massive heart attack. Followed a few years later by the surprise news that my mom had met a nice family man from another town and I was getting a new stepfather. Which was then followed by the further surprise of seeing her with a black eye for the first time. Then, not long afterward, a broken arm.

There were other surprises, too, culminating in the most horrific of them all on that day nine years ago.

I've gone quiet, lost in troubling memories, and, of course Nick doesn't miss the change in my mood. The hand resting lightly on my thigh now lifts to my cheek. His touch is so tender it nearly breaks me.

"You'll like this surprise, I promise."

I don't know if he understands how profoundly his reassurance affects me. He can't, of course, and if I'm being honest with myself, I hope to hell he never does. I hope he never learns how ugly my past is—or how brutally it all came crashing down.

I want to pretend, even for just a little while, that this is my reality. I want to imagine that I know what it's like to be unburdened with secrets and lies. More than anything, I want to savor whatever Nick has in store for us and pretend that we are simply a normal couple enjoying a normal date together.

Determined to do just that, I settle back as we continue the drive through Queens. When we approach Cross Bay Boulevard, I think I've got his plan figured out.

"So, we're going out to eat at Howard beach?"

He grins. "Not that beach."

And, damn the man, his cryptic answer is all I get out of him. Soon, though, I see signs for the airport, and Nick merges into the exit lane for JFK. Without a word of explanation, he takes the turn and heads directly for the airport.

"Nick." I gape at him, confused and anxious and excited all at the same time. "Seriously. Where are we going?"

"Trust me." He glances at me, and while he's clearly enjoying his game, I also see sincerity written in his soul-searching blue eyes. "Can you do that, Avery?"

I stare back at him, feeling the weight of this moment all the way to my bones. He's not just talking about today, this mystery excursion. I can see that in the solemnity of his handsome face. He's asking for my trust in a much more meaningful way. One I'm not certain I fully understand yet.

Can I trust him?

I've never felt I needed a man to walk me through the rough patches in my life. I still don't, but I have to admit there is something comforting in being with Nick. I like the way he looks at me, the way he treats me. There is something deeply fortifying in being able to look across the small cabin of the vehicle and know that I'm not alone. To believe that with this man, I am protected. I am safe.

And yes, I do trust him.

The realization is so foreign, so out of my realm of experience, it takes me aback.

I nod, and his answering smile is my reward.

He avoids the main artery to the airport terminal.

Instead, we follow a service drive to a separate terminal reserved for private aircraft. He parks the car in the small lot and kills the engine.

"Shall we?"

"You're still not going to tell me where we're going?"

Instead of answering, he leans across the seat and drags me into a bone-melting kiss. When he releases me, I'm breathless, caught up in the oceans of his searching eyes. His deep voice caresses my senses like velvet. "Trust, Ms. Ross."

"Right," I murmur, my veins buzzing from just that brief joining of our mouths. "Am I at least dressed all right for wherever it is you're taking me?"

He pulls back to look at me in my low-cut black top, black jeans and heels. "You're more than dressed all right. You're sexy as hell. But you might be a little warm where we're going, so I'll phone ahead and make sure you have everything you need when we arrive."

I narrow my eyes at him. "You're going to phone ahead for clothes for me?"

"Unless I decide to keep you naked instead."

I smile and shake my head. "Are you this controlling in all aspects of your life, Mr. Baine, or just when it comes to me?"

"Are you truly ready to find out?"

A tingle runs over all of my nerve endings at his dark invitation. Although I spoke with humor, there is none in Nick's voice. His brilliant blue eyes hold me in a piercing, probing stare that I can't break even if I wanted to. The hungry way he looks at me makes my stomach flutter and my sex ache to have him inside me.

I can't help feeling that he's preparing me for something . . . that if I step out of this car with him now—if I allow him to lead me away from the life I knew before him—there will be no turning back.

He's telling me this now, giving me the chance to escape.

But that's not what I want.

He knows this, just as surely as I do.

I'm already in too deep. I have been from the start with him. And I don't want out.

"All right," I tell him. "Yes. I'm ready, Nick."

~ ~ ~

"So, was I right?" he asks, walking up behind me as I gaze out over the beginnings of a spectacular Miami sunset.

We're high atop the city on the wraparound terrace of a luxury penthouse, surrounded by open sky, endless water, and a soothing, warm ocean breeze. With nothing but a hip-high railing of clear Plexiglas in front of us, I feel as if we're part of the sky itself, suspended eighteen stories above the earth.

Nick rests his chin lightly on my shoulder, his deep voice curling through my senses. "How do you like this surprise?"

"It's incredible."

From our vantage point on the top floor of the sleek white residential tower, the sky seems close enough to touch, its smattering wisps of clouds lit up with a hundred shades of pink, lavender, coral, and gold. In front of us, the Atlantic stretches endlessly from the beach and boardwalk far below, to the distant horizon. Over my shoulder in the opposite direction, the sunset is even more brilliant, silhouetting the teeming, vibrant colors of Miami's downtown on the other side of Biscayne Bay.

We arrived a short time ago on board the piloted private jet Nick paid to charter on the spot at JFK. For all of our three hours in the air, he kept me in suspense over where we were going. And while a spontaneous trip to Miami Beach is more adventure than I've ever known, it turns out that was only part of his surprise. This penthouse condo—yet another of his impressive properties—is the icing on an already fabulous cake.

"I can't get over this view."

He presses a kiss to the side of my neck, just below my earlobe. "Wait until you see the sunrise from up here."

Wrapping his arms around me, he draws me closer to him, against the firm muscles of his chest and thighs. The flirty, above-the-knee, spaghetti-strap sundress I'm wearing—also courtesy of Nick—sways around my legs as I pivot in his embrace. "Are we staying overnight?"

"We can stay as long as you like."

Forever, I think, as he gently sweeps aside some of my hair that's blown loose from my ponytail, then caresses my cheek. Desire licks across my senses at that tender touch. I sigh, feeling all of my tension and uncertainty from earlier today begin to melt away from me.

Our bodies brush together only lightly as we stand here, but it's enough for me to feel the solid bulge of his erection at my abdomen. The fact that he wants me now like I want him sends a shiver of heat and awareness spiraling through me, straight to my core.

How can his slightest touch always arouse me so easily? How can it be that when we're together the rest of the world simply peels away?

He knows what he does to me, and from the slow smirk he gives me now, there's no denying that he enjoys how readily my body responds to him.

"Christ, you are a temptation," he murmurs, lowering his head to nip at my lower lip.

As he teases me with his kiss, his hand skims between my bare thighs under the fluttery fabric of my skirt where I am totally naked. Of the half-dozen dresses Nick arranged to have waiting for me, the thin-strapped bodice of the one I selected isn't made for a bra, so I'm not wearing one. And, at Nick's insistence when we changed clothes on our arrival, I'm not wearing panties either. I smile at the thought, because his erotic demand nearly undid him when he watched me slip into the silky little dress, and I know it's going to prove a distraction to him, too, until he's able to take it off me again.

He groans when his fingers reach my sex. I'm already wet just from being held in his arms, and from the kiss that turns possessive now, as he cleaves between my folds and strokes me without shame or mercy. I whimper helplessly at the first graze of his thumb over my clit, my hands fisting in his thick black hair as he pushes his tongue into my mouth and two fingers plunge deep into my body.

"Nick." His name is a gasp as I let my head tip back while he drives me toward madness with his wicked caresses. "Oh, shit . . . I could come like this."

"And you will, baby." He kisses my exposed throat, his tongue playing in the hollow at the base of my neck. "But not yet."

To my dismay, I feel his hand start to withdraw from me. I can't contain my disappointed moan. My skirt falls back down around my thighs, and when I look at him, he is grinning like the devil himself. Unabashedly carnal, he puts the two fingers that were inside me into his mouth and sucks on them.

"I'm ravenous," he growls darkly, a sinful curve to those lips I want to feel on mine, on every naked inch of my body. "Before I devour you the way I fully intend to, I should make good on that promise to feed you."

26

Nick's favorite place for seafood is a small, tucked-away beachfront restaurant about forty-five minutes south of Miami. We drive up in a metallic red Lamborghini Aventador rental that he arranged for at the airport upon our arrival earlier today, a sexy beast of a car that's turned every head we've passed. Although I've never been someone who craves the spotlight, I can't deny that I feel like a princess as Nick helps me out of the roadster and escorts me to the restaurant at his side.

The squat little building doesn't look like much from the outside, but it's crowded and more people are waiting under the arched portico of the entrance. As soon as the hostess spots Nick, however, she nods in greeting and steps through the waiting patrons to retrieve us.

"How nice to see you, sir," she offers, discreetly avoiding saying his name among the other patrons. I am granted an equally welcoming smile. "And good evening, ma'am. Right this way, please. We have your table waiting."

We follow her out to a garden patio area illuminated by flaming tiki torches and palm trees aglow with winding ropes of tiny white lights. Twenty-odd tables covered in elegant white linens, gleaming silverware, and crystal glasses fill the small concrete space overlooking a round lagoon and sandy beach. Beyond that are the glittering waters of Biscayne Bay and the open Atlantic.

The last moments of sunset paint the darkening sky in vivid colors as we make our way to the far end of the patio and the only open table—which also happens to be the one with the most romantic view of the water and skyline through the sheltering palms.

As we settle in at our table, Nick sends the hostess away with a request for a bottle of champagne. I notice he doesn't specify the label, nor does she ask.

"Are we celebrating?" I ask, glancing across to him while I unfold my white linen napkin and place it on my lap.

"Rumor has it someone quit their job today." He arches a brow in question. "I'd say that calls for celebration or consolation. Champagne seems a good accompaniment for either one."

I swallow, caught off guard by the reminder of what happened today. "It's cause for celebration," I say, unsure if I'm resolved or merely hopeful. "My boss is a jerk. If I'd had the nerve, I would've quit long before now."

Nick listens silently, his gaze never leaving me as I speak. "Sometimes it's hard to see the things that are holding us back. Sometimes it takes a push to make us truly open our eyes."

I nod, acknowledging to myself just how right he is about that. How long would I have endured Joel's overbearing treatment if I hadn't been forced to confront him? Would I have accepted his domineering attitude if it hadn't been for the sense of self-worth and power that being with Nick these past several weeks has instilled in me?

Our champagne arrives, a 1998 Dom Perignon that I'm certain I won't find on the general wine list. The wine steward carrying the four-hundred-dollar bottle waits for Nick's approval, then pours it for us. After the bottle is placed on ice and the steward is gone, Nick raises his glass.

"To opened eyes," he says.

I smile and touch my glass to his. "To good surprises and spectacular sunsets too."

"Indeed."

A broad grin breaks over his face, and for an instant I'm spellbound. I am well aware that Dominic Baine is handsome. Arrestingly so. But the impact of his smile on me in the middle of this crowded restaurant patio, with the unshakable awareness that everyone here is looking at us—wishing they could be us—is like something out of a dream.

He is like something out of a dream, and I barely resist the urge to pinch myself to make sure I'm actually awake and living this moment, not merely wishing I am.

My first sip of the crisp champagne tingles all the way down my throat. Nick doesn't take his gaze off me, not even to watch the final explosion of color that fills the sky in the moments before the sun is doused and the brilliant colors over the water give way to a starlit night.

We place our dinner orders—for Nick, the Chilean sea bass, and, for me, a Caribbean style red snapper—then settle back to share a ceviche appetizer of baby octopus, shrimp, white fish, and julienned vegetables sprinkled with cilantro and drizzled with a spicy cream sauce.

Nick pops a shrimp into his mouth, then watches as I push one of the small, many tentacled morsels to the other side of the plate with my fork. He shakes his head at me. "That piece is yours. Take it."

I wrinkle my nose, skepticism surely written all over my face. "Hmm, no, thanks."

"It's the best part of this dish." He stabs it on the end of his fork and holds it out to me over the plate. When I only stare at the decapitated little creature, Nick cocks his head. "Don't tell me this is your first time?"

"Isn't it obvious?"

He doesn't move his hand. And now, more than one person is staring our way while I sit frozen, and not a little repulsed, by Nick's gentlemanly but unwanted offering.

"Try it, Avery. Don't let fear keep you from pushing your personal boundaries. If you do, you'll miss out on some of the most pleasurable things in life."

I can't look away from his intense gaze and something dark—something wicked—unfurls deep inside me at his low-voiced enticement. "Why do I get the feeling you're not only talking about dinner?"

His answering smile is decadent, carnal. "Trust, Ms. Ross. Remember? You have my word, I won't introduce you to anything you won't enjoy. Immensely."

After everything he's shown me so far, I don't doubt that for a second.

Given little choice, I lean forward and close my mouth around his fork. The octopus feels strange on my tongue, tender yet firm. As I chew, I discover the flavor is actually quite good. Citrus and spice and creamy sweet sauce mingle wonderfully with the delicate taste of the octopus.

"You like it?" At my nod, Nick smiles approvingly, still leaned forward in his chair, his gaze riveted on my mouth. "I can't wait to expand your horizons even further."

I arch a brow at him. "Care to elaborate, Mr. Baine?"

He chuckles. "I'll do better than that. I'll demonstrate. Later."

I swallow and lick my lips while my stomach flips wildly at his erotic promise. Between my legs, I am suddenly very much aware of my nakedness and of the coil of heat that blooms there as he stares at me as if the rest of the people around us don't exist.

God help me, but I can't wait to find out what other things he has in mind for me.

I'm so caught up in my thoughts and Nick's scorching attention that I hardly register the fact that my phone is ringing in my handbag. Once I do hear it, the trill seems as loud as a siren in the tranquil little patio dining area.

"Sorry," I say and reach for my purse by my sandaled feet. "It's probably my friend, Tasha, from work calling to check in with me. I told her I'd call her later today."

As I grab the phone to silence the ring, I see the number there and feel my face lose some of its color.

"Go ahead and take it, if you want to," Nick says.

"No." I shake my head as I send my mother's call to voice mail. "It's not Tasha."

"Oh," Nick replies. His level tone is unreadable, but his face darkens with suspicion. "Do I have to be concerned about another man?"

"What? No." I frown, shaking my head. "No, nothing like that."

"Good." He doesn't smile. Nor does he press me for more details.

Dammit, I should be thankful for that reprieve and go back to our conversation as if the call never happened. But for some reason—one I don't care to examine—I feel compelled to let him peer inside my life, my real life, if only a glimpse.

I slide the phone back into my purse, then take a sip of my champagne. "That was my mom."

His dark brows rise a bit. "You didn't want to talk to her?"

"Not right now."

He says nothing for a long moment. Then, when he does speak, his words seem to be chosen carefully, as if he senses that he's treading on shaky ground. "You and your mother aren't close?"

"We're very close. I adore her."

"But you haven't told her about me."

"No." I set down my empty glass. Mindful of curious ears, I keep my voice quiet. "What would I tell her? That for the past several weeks, I've been sleeping with one of the richest men in New York—possibly the whole country? Or that I've just quit my job and now I'm sitting in Miami eating octopus and drinking champagne without a care in the world?"

Nick smirks. "I know a lot of enterprising mothers who would like nothing more than to hear those words."

"Not my mother. She'll think I've lost my mind—

and maybe she'd be right about that." I shake my head slowly. "If I tell her anything about us, it will only make her worry about me. I won't do that."

"Because you're protective of her," he says, directly hitting the mark.

"The same way she's always been protective of me. She's had a . . . difficult life. She still does. I try not to add to her burdens." I glance down as I exhale and fidget with my hands in my lap. "My mom is all the family I have left."

"I'm sorry." I lift my head and find nothing but sincerity in his face. "I'm sorry if things haven't been easy for you."

His words touch me, cracking something open inside me that I can't afford to let break. I shouldn't let him see me so clearly. I shouldn't want him to understand my pain, or the secrets I can never fully release. Not even to him.

"What about you, Nick? I don't think your life has always been easy either."

I can't keep my gaze from drifting to his right hand and arm, to his scars. He's wearing light tan slacks and a pale blue button-down, the cuffs rolled up over his muscular forearms. To anyone merely glancing at him, his imperfections are the last thing they'll notice. But I've seen the evidence of his injuries. I know he suffered something awful—something brutal—at some point in his life.

When I glance back up to meet his eyes, they seem to have hardened somewhat. He lifts his shoulder, one corner of his mouth tugging into a mirthless smile.

"When I was eighteen, I had the bad sense one night to get in the way of a drunk who was spoiling for a fight.

I thought I was a hardass. I thought I could handle the situation. The bastard sent me through a plate glass window. I woke up in the hospital a week later with a shredded arm and a nearly severed hand."

I gasp, my hand flying to my mouth. "Oh, my God. Nick, that's awful."

He shrugs, yet there is something in his eyes that seems anything but nonchalant. "I survived. The scars are just a reminder of my stupidity and arrogance. Anyway, I doubt I could find many people to feel sorry for me now."

I do, but I don't say the words. I know he would reject my sympathy. He sure as hell doesn't want pity. But my heart aches for what he must have suffered. The horror of the accident. The pain of the recovery. The permanent reminder of all of it.

I reach across the table and rest my hand over his damaged one. He doesn't pull away, but the look he gives me is flinty and forbidding. It's shuttered, as if he's given me all he intends to right now and if I push, I'll never hear anything more.

I'm spared from the temptation when our dinners arrive. They are every bit as delicious as our appetizer, and, for a while, Nick and I content ourselves with savoring our meals. Nick orders a bottle of white wine for us even though a quarter of the bottle of champagne still sits on ice in the bucket beside our table.

We chat about small things as we eat and drink our wine. To my delight, halfway through our meal, a five-piece Cuban band arrives and sets up nearby. I guess the youngest of the musicians to be in his fifties, with the rest of the group seeming at least a decade or two older than him.

The men begin playing a sultry song that sets my sandaled foot tapping beneath the table and my shoulders swaying slightly to the melody. When I catch Nick watching, a wave of self-consciousness sweeps over me.

"Sorry."

"Don't be." He considers me for a moment, then sets his napkin next to his plate and stands up. He holds his hand out, palm up. "Come with me."

"Uh, what?"

"Dance with me."

We're not the only ones who've decided to enjoy the music on the small area of the patio cleared for dancing, but I still feel every pair of eyes on us as Nick waits for me to take his hand and join him. Reluctantly, because I can't imagine refusing, I ease up from my seat and place my hand in his.

He leads me over and draws me against him, his hand resting lightly at my back, the other clasped loosely around mine. Neither one of us are going to win any rumba awards, but then, it's not as if we're trying to impress anyone. We move together, gazes locked, bodies brushing to the rhythm of the sexy song.

It feels good to be close to him, moving with him as one. His eyes hold me captive in flickering light of the tiki torches, his scent intoxicating me even more than the wine. I want him desperately, and I can sense his arousal, too, even before I feel the growing evidence of it at my hip.

His hand slides down my spine, then over the curve of my ass. I know what he's thinking as his touch lingers there, possessive and unapologetic. My bare flesh trembles beneath my short skirt, every inch of me aching for him.

Nick lowers his head beside mine, and his lips graze the shell of my ear. His words send desire jolting through me. "Let's get out of here."

27

We speed through the city on our return to the beachfront penthouse. Nick's left hand is draped over the wheel, his right hand resting on the Aventador's gear shift as the agile roadster prowls Miami's brightly lit, teeming streets. I'm vaguely aware of the envious looks we inspire along the way, but all of my attention is fixed on the sexy-as-sin man seated beside me.

I'm leaned toward Nick as best I can in the deep bucket seat, my hand splayed over his powerful thigh. Each flex of his muscles as he accelerates or downshifts makes me hotter to have him. Every brief, fevered glance he sends my way makes my stomach flutter eagerly and my sex coil with hungered anticipation of the moment I can have him inside me again.

"Are we almost there?" I ask, hearing the rasp of desire in my own voice.

"Oh, baby, we're not even close." Nick slants me a

dark, devilish look. "The apartment, however, is only ten minutes away."

I smile at his teasing and decide to do a little of my own.

"Ten whole minutes? I'm not sure I can last that long without touching you."

I run my palm higher on the inside of his firm thigh until my hand grazes the bulge of his erection. I caress between his legs, cupping his balls and relishing the sudden kick of his breathing. His shaft swells even harder under my roving touch, his thigh muscles quivering as I move my fingers over him. His reaction makes me bolder, so I lift my arm out from under the shoulder strap of my seat belt and pivot closer, my caress growing shameless.

As we roll to a red light at an intersection crowded with people, my mouth is only inches from his ear. "I'm not sure I can last ten more minutes without tasting you, Mr. Baine."

He makes a sound that seems more growl than reply. When I unfasten his zipper and pull his erect cock out of his pants, his blue eyes pierce me with carnal heat.

"You are very naughty, Ms. Ross."

I press my lips against the squared line of his jaw. "Actually, I'm ravenous."

He grins at my reminder of earlier tonight, but his body goes tense under my touch. As we wait for the light to change, I stroke his thick, jutting shaft. I don't miss the fact that his molars are clamped tight, tendons straining in his neck while I run my hand along his length. His eyes flick over to mine and I give him a saucy smile, then lower myself down onto his lap. He grates out a sharp curse at the first swirl of my tongue over the tip of his penis.

"Good thing we didn't stay for dessert," I murmur. "I like this much better."

I wrap my lips around the head of his cock, and he groans.

"Ah, fuck . . . baby," he rasps, looking down at me as traffic and street noise buzzes all around us at the intersection. "You get me so fucking hard."

I can't deny my thrill at hearing those words, at feeling the solid evidence of his response to me as his rigid flesh slides so deliciously against my tongue. I tease the broad head of him, tracing the smooth rim and crown, then licking along the tender underside. Tasting, but not taking.

And God, does he taste good. Silky, salty, satiny smooth as I slide up and down on his rigid flesh. But beneath all of that velvet is pure, masculine power. And my small taste of him only makes me crave more. I part my lips and take him into my mouth, sucking him deep.

Nick's hips thrust up in response, in demand. He hisses sharply, his right hand coming down onto the back of my head. His fingers sift through my long ponytail as I lick and suck on him without mercy.

"Christ," he snarls. "I'm not going to last ten damn minutes without fucking you either."

I know the instant the light turns green. Nick shifts into gear and stomps on the accelerator, sending the Aventador leaping away from the intersection with a thunderous roar of the engine and a scream of spinning tires.

I don't think it takes even five minutes for us to reach the apartment building. I'm still enjoying Nick's cock as he parks the Lambo in the underground garage and cuts the engine.

On a guttural curse, he pulls me off him and hastily zips up. "You don't play fair, Ms. Ross."

His grim smile sends ten kinds of shivers through my body as he coils my ponytail around his fist and drags me roughly across the seats. His eyes scorch me with barely restrained need as he holds me immobile, our faces less than an inch apart. "I can think of any number of ways I'd like to punish you for that."

Punish. The word startles me on some basic, primal level. It's not one I've ever heard from a lover before. Certainly not one I'd expect to turn me on. But it does, the way everything about this man stirs something bold and reckless in me. Things I've never been, or thought I could be, with anyone else.

With Nick, I have no fear. No, with him, none of my old rules apply. He's been tempting me to bend or break them all from the very beginning. I lick my lips, which are swollen and still carrying the erotic scent and taste of him.

He takes me into a kiss that is hard and urgent and raw. I moan with the intensity of it, my sex clenching in animal response to every claiming thrust of his tongue inside my mouth. I bring my hands up to his face, my fingers rasping over the faint stubble of his jaw, then tunneling deeply into his soft black hair so I can hold him closer.

I want this bruising kiss to go on forever. What I really want to do is drop back down on him and suck him until he comes, but Nick releases me on a low growl, and it's plain from the stormy heat of his eyes that he has other plans.

We barely make it into the penthouse apartment

before he pounces on me. His kiss is carnal, his body hard against my curves, dominating me in a way that leaves me breathless.

I'm not sure how we end up moving to the terrace. Nick's command of my mouth and my body is so consuming, I don't register that we're outside until I feel the first cool brush of night air on my bare arms and legs. My short, lightweight skirt dances around my thighs. The ocean breeze is cool against my naked sex, a delicious contrast to the molten heat Nick has ignited in every cell of my being.

Nick reaches between my legs and draws in a breath through clenched teeth. "I shouldn't play fair with you, either. I should tease," he says, his fingertips barely skimming my drenched cleft. "I should torment."

He gives my sensitized clit only the briefest stroke of his thumb—a there-and-gone caress that wrings a broken cry from my parted lips. I gaze up at him helplessly, prepared to beg for more.

"I should punish you," he murmurs, his voice harsh with lust.

As he says this, I realize I'm holding my breath, suspended in a dark anticipation that sends my heart galloping in my breast. I am waiting for his touch, for his kiss, for whatever he desires from me. I am his for the taking, however he wants me. I have been from the moment our eyes first met weeks ago, and he knows it.

"Yes," I answer.

My admission is so quiet, at first, I think the breeze has carried it away. But then I watch Nick's eyes darken under the hard slashes of his brows. I watch his achingly handsome face take on a dangerous edge now, a look that unnerves me, excites me . . . makes me tremble with need.

"You trust me," he says, less question than confident statement of fact.

I nod, too caught up in my desire to summon words.

"Turn around."

I obey his low command, and find that I am standing at the very edge of the open terrace. The Plexiglas railing is only inches in front of me, the hip-high barrier between my body and an eighteen-story drop practically invisible in the starlit darkness. It steals my breath to be so close to the inky, endless space below me. Farther out, the moonlit, spangled water ripples away from the dark shore as far as my eyes can see.

Nick's strong hands come to rest on my shoulders. His warmth seeps through my skin and bones, and I can't keep from settling back into him as he moves up close behind me. I want to feel his arms around me, to know that I am anchored to something safe and solid, but he denies me that comfort.

"Hold on to the railing," he instructs me, his tone authoritative and calm. "Don't take your hands off of it, Avery. Not unless I tell you to."

I nod, swallowing on a dry throat. The arced perimeter of Plexi is topped by a broad strip of polished steel. I curl my fingers over it, holding on like I've been told. The short, swishy skirt of my dress flutters in the night breeze, tickling my thighs. Behind me, I feel a stirring of even cooler air as Nick backs away slightly.

"Spread your legs for me, baby." He makes a low sound of approval when I comply. "Good girl. Now bend forward. Lower, baby . . . That's it, all the way down. I want to see your fine ass and sweet pussy bared and ready for me. Ready for anything I want to do."

Oh, God. My sex clenches at his erotic threat. I draw a shaky breath and try to glance over my shoulder at him. When his palm smacks my behind, I yelp at the unexpected shock of it, staggering a bit on my high-heeled sandals.

"Face forward, Ms. Ross." His deep voice vibrates into my bones. "You earned this, remember?"

The lingering sting of his spank is a lick of flame on my ass, but his fingers are right there an instant later, skimming over me feather-light, soothing the bite. Shivers grip me in the wake of that teasing touch, and my pulse becomes a throb, one that seems rooted in my clit.

"You're mine to torment now," he reminds me. His caress dips lower, into the slick heat between my parted thighs. "I'll tell you when you can move."

Given no choice but to submit, I drop my head and wait breathlessly, eagerly, for the next morsel of pleasure—or pain—that he decides to grant me.

I moan when he dips two fingers inside me, plunging deep. He thrusts once, twice, a slow rhythm that drives me mad. I need more. To ease the ache, I need it harder and faster.

"Nick, please . . ."

"Please, what?"

He drives another finger into me, but it's still not enough. "Fuck me."

"Oh, baby." He chuckles darkly, a sound so purely sexual I nearly come on the spot. "Don't cry for mercy so soon. I'm not even close to finished with you yet."

As if to demonstrate that this is punishment I volunteered for, he withdraws his fingers completely, ignoring my whimper of protest. My skirt is tossed up and over my back, exposing me fully from the waist down. His palms caress my ass cheeks, massaging them. Parting them in the instant before I feel the first wet flick of his tongue at my anus.

"Nick." His name shudders out of me on a ragged gasp. It's all I can do to remain standing as he licks and sucks and tongues my ass. I'm squirming helplessly, my muscles quivering from the arches of my spread feet to the tendons of my fingers clutched for dear life to the terrace railing.

My orgasm builds swiftly as he gathers me closer to his mouth and greedily feasts on me. When his fingers slide into my wetness to stroke my tender flesh, his thumb rolling over my clit in a demanding tempo, I can't hold back my pleasured cry. My spine arcs, and a spasm shakes me. And suddenly I'm coming harder than I ever have, sensation pouring over me, racking me to the core.

His teeth nip my ass hard, spiking the last aftershocks of my release into the stratosphere. I feel him shift behind me. I hear the metallic jangle of his belt as he unbuckles it, followed by the urgent rasp of his zipper. Foil crinkles, then rips as he tears open a condom packet.

His hands are hot on my bare pelvis, his fingers like iron as he yanks my ass toward him. His shaft is hard and thick against the cleft of my body, and my sex responds with renewed need. I whimper impatiently, tilting my hips to receive him.

I want to cry for mercy, dammit. I want to scream for him to drive home to the hilt. Instead, I clamp my teeth down so hard on my lower lip that I taste blood. Just when I think I can't possibly take another second of this torment, Nick's cock slides between my legs.

"Forget the punishment. I need to fuck you." He slips one hand between us, seating the blunt head of his penis at my body's entrance. "Hang on now, baby. Don't you let go."

He rams into me with a thrust that has me seeing stars behind my closed eyelids. There is no gentleness to his rhythm, only need. Hot and fast and slick and raw. The pleasure and pain is so intense, so exquisitely entwined, it nearly makes me weep.

And each savage pound of his body drives me closer to the steep fall below. The railing is secure, solid as steel, but I can't deny my fear as my shoulders and chest drape over it, fully at Nick's mercy. My breath gusts out of me in shaky gasps and blood rushes to my lowered head, my body rocking hard against the low wall as I absorb the impact of his possessive, dominating thrusts.

He's taking me someplace tonight that I've never been. Someplace exhilarating and intense, where adrenaline is fuel to pleasure and punishment is its own sweet reward.

And I can't get enough.

I grasp the railing like he told me to do, but in spite of his command I can feel that it's really his firm hold on my hips that's keeping me tethered. In spite of the danger he may one day pose to my heart, his strong hands are the ones keeping me safe now. It is his control that's giving me the freedom to feel this intense pleasure, this ecstasy that's made all the more explosive because of the fear, because of the risk.

As much as I crave this wildness, every clash of our bodies tells me that he craves it too, that he is as ruled as I am by this passion that exists between us.

He snarls with it now, hammering hard and furious.

Desperate for my own release again, I widen my stance and cant my hips to take him deeper, and the leash he holds on his control snaps. As he comes, he utters my name like a curse, one hand leaving my hip to twist in the length of my thrashing ponytail as his thrusts go deeper. As if he can't get far enough inside me.

His climax trips my own. I splinter apart on a pleasured scream.

And when my hands start to give out from the blissful bonelessness of my spent body, Nick's arms wrap solidly around me. He pulls me back from the edge and turns me around in his embrace, his eyes tender on me but dark with erotic intent. He scoops me up into his arms, then carries me back into the penthouse and to his waiting bed inside.

28

Sunrise, as promised, is nothing short of spectacular from Nick's penthouse terrace. While he's on a call with a colleague in London, I wander outside with my cell phone to snap some photos of nature's glorious pastel light show. My work may not be worthy of Nick's gallery—a fact that stings more than I care to admit—but I want to remember these colors for the next time I paint. On a whim, I take another shot, one that also captures a pretty white sailboat cruising about a mile out from shore.

Recalling now my promise to touch base with Tasha, I select one of my new photos and text it to her.

Sorry I didn't call yesterday, but this happened.

Here with Nick. All good.

Her reply buzzes back almost instantly. *Are those friggin palm trees, bitch?! I really need to rethink this friendship with you...*

I laugh and send a smiley face. *Love you too. Be in touch*

when I can.

Glad you're all right, she texts back. *Call me soon! P.S. Work sucks even worse without you!*

I can't believe it was only yesterday that I walked out of Vendange. Less than twenty-four hours with Nick on this fantasy getaway makes Joel and the restaurant seem like a distant dream.

All the rest of my problems seem far off, too, held at bay by the pleasure Nick has given me and by the feeling of safety I know when I am in his arms. It's not something I've had with anyone else—this sense that I am truly protected and secure.

That I am sheltered from everything. Even my past.

Hidden away up here with Nick in his paradise in the clouds, I can almost believe that nothing bad can touch me.

Only an illusion, I know. Right now, I am too content to care about reality.

As I take in the awe-inspiring view, I snuggle deeper into the white bathrobe Nick gave me to wear when I stepped out of the shower with him a few minutes ago. The thick cotton terrycloth carries his scent. The indescribable blend of clean, masculine skin and spicy sensuality has become my favorite drug, arousing everything female in me and stirring a deep possessiveness I cannot deny. Crossing my arms over my breasts, I tilt my chin down to nestle my nose into the plush lapel and I inhale slowly, savoring this sensory reminder of him.

As beautiful as this morning is, I don't want to let go of the night we shared. I don't want to go back to New York, where everything Nick has whisked me away from still awaits.

Including the many lies I'll have to explain to him.

"I thought you'd be dressed by now."

At the sound of his voice, I glance over my shoulder and see him walking up behind me in nothing but a large white towel fastened around his hips. My mouth waters as I watch him moving with predatory grace across the terrace. I've had my lips and tongue all over every inch of that tan, muscular body, and just the sight of Nick striding toward me now makes me hungry to do it again.

I smile, unable to keep the joy off my face. "I can get dressed anytime. I don't know when I'll have another chance to see the sun come up from such an amazing vantage point."

"Glad to know you have your priorities straight. Clothing is highly overrated anyway." He grins, drawing up beside me and leaning his hip against the railing. "After last night, I doubt I'll ever be able to stand out here again without getting a raging hard-on."

As evidence of that fact, I can't help noticing how enticingly his towel is bulging at his groin. He has no shame, of course, standing there half-naked and looking hot enough to melt me on the spot. My sex responds with a tingling surge of wet heat, spreading flame into my limbs and beading my nipples against the soft fabric of the robe.

I'm sure Nick sees my reaction. He's become attuned to my body's needs even more than I am myself. Blue eyes darkening, he reaches out and takes the tail end of the robe's long sash, pulling me against him. I don't fight it. More than anything, I want to feel his hands on me again. I want to feel him inside me now, again . . . for as long as I possibly can.

He kisses me, wrapping his arms around my back.

"Have you decided what you'd like to do today?"

"I can think of a few things."

His dark brows wing up with the slow curve of his lips. "Oh, trust me, Ms. Ross, so can I. And we will, I promise." His lips brush mine again, ending with a deliberate nip that makes me gasp. "Don't think I've forgotten that I still owe you some form of punishment."

"If last night was any indication, I can hardly wait for more."

He chuckles at my challenge and the hands clasped loosely at my back slide down to squeeze my ass. He draws my pelvis against the now massive ridge of his erection. "Feeling daring, are you?"

"I can't help it. You're a very bad influence, Mr. Baine. I'm a shameless harlot around you."

"Shameless happens to be my favorite kind of harlot," he growls as he kisses me again, grinding his cock against me in a hard demand that fires up all of my nerve endings. I moan at the arousing feel of him, already half-drunk with desire. He tears his mouth away from mine on a ragged curse. "Jesus, what you do to me. You get me so damn turned on, I think I could fuck you for weeks without coming up for breath."

I sigh with pleasure at the very idea. "Mmm, sounds good to me."

His hands slip inside my robe. I drop my head back on a soft cry as his fingers trace up my rib cage, then begin to caress my naked breasts. My thighs are straddling his leg, and I can't resist moving against him, my sex wet with arousal and aching for contact. Nick doesn't keep me waiting for long. One hand skims down my body and into my swollen cleft. He delves between my folds, stroking the hard bud of my clit before penetrating me with his finger.

"Oh, God." My breath is rushing in and out of my lungs as he thrusts and withdraws, driving me mad with rising need. "Nick, that feels so good."

His eyes deepen to a stormy blue as he watches me writhe and squirm on his hand. When he speaks, his voice is rough as gravel. "Now who's the bad influence, Ms. Ross? Here I was planning to take you out for coffee and a nice breakfast before I made you come again today."

I laugh and shake my head. "Coffee and breakfast later. Right now, I just want you to fuck me."

"Shameless *and* demanding," he replies, lowering his head to claim my mouth in a deep, dominatingly possessive kiss. Then he withdraws his fingers from inside me and gives my clit a light pinch. "Get your sweet ass in my bed, Ms. Ross. Unless you want me to take you right here in broad daylight."

~ ~ ~

We don't make it out of Nick's apartment to look for breakfast until sometime after ten. I would be happy spending the entire day in his bed, but, unfortunately, our empty stomachs refuse to be ignored. While I have to admit I was looking forward to another of his amazing home-cooked breakfasts, I can hardly be disappointed when I see the cheery waterfront cafe he's taking me to in Coconut Grove.

Overlooking a marina filled with sleek megayachts and tall-masted sailboats of all sizes, the outdoor restaurant is filled with a mix of people. Some drip with jewelry and logoed resort wear, while others are dressed in the tourist-casual staples of cargo shorts and T-shirts. Nick and I fall somewhere in the middle. He looks laid-back but unmistakably affluent in navy Bermuda shorts, deck shoes, and a white polo shirt.

As for me, I'm feeling feminine and pretty on his arm in my sleeveless, sky-blue linen wrap dress and flat sandals—my entire outfit high-end designer label, compliments of the Dominic Baine fantasy getaway collection. I've never had such fine, expensive clothes, but I know the heads turning in my direction are not so much about the way I'm dressed as they are about the man I'm with. The people here may not recognize him for the business titan he is, but I've witnessed more than once how Nick's presence commands attention wherever he goes.

It's impossible to ignore the hungered looks of more than a few of the other women who watch him now, nor their thin, envious glances that slide my way as an afterthought. As if he senses my anxiety, Nick's palm comes to rest possessively at my lower back as we move through the restaurant with the hostess in front of us.

We're shown to a table near the perimeter of the restaurant where thick nautical ropes section off the dining area from the walkway leading out to the docks. Seagulls glide over the boats, their cries mingling with the buzz of conversations around us.

Nick and I settle in and place our orders, then soon enjoy fresh fruit plates and light-as-air crepes, all served under a cloudless, sunny sky that couldn't be more perfect. Even though the place is busy with boaters coming and going, it feels incredibly intimate being seated across from him, having breakfast at our thatch umbrella-covered table.

Somewhere along the way these past several weeks, it's begun to feel natural and comfortable to be with him no matter where we are. It feels safe to be with him.

It feels . . . right.

That realization alone should fire off all kinds of warning bells inside me. Instead, it fills me with a joy that's been missing from my life for so long, I'm astonished that it might truly be real.

Nick catches me smiling as I sip my coffee. "What are you thinking about?"

I shrug with the intent to evade the question, but it blurts off my tongue anyway. "I'm thinking that I'm happy." I swallow, caught up in the oceanic blue of his gaze. "I haven't been happy like this in a really long time. Maybe never."

He reaches across the table for my hand and brings my fingers to his lips for a tender kiss. "Someday, Avery, you're going to tell me why that is."

He says it as if it will be my choice, but there is an unspoken demand in the intensity of his studying gaze. A shot of panic races through me at the thought. I can't tell him more, no matter how far things end up going between us. There are some things he can't ever know.

Aside from the lies I've told him about my personal life, the secrets I'm keeping about my past will make him either pity me or despise me. I couldn't bear to see either of those things in his eyes. It's hard enough seeing the question in his eyes now, as my silence lengthens.

To my relief, our waitress chooses this moment to come over and ask if we'd like anything else. The moment broken, I tuck my hands in my lap and decline her offer of more coffee. After our plates are cleared away and Nick has sent her for the check, I attempt to steer us toward safer conversation.

"Some of these boats are really incredible, aren't they?"

I can see that he suspects my dodge, but he indulges me with a nod of agreement. I gesture to a blocky, gunmetal gray beast of a speedboat that's just motoring in to dock. "Check that one out. It looks like something a James Bond villain would own."

Nick chuckles when I wrinkle my nose. "You don't like it?"

"It's all right. Call me old-fashioned, but I like the sailboats best."

His brows rise. "A woman after my own heart."

His easy smile is devastating and his casual remark makes the air seem a little warmer, a little more electric. I take a sip of my coffee and try to pretend he's not turning me on just by sitting across the table from me. "So, you like to sail, Nick?"

"I've puttered around from time to time," he says. "When's the last time you were out on the water?"

I wave my hand dismissively. "Oh, a long time ago. And never on anything like these boats. My grandpa had a Sunfish on the lake where they used to live. He'd take me out on that when I was little, and taught me a bit about sailing."

"Sounds like a good time."

I nod. "It was. Sometimes he'd let me help turn the sail. Mostly I just liked being out on the boat with him." I release a slow sigh, reflecting on the time when things were different for me back home. When things were good. "It's been a long time since I thought about those days."

"Your grandfather doesn't sail anymore?"

"He died when I was in my teens." I could leave it at that, and probably should. But the wound is still fresh even after all this time and the words leak out of me in a quiet voice. "He'd been drinking late one night and made the mistake of getting in his car. He hit a tree on one of the back roads by the lake. Fortunately, no one was with him or on the road when he had the accident."

"Jesus." Nick's face grows solemn as I speak, almost stern. "I'm sorry you had to lose him like that."

"It was a hard blow for all of my family. One of many," I admit, knowing I can't go any further with this memory than I already have.

I can't tell Nick that my grandfather's alcoholism came on the heels of losing his cherished daughter to the Pennsylvania prison system on a life sentence for murder. I can't tell him that after my mother was convicted and my grandpa was dead, the only person I had left was my grandmother—a woman whom I know wanted to care for me, but couldn't because of her sorrow for the daughter she'd been forced to watch be taken away.

I can't tell him about the deeper secrets that have been eating away at my soul for nearly a decade. Secrets that are like poison, eroding me from within the longer I keep them, but certain to destroy me if I ever let them out.

Our server comes to my rescue again, bringing our check and presenting it to Nick with a smile that seems less about winning a big tip than catching his eye. If he notices the attractive girl's attention, he handles it with the same cool confidence that he handles everything else that comes his way.

Discreetly placing a large bill inside the check wallet, he hands it back and politely tells her to keep the change.

"Want to take a walk?" he asks me, training the full measure of his smile on me alone.

"I'd love to."

We head out onto the boardwalk and begin a leisurely stroll along the docks to look at the rows of flashy, large-engined speedboats with groan-inducing names like *Pier Pressure* and *Liquid Assets* and *Feelin' Nauti*. A few minutes into our tour of the marina, I spot the futuristic looking gray yacht from earlier. When I snort out loud, Nick turns a curious glance at me.

"What'd I tell you?" I gesture to the name emblazoned on its stern. *"Double-Oh-Heaven."*

He laughs, too, then takes my hand and we begin making our way over to the quieter area of the marina where most of the sailboats are docked.

As we walk, my phone rings in my purse. I don't have to guess who's calling. Given that my mother wasn't able to reach me last night, she's using precious time during her lunch break to try again. As much as I don't want anything to intrude on the nice time I'm having with him, I hate leaving my mom to wonder or worry about me.

Nick pauses. "Do you need to get that? Go ahead, if you want. I'm going to run over to the marina shop and get us a couple bottles of water."

Although I'm certain it's only a polite excuse to give me privacy, as soon as he steps away I reach into my bag and swipe the screen to answer. "Yes, I accept," I quietly tell the automated collect calling message. "Hi, Mom."

We fall into an easy conversation, picking up right where we left off a few days ago. After assuring me that her parole board interview is still on track with no anticipated snags, she happily informs me that she's finished the mystery novel she was reading when we last spoke and has now started a juicy romance about a vampire, of all things. She tells me how glad she is that spring is coming and how pretty the blossoming trees look outside her cell's window.

I listen and respond accordingly, while guiltily staring out at the boats gleaming in the blue water of the marina and the white gulls swooping through the sun-filled sky—a freedom my mother will likely never experience for herself again.

I want to tell her about Nick. I want to tell her that I've met someone special, someone who makes me happy. But our fifteen minutes have dwindled to less than five, and, besides, I know that's a conversation that won't be easy for her to hear. She'll worry for me. She'll need to be reassured that I'm safe with this man she doesn't know. That I'm being careful.

As we say our goodbyes, I see Nick walking toward me across the dock. He's carrying a plastic shopping bag with the marina's logo on it in one hand and a couple bottles of water in the other hand. By the time I end my call, he's striding up to me with an enigmatic grin on his face.

"What's all this?" I ask.

He passes me the water. "Provisions."

While I stare in confusion, he reaches into the bag and pulls out a sailor's cap. The blue and white captain's hat is made for a child, but Nick leans in to kiss me as he places it on my head. "Are you ready to go?"

"Ready to go where?"

Instead of answering, he starts walking up one of the

docks. I hurry after him, watching as he approaches the prettiest vessel in the marina—a large, two-masted, teak-trimmed white sailboat named *Icarus.* Nick sets his shopping bag down on the deck and motions for me to join him.

I eye him warily. "You can't be serious. Don't tell me you just chartered this boat for us."

"I didn't." His grin is positively boyish. "I own her. She was one of the first things I bought for myself once I could afford to be stupid with money. Come on aboard, Avery. Let's go sailing."

29

For the rest of the day, my world consists of billowing white sails, crystalline blue water, balmy ocean air . . . and Nick, expertly mastering them all. After motoring out of the marina into Biscayne Bay, we raised the sails and headed south. I don't know how many hours we've been sailing or even where we'll end up.

Frankly, it doesn't much matter to me.

With the breeze in my face and the sun warm on my skin, I'm in heaven. It doesn't hurt that I'm sharing this little piece of bliss with a gorgeous man who looks like something out of a swashbuckling dream. Nick's dark hair is tousled and wild as he stands shirtless and barefoot in the cockpit, his tan skin turning an even richer shade of bronze in the hours since we set sail.

For what isn't the first time, he catches me staring at him. His answering grin is relaxed and carefree, and it does strange things to my heartbeat. "Ready to take the helm for a while?"

"Sure." I step next to him in the cockpit, eager to pitch in. Although my grandfather taught me the basics of sailing, my skills are rusty and Nick's boat is like nothing I've ever handled before. "What do I need to do?"

He moves in behind me at the wheel and points forward, his arm stretched out over my shoulder. The heat of his body, the sun-kissed scent of his skin, all conspire to make me dizzy with sensory overload. And he knows his effect on me, dammit.

"Just hold her steady," he tells me, his hot breath tickling the shell of my ear. I feel his lips brush the tender skin below my earlobe as his low voice rumbles against my back. When I shudder with kindling arousal, he compounds my body's reaction by pressing a soft kiss to the side of my neck. "Steady now, I said. A good first mate can take any distraction in stride."

I smile and pivot a wry look at him. "I doubt most first mates have to deal with the kind of distractions I do."

He arches a brow. "Complaining, Ms. Ross?"

"Hardly."

"Good." His mouth curves in an unrepentant smile. With gentle fingers, he turns my face forward. "Now, just keep our bow aimed at that buoy over there."

I give him a cheeky salute. "Aye, aye, Captain."

Barefoot and agile as a cat, he hops topside to trim the sails while I hold our course. I do my best to follow his instructions, but it's damn hard to stare at a bobbing marker in the distance when Nick's near-naked body and effortless athleticism are on full display. He manages the sails singlehandedly and with a level of skill that leaves me more than impressed. Not to mention, hopelessly turned on.

He returns, raking his scarred hand through his wind-blown hair as he hops into the cockpit. When I step back to give him the helm, he shakes his head.

"You keep her. The wind is steady and we're on a straight course now. You're doing great." He gives my ass a firm squeeze as he leans around me and steals a kiss. "Besides, it's my turn to watch you for a while."

He takes a seat on the slatted-teak bench on the starboard side of the cockpit and lets me take us farther into the bay. When I glance over my right shoulder I find his arms draped casually along the back of the bench, one ankle resting on his knee. Beneath the dark slashes of his brows, his bright blue eyes burn steady as he appraises me.

I clear my throat, needing something else to focus on besides the inviting heat I see in his gaze. "So, you just putter around on boats from time to time, hmm?"

He smirks. "More or less."

"After seeing you out here today, my money's on *more*. How long have you been sailing?"

"Long time. I was practically born on the water." It's a vague answer, and I assume that's all he intends to tell me when he shrugs, glancing out at the waves as we cut through them. "I actually grew up here in Florida. Started sailing even before I learned to ride a bike."

"Oh." I can't hide my surprise, not even when Nick looks back at me. "Sorry. I guess I just assumed you were born and raised in New York."

"Ah. That's right." He grunts, studying me. "One of those insufferable trust fund brats."

I laugh, shocked that he remembers what I said to

him the night we met at the gallery. Now I wonder if my offhanded remark had struck a nerve in him or if he's just so exacting that no detail ever escapes him.

And now my own thoughts roll back to a comment he said back at the docks. I check our course and venture another brief glance in Nick's direction. "And this boat was one of the first things you bought for yourself after you became successful?"

He nods, idly petting the gleaming mahogany trim. "Custom-built, forty-five foot Sparkman and Stephens yawl. I'd wanted one since I was ten years old and saw an old photo of JFK on his S and S. So, after I cleared my first couple million in investments, I spent half of it on the *Icarus*."

My brows shoot up. "You're trusting me with your million-dollar baby? Oh my God. Please, come here and take the wheel now."

He chuckles, but doesn't make a move to relieve me. "I have no doubt she's in good hands. After all, I speak from personal experience."

I return his smile and go back to my duty at the helm with even more focus, now that I'm aware of what I'm steering. Although I'm not an expert in the subject, even I could tell that this boat was special. That it was classic, one of the best money could buy.

And isn't that one of the constants I've come to understand about him? Dominic Baine surrounds himself with fine things. Beautiful, expensive things. How I ended up in that equation, I have no idea.

No, not true. I do know. And the taste of it is sharp and sour in my throat—especially when he's letting his guard down with me since we arrived in Miami. He's letting me in, little by little. And the only reason I'm here in the first place is because all this time, I've led him to believe I'm someone I'm not. I've pretended to be someone better. Someone who could actually belong with him.

How long I can expect my lies to hold, I don't even want to guess. I've gone far past the point of no return, and I don't know how I can ever hope to put things right.

I force my guilt and worry behind me as I glance at him. It's often so easy for me to think of Nick in terms of how he projects himself to the world at large. The formidable business magnate. The super-rich financier. The commanding man who with a snap of his fingers can have anything, and anyone, he desires.

Right now, seated on board his sailboat in nothing but a pair of shorts, the wind ruffling his black hair as he stares out at the horizon lost in his thoughts, instead of the powerful force of nature who slices through all of life's obstacles the way the *Icarus* cleaves the waves, I see Nick as a boy, fixating on something he wanted and resolved to make it his.

He's never looked more mortal. With the scars that riddle his right arm and hand, he's never looked more real, nor more earthbound.

"Why the name *Icarus*?"

"Are you familiar with the myth?"

I shrug. "Maybe. Wasn't he the god whose wings were burned by the sun?"

"Not a god. Just a man. Icarus was imprisoned on an island with his father. To escape, his father made them each a pair of feathered wax wings and warned Icarus not to fly too close to the sun, nor too close to the sea. But Icarus didn't listen. He got his first taste of freedom and it went to his head. He flapped so high, the sun melted the wax. He flapped some more, then all the feathers fell off and he dropped into the sea and drowned."

I tilt my head. "So is this boat a warning, or a lesson?"

His slight smile is pensive, cryptic. "Both, I suppose."

"Someday, Nick, you can tell me why that is." I see the flicker of surprise in his gaze as I serve his words from our breakfast this morning back to him now. He doesn't answer me, of course. "Did you ever doubt you'd be able to get your boat one day? Or at ten years old were you just a younger version of this driven, relentless man I'm looking at now?"

His mouth curves in an unrepentant smile. "What do you think?"

I laugh, shaking my head. "Nothing has ever been out of reach for the indomitable Dominic Baine. Is that it?"

"Nothing that I truly want, no."

Including me. Although he doesn't say the words, there is no mistaking the message in his darkening eyes. And I cannot deny the current of awareness that arrows through me as he holds my gaze.

He stands up and steps over to join me at the helm. His nearness unnerves me. At the same time, it sends my senses scattering with the giddy anticipation of his touch.

"Come a bit starboard now," he instructs me, calmly letting me know I'm neglecting my post. "Yes, there you go. That's my girl," he says as I adjust the wheel. "Eyes up front."

I nod, watching our course and the ribbon "telltale"

on the sail to keep us moving in the right direction. Nick moves behind me, resting his hands on my shoulders. I sigh the instant I feel his hands sweep aside my long ponytail. I moan when his mouth presses warmly against the back of my neck.

"I want to take you somewhere new tonight," he murmurs. "But only if you want to go there with me. And only if you trust me."

On its own, the statement shouldn't make my pulse throb with desire. But coupled with Nick's smoldering gaze and growling voice, it's edged with sensual promise. I swallow, my heart kicking into a faster tempo as his hands move down my sides, then around to caress my breasts.

"If you want to return to a safe port tonight instead, tell me now, baby."

"N-no." My denial is a shaky sigh, followed by a soft cry as Nick's hands slide down the front of my body and into the V of my legs. He starts gathering my skirt, lifting it above my knees, up over my thighs. "Nick . . . you can't—"

"Just a touch," he says, sweeping aside the lace of my panties and finding my sex. He fingers me deeply, making me squirm with pleasure. "Jesus, you're drenched. So snug and hot. I can't get enough of this pussy. And now I need to make you come."

Before I can protest—before I can even attempt to refuse him—he strokes me relentlessly from my clit to the cleft of my ass. Lifting my foot onto the edge of the cockpit bench beside me, he spreads me open and fills my sex with his fingers.

"Oh my God."

Nervously, I glance at the smattering of other boats

in the bay with us. There is no one close enough to see what we're doing, but the delicious risk of people seeing Nick's hand between my legs as I steer a million dollars' worth of luxury watercraft toward the open Atlantic is a thrill I never expected.

My vision blurs as pleasure spikes through me with every wicked flick of his thumb and deep plunge of his fingers. He shows me no mercy, though I hardly expect that from him anymore. No more than I can expect myself to resist him. I fall willingly, happily, into the vortex of sensation he's stoking within me.

It's all I can do to keep my hands on the wheel and my eyes on our course. My limbs feel boneless, but Nick's bare chest and strong body at my back keep me rooted, centered, safe.

And he doesn't let up until I come.

Not until a cry of release tears loose from my throat and flies up into the billowing sails in a scream.

30

As night falls, Nick navigates the boat into Florida Bay where we moor about a mile out from what he informs me is Islamorada in the Keys. After so many hours on the water, it feels good to pause and take down the sails for a while. I'm exhausted for a variety of reasons, but I've never felt more alive.

"Hungry?" Nick asks, bringing me down to the galley with him where I discover the provisions he'd purchased back in Miami include a loaf of fresh bread, a bottle of white wine, and the basics for a romantic dinner for two. I watch him gather a box of pasta, olive oil, plum tomatoes, zucchini, a small container of grated parmesan cheese, and a clove of garlic. "Pasta primavera sound all right to you?"

"Sounds perfect."

He hands me the bottle of Pinot Grigio then pulls a corkscrew out of a drawer. "Glasses are behind you in the cabinet. You pour the wine. I've got dinner handled."

"Aye, aye, Captain Baine." I tilt my head, smiling as I take the wine opener from his grasp. "Or do you prefer I call you Chef Baine?"

He chuckles, but his expression is pure heat. "What I really want to hear you say to me tonight is 'Yes, sir.'"

I freeze, startled by the weight of that single word.

He holds my gaze and those deep, ocean-blue eyes are possessive and hot on me, stripping me bare without permission or apology. There's no mistaking the erotic implication in his reply. And even though his tone has a playful edge to it, my pulse responds with full awareness of what he's suggesting. Control and capitulation. Domination and surrender. Master and submissive.

"Is that what you want from me?" I ask, my voice soft.

Nick slowly turns away from the counter to face me full on. "I want everything from you, Avery. Not as my submissive, or because I want you to serve me as anything close to that. That's not where I'm at in my life."

My heart stutters when I hear the admission he's not putting into words. "But you were."

"Not for a long time."

"With Kathryn?" I can't help how quickly her name leaps to my tongue. I've been trying to puzzle out what she means to him. Now that I've finally dared to ask, I dread the answer.

I see Nick's displeasure at her mention and I swallow, wishing I could take it back.

His eyes harden. "Kathryn was in my life for a short time, years ago, when I first got to New York. The other part of my life has nothing to do with her, and never did.

She has nothing to do with us either."

Some of my wariness eases at that. I believe she's not part of who he is now, or who he is with me. I want to believe there's nothing more to the story about this other woman and him, but I can see from his forbidding gaze that, at least for now, the subject of Kathryn is firmly closed.

He steps closer, the tight confines of the galley kitchen shrinking around us, until there is less than an inch of space between our bodies. His sculpted, bare chest and bronzed, broad shoulders fill my field of vision, crowding me with the warmth of him, with the enticing scent of his skin.

"I want more from you than you've ever given another man, Avery. More than you'll ever want to give another." He caresses my cheek, and I lift my gaze up to his. To the handsome, often unreadable, face of this man who's becoming a vital part of my life whether I want to allow it or not. "I want your pleasure—your complete surrender—and to truly give that to you, I need your trust. You won't need a safe word with me. Tell me no, tell me to stop, and I will. I promise you that. But if you trust me, I will take you to the edge of your steepest, most private desires."

Memories of last night on his terrace balcony flood my mind—the way he asked for my trust, then took me to the dizzying edge of pleasure, pain, and fear.

Then again, today when we were sailing, the way he commanded both my body and my release. The way he asked if I was ready to go further with him—away from safe ports.

Now, the sum of all these things sends a deliciously dark shiver over my nerve endings. If he were still into that lifestyle, I'm sure I'd know it by now. But that doesn't make his suggestion any less unsettling. Nick is dominant by nature, alpha to the core. Given my background—my broken past—I should find fear in that part of him. Yet there is no fear with Nick. Only delicious, dark anticipation.

And the thought of submitting to him sexually—in all ways—makes everything female in me quicken with curiosity . . . and desire.

"No limits between us," he says, his voice quiet with demand and promise. "No boundaries. No holding back. Not ever, Avery. Not with me."

God help me, the way his gaze is burning me up—the way my body recalls in vivid, sensual detail how masterfully he knows how to please me—I would be willing to try anything and everything with him. I'm starving for the kind of freedom he's describing. I'm terrified of it, too, even though in a distant corner of my conscience, I realize I've been heading down this path with Nick from the very beginning. Ready to submit my body and my pleasure . . . if not my soul. Eager to entrust all of myself to him, regardless of any warnings. Regardless of all the risks.

I lick my lips, and watch his eyes drift to my mouth and stay there. His jaw tenses and then his inky lashes lift, and I'm drowning in a storm of turbulent blue.

"I want more than you think you're capable of giving to anyone, Avery. But you'll give it all to me."

It's not phrased as a question, but I nod, the only movement I'm capable of when he's looking at me with such raw hunger. His mouth curves at my almost instinctual agreement to his demands. I am his. Since the moment we met, I have belonged to him and no other, and he knows it as well as I do.

"I want to hear it," he murmurs, his voice rasping over my senses like silk, decadent and seductive. "Say it, baby."

"Yes."

His brows lift slightly, expectantly. The unspoken, but gentle command sends a dark thrill through me.

"Yes, sir."

"Good girl."

He steps back a bit, even though I long for him to kiss me, to touch me, to toss me down and take me right where I stand. But he denies me. Devil that he is, he purses his lips in wicked amusement and studies me for a long moment.

I know he wants me right now too. I can see it in his eyes. I hear it in the rising tempo of his breathing. I can feel it in the electric charge of the air between us, so potent and palpable it makes my nipples tighten and sends goose bumps prickling to life on my bare arms. My gaze drifts downward, and it's no surprise to find his erection straining against the dark fabric of his shorts.

He wants me, but, damn him, he's going to make me wait.

He lifts my chin and gives me a brief, teasing kiss. "Pour the wine, baby. I'll decide over dinner just how far I'm going to take you tonight."

~ ~ ~

We enjoy Nick's pasta primavera and our bottle of wine by candlelight at the fold-out table in the cockpit, canopied by a black velvet sky pierced with countless stars. The meal is wonderful, the evening tranquil and warm, yet I spend all of it in a state of heightened anticipation of what awaits me once it's over.

Each glance he sends my way kicks my pulse into a harder tempo. Every time he reaches over to refill my glass or brushes his fingers across mine, the embers still smoldering in my core leap to new life, fueling the wet heat between my thighs and making me fidget on the cushioned seat across from him.

And because he knows me so well, I don't think for a minute that Nick isn't aware of my restless curiosity. Or my need. No, he's enjoying every second of it.

I can't take the tension or the wondering, and if I think about being naked and at his mercy for another moment, I'm going to scream. Either that, or combust on the spot.

I shake my head when he offers me the last of the wine after we finish our meal. "I'd better not. We both know I tend to do reckless things when I've had too much to drink."

He smirks. "Like leaving art exhibits with a man you just met?"

"Yes, there is that. And then running away with him to Miami and sailing off on a whim to points unknown."

"I happen to know exactly where we are," he says, pouring the rest of the Pinot Grigio into his glass. "You have nothing to worry about as long as you're with me."

I laugh. "Oh, I seriously doubt that's true."

He cocks his head, a frown creasing his forehead. "Are you worried now?"

"No." I lick my lips, watching him in the low light of the guttering candle, his sculpted features and square jaw cast in shadows and harsh angles. Dominic Baine is profanely handsome, infinitely seductive. In his expensive, tailored suits and polished luxury, he is the epitome of elegance and class. Tonight, dressed only in his shorts, with his short black hair windswept and wild, his jaw grizzled with the first rough hints of his beard, he is jagged and beautiful, a dark, wicked angel.

And right now—in this place, in this moment—he is mine.

Looking at him now, after our day together on the water and our romantic dinner alone on the boat, I can almost forget that he's a titan of the corporate world with a net worth that exceeds the economy of a small country.

I can almost forget that I've been warned to be careful around him, to protect my heart.

That if I'm foolish enough to get too close, he'll only cut me loose like he has so many others before me.

It isn't until I think of them—the women who came, and went, before me—that doubt begins to seep under my skin, despite his earlier reassurances about Kathryn, at least. My pleasant bubble broken, I glance away from his stare, turning my head to look out at the glistening black water and the smattering of lights that glow on the key across the bay.

"How long have you had the *Icarus*?" I ask him, desperate for conversation that won't have me wondering when he's going to make love to me again or how many other women might have found themselves seated in this same place with him.

"I had her built eleven years ago. I was twenty-two and had just gotten my first taste of success in real estate investment. Needless to say, I was hooked."

I glance at him and find him leaning back in his seat, his wineglass held loosely in his hand. He looks so young like this, almost carefree. I can't help but smile. "And now here you are, thirty-three years old and two-point-four billion later." I see the flicker of surprise chase across his features and I flush with embarrassment. "I'm sorry. I shouldn't know that about you unless you wanted to tell me. My friend, Tasha, looked you up online without asking me first and relayed some of the highlights."

"The friend in Queens with the new baby?"

"Yeah. Tasha was also with me when I almost crashed into you in the lobby elevator."

Nick's brows lift. "Was she? Funny, I don't recall anyone else once I saw you."

It's blatant flattery, but, coming from him, I'm not entirely immune. I don't even try to hold back my smile. "Tasha thought you were arrogant. She didn't want to like you, but I think you may have won her over with the bouquet you sent for Zoe's baptism several weeks ago."

"Actually, I was aiming to win over a different woman that day." He finishes off his wine and sets the glass down on the table. "So what other internet highlights did Tasha share with you about me?"

I shrug. "Only that you're very successful. And that you're known for how fiercely you guard your privacy."

"Dominic Baine, 'the shadow mogul,'" he says, sounding vaguely amused. But I know him too well to be fooled by his casual dismissal. He's irritated by his public reputation. He's defensive. "If there's one thing the press can't stand, it's someone who refuses to dance in their spotlight. Then they start looking for weaknesses, dents in the armor. They start digging for secrets."

"Will they find any?"

The question blurts out of me before I can stop it. Nick's gaze sharpens on me, his jaw hardening. I want to reel my words back in, but they hang between us like a challenge. I know he feels so too. I can sense the flare of displeasure in him as he leans forward, placing his elbows on the table as he holds me in his hard stare. Against my will, my gaze drops to the numerous jagged scars that slash across Nick's right arm and hand.

"Everyone has secrets, Avery. If you don't want them to rise up again, you have to be careful to remember where you bury the bodies."

Although he says it reflectively, with an edge that makes me wary to push him, I realize he could just as easily be speaking about me. I feel my face drain of color under his scrutiny, a jolt of pure panic rushing through me. Does he know? Can he possibly have any idea about my past?

No, he can't be. I'm certain of it.

Because I was a minor, there was never any mention of my name after my stepfather's death. There's nothing to link me to those news stories, then or now. It's one of the many reasons I'm thankful to have kept my daddy's last name, even when Martin Coyle first married my mother and pressed her to let him formally adopt me.

My skin crawls at the memory, and I can't suppress the shiver that sweeps over me. I know where the bodies of my secrets are buried, but no matter how far I've run from them, they still hold me in their icy grasp.

Nick's touch draws me back to the present, his fingers tender as he covers my hand with his. He rises to his feet now, his expression softened. "We're done here. Stand up, baby, and come with me."

When I hesitate, uncertain, he holds out his hand in silent demand. As soon as I'm standing, he gently turns me around and begins unfastening my dress.

"Nick, what are you—"

"You won't need this anymore tonight." He makes quick work of it, leaving me standing in just my bra and panties. "Now, come with me."

31

Nick, where are we going?"

He doesn't answer, just wraps his fingers around mine and leads me away from the table. I expect him to take me into the cabin. Instead he steps onto the gunwale and grabs hold of a line with his free hand.

"One hand for me and one for the boat," he tells me as he helps me up beside him. "Watch your step. The salt spray can make the deck slippery."

Together under the moonlight, barefoot, we make our way to the bow. Nick parks me on the broad wooden deck, then walks over to one of the hatches and retrieves a pair of long, folded cushions. He lays them out next to each other beneath the stowed mainsail.

"Right here," he says, indicating the cushion beside him as he sits on the other one.

As soon as I sink down next to him, he pivots toward me and his mouth covers mine. His tongue delves inside in a possessive kiss that scatters all of my thoughts, even the most troubling ones. I sigh as his lips draw back from mine, all of my tension flowing away like the tide.

"Better?" he asks as if he knows I needed the change of scenery as much as I needed his mouth on me.

I gaze at him in a state of sensual intoxication. "Much better. I've been waiting for you to do that all night."

Even in the darkness, I can see the satisfied curve of his smile. "Good things come to those who wait."

I snort, unable to help myself. "You don't believe that for a second. You take what you want, remember?"

"Yes," he agrees, unrepentant. "But we're not talking about me right now."

"Okay, then prove it."

"Prove it?"

"Show me all the good things you have in mind for me." I lick my lips and add a belated, "Sir."

His brows rise, whether in amusement or challenge, I'm not sure. "Evidently, I haven't sufficiently explained the concept of how this is supposed to work tonight. You don't get to make the demands."

Before I know what he's doing, he reaches around me and unfastens my bra. I yelp in shock as it pops loose. Nick sweeps the lacy fabric off me, tossing it onto the cushions. When I raise my hands reflexively to cover myself, his fingers close around mine.

He shakes his head in firm reprimand. "You don't hide yourself from me either."

Placing my hands at my sides, he sits back and simply looks at me for a long moment. My breasts and torso are fully exposed to him, and he seems intent on taking his sweet, maddening time admiring every inch of me. I shiver, even though the night air is warm on my bare skin. Waves lap against the boat as it rocks gently in the water, lulling me into an almost trancelike state as I hang suspended in mounting anticipation, yearning for his touch. For his kiss.

For whatever this provocative man desires of me.

When he finally reaches out, brushing his fingertips along the tender undersides of my breasts, I exhale a tremulous sigh.

His voice is a dark, wicked whisper. "You see, Ms. Ross, the way this works is, your body—your pleasure—belongs to me."

His caress grows bolder, his palms firm on me, his thumbs rolling over my beaded nipples, pinching their hyperaware tips. Arousal pours through me at his rough handling of my sensitive flesh, and I let out a soft moan of surrender, leaning my weight onto my braced hands to grant him total access to my body.

"Yes," he murmurs thickly, approvingly. "Now, you're getting the idea."

His mouth covers one of my nipples, drawing it deep. I hiss in pure, unabashed need as his tongue circles slowly, flicking and suckling. Heat rushes under my skin with every delicious suction, every sharp, unexpected graze of his teeth.

I whimper and squirm where I sit, loosely cross-legged, my sex growing damp and hot inside my panties. I want Nick's hands down there too. I want his mouth on my clit, his tongue buried in my cleft. I want it so badly, my sex clenches, the scent of my own arousal rising warm and sweet on the soft ocean breeze.

It's all I can do not to reach for Nick and push his head down between my parted thighs. I gasp his name, arching back further on my palms, my spine bowed toward him, my breasts thrust forward as he continues his sensual assault on them. "Nick, please . . ."

His answering snarl vibrates into my bones. Lifting his gaze from my breasts, he gives me a ruthless smile. "Begging is nice, sweetheart. But tonight it's only going to make you wait even longer for what you really want." As he speaks, the backs of his knuckles skim down the center of my body, a slow descent that pauses as he reaches my navel. "Unless you ask me very nicely."

"Please, sir," I whisper, a tremor building from just that brief, teasing touch. "I want . . . Oh, God, I need to feel your hands on me. Please."

"In that case, how can I possibly refuse?" He leans forward and kisses me. At the same time, his palm slides between my legs to cup my mound.

I cry out at the glorious pressure and powerful possession of his hand as it curves around my aching sex. My cleft is drenched, and as he caresses me, his fingers slip past the edge of my panties into my wet slit. He groans, his strong fingers flexing, stroking my naked flesh.

I want him to rub my throbbing clit. I want him to push his fingers inside me and give my empty channel something to hold on to. I want to feel his cock filling me, fucking me.

I am already panting with want, desperate for anything he'll give me, but all too soon, his touch is gone. He ignores my protesting moan and pushes me down onto my back on the cushion.

He carefully straightens my legs, then peels off my wet panties. I lay before him, naked and trembling, my nerve endings on fire as I watch him rise up on his knees to unfasten his shorts. He takes them off, pushing his boxer briefs down along with them. His erection springs free, heavy and enormous.

My mouth waters as my gaze fixes on him, and when my tongue darts out to wet my lips in response, Nick's smoldering expression turns molten. "The feeling is mutual, baby. Before the night is over, I'm going to have my mouth on every delicious curve and crevice of your body." A coarse, purely sexual growl curls up his throat as he looks at me. "And I promise you, that sweet mouth of yours is going to be all over me too."

He sets his shorts aside and moves in close to my side. When I reach for him, he catches my hand and stretches it up above my head. Then he brings the other one up, and places one of my palms atop the other. He holds them there for a moment, before his fingers run slowly down the length of my arm, then along my rib cage.

"All of this is mine," he says. "Every perfect inch."

I shiver under his light caress, goose bumps racing in the wake of his touch. It's torture keeping my hands above my head, but I know that's what he wants. It's what he's demanded, even if he hasn't said the words.

His touch descends, lingering along the buoyant curves of my breasts, then down the center of my rib cage. He strokes my belly, his finger tracing the rim of my navel, sending electric sparks into my limbs. Then his touch travels farther, over my hip bones, then along the line of trimmed blonde hair on my pubis. When his fingers sink delectably into the soaked V of my thighs, my answering sigh leaks out of me, thin and shaky with desire.

"This," he says, his eyes locked on mine as he cleaves

my slick folds. "This especially is mine. Any way I want it. Whenever and however I choose. Isn't that right?"

I nod, all I can manage as his touch slides all along my sex, his fingertips alternating between stroking my clit and teasing the entrance of my body. I moan helplessly, yearning for him to penetrate me, to fill me.

"I need to hear you say it, baby."

"Yes." My answer is a threadbare gasp.

"Hmm." He slowly shakes his head. He draws his fingers away from me and I whimper at the loss. "You know what I want to hear, Avery. Say it for me. Let me know I have your surrender."

"Yes," I answer breathlessly, eager in spite of my uncertainty about where he might take me tonight. "Yes, sir."

"Very good. For that, you deserve a reward."

He moves between my legs, then spreads them wide. His heated palms skate down my thighs and behind my knees, bending them so that the soles of my feet are flat on the cushions. His gaze rakes over me, from my fully exposed sex, to my naked torso, which glows milky pale under the moon and stars above us.

Then his eyes lift to my face and I see so much desire in his expression, it staggers me.

"Jesus Christ, you are stunning, Avery. You have no idea, do you?" His deep voice is rough, a jagged scrape of words from his throat. "If I were a painter, this is the only muse I'd ever need."

He kisses the shallow dip of my stomach, his mouth hot against my skin. His tongue is deliciously soft as he licks and sucks a dizzying path to one side of my pelvis, then the other. My spine arches in reflex to his kisses, and it takes all of my concentration to keep my hands obediently clasped above me as he proceeds to taste every bare inch of my abdomen.

I'm already soaked and quivering even before his palms slide under my ass, lifting me to his mouth. The first flick of his tongue along the seam of my body nearly unravels me. But I ride it out, wanting to obey him. Wanting to please Nick with my submission as much as he is pleasing me now with his dominance and control.

He plunders my sex with his mouth and tongue, stroking my clit, licking and sucking my pussy as if he means to devour me. Tremors ripple through me, spreading fire across my senses as my climax swells to life. I can't contain it. I can't hold back my sharp cry of release as he sucks my clit between his teeth and penetrates me with his fingers, my walls squeezing around him, greedy and demanding.

"Oh, God." My hips buck in his hands, but he doesn't relent. He keeps kissing me, keeps stroking me mercilessly with his tongue until I fear I'll pass out from sheer ecstasy. "Oh, fuck . . . Nick."

I'm still coming, still shuddering with the aftershocks of my release when he finally eases me back down onto the cushion. "Don't move. Keep your hands where they are."

"Yes, sir." My agreement boils past my lips, not even a hint of hesitation. Right now, I'll say anything—submit to anything—for another chance to feel his mouth on my needy flesh.

Straddling me, he rises up over my torso. His cock is fully engorged and immense, riveting my gaze to it as a droplet of hot, silken fluid drips from the broad crown onto my belly while Nick reaches over my head. I have no idea what he's doing. My mind is blissfully drugged on adrenaline and endorphins, and my senses are still hazy as I slowly float back down from somewhere in the clouds.

I hear him withdraw something from a hatch near our heads. The soft slither doesn't fully register until I feel the cool abrasion of rope being wound around my wrists.

Alarm shoots through me, jolting me back to full awareness. "Nick—"

"Shh." He pauses what he's doing and reaches down to gently stroke my cheek. His gaze holds my wary eyes, firm and calm. "Do you trust me?"

I swallow. "You're tying me up . . ."

"Yes. But only because I think you'll enjoy it."

"I don't know." I try to pull my hands down and find he's already bound them. Although there is slack in the line, I am tied securely to a metal cleat. "Nick, I've never . . ."

"I know, baby." His voice is as gentle as I've ever heard it. "But you can trust me. And you know how you can stop this if we go too far for you. Just tell me to stop. Anytime, at any moment, and I will." He caresses my cheek, then leans down and brushes a tender kiss over my lips. "Let me take you somewhere you've never been. Let me show you how good it can be to let go, to lose yourself to something you can't control. Lose yourself to me, Avery."

He's not asking so much as commanding, yet I don't bristle. I do trust him. I want to do things with him I'd never dare try and never in my life wanted to share with anyone else.

I agreed to let him take me away from safe ports today, and I can think of nothing more enticing than to do what he's asking of me now—to lose myself to him and to this unquenchable passion that seems to obsess us both.

"Trust me," he says, and I nod. "Not good enough, baby. I need you to say it."

"Yes, sir."

He shakes his head. Strokes my cheek with tender care. "No more *sir.* Not now."

He kisses me again, a slow, soul-searing tangle of our lips and tongues. My arousal kindles to new life again, fueled by the erotic pressure of Nick's erect cock resting against my stomach as he straddles me. His shaft twitches and swells as we kiss, his breath rasping into my open mouth.

He slides his palms down the length of my outstretched arms. "Do you have any idea how much you turn me on?" His caress moves to my breasts, then lower, as he eases himself back down between my parted thighs. "I could fuck you for days, baby. Weeks."

I sigh at how good that sounds. "Promises, promises, Mr. Baine."

He chuckles darkly. "I would say don't tempt me, but there's no point in pretending that where you're concerned."

"Then fuck me now," I order him, but my attempt at control is lost when his fingers slide into my cleft and push deep inside me. "Oh, God, Nick."

I feel him lean back and grab for his shorts with his free hand, his other still driving me wild and making me squirm in needy anticipation. I hear the tear of a condom wrapper, followed a moment later by the delicious pressure of Nick stroking his cock along the wet seam of my sex. I arch to greet him, and he thrusts home on a coarse grunt.

We slip into a deep, urgent rhythm, both of us hungry for the contact, our bodies fitting together as if they were made for each other. He pushes deep, filling me until I can hardly breathe. Bound at my wrists, I can only use the tension of the rope to steady myself as he pounds into me in a frenzied tempo, driving me toward the crest of a fierce orgasm.

Nick watches me as I start to break apart once more, his eyes scorching me with the ferocity I see in them. "That's it, baby. Come for me again. I want to see it. I can feel your tight pussy milking me. I know you're close."

"Yes," I gasp, my breath heaving as I rock on the cushion, totally at his mercy.

The rope is a sweet abrasion against my skin, reminding me that I have no control with this man. Nor do I want it, not when the pleasure is as intense as this. I bite my lower lip as a whimper starts to boil up the back of my throat.

"You're so pretty when you come," Nick praises me. "You make the sexiest sounds. It makes me so damn hard to hear your little cries."

He fucks me deeper, powering into me relentlessly, mastering me completely. I bear down to take the full measure of his battering thrusts, loving the animal intensity of him. Loving how raw and primal he can make me feel, while still managing to make me feel safe, even cherished.

My orgasm explodes an instant later, breaking over me in wave after wave, drowning me in pleasure. Dimly, as I'm spinning out to orbit, I feel Nick's pace slow to a pause. He pulls out of me, still fully erect.

"Flip over, baby." His voice is gravel, rough and jagged. "I need you on your knees. Now."

Because I'm boneless now, in addition to being bound, he helps me turn. His strong hands are shaking a bit as he takes hold of my hips and twists me so that I'm no longer on my back, but positioned before him on my knees on the cushion. The length of white rope is coiled tighter around my wrists now that I've flipped over, locking me in place with my ass in the air and my hands stretched out in front of me.

"Ah, fuck," Nick growls. "What are you doing to me? I've never seen anything as hot as you."

His palm lands sharply on my ass. I wince and bite my lip, my soft cry sounding more like a desperate, wanton mewl. Nick seizes my hips and hauls them higher, pulling my arms tauter and making my spine bow. His cock nudges thickly at the mouth of my sex, then slides home.

My breath rushes out of me as he fills me, stroking into me long and hard. His cock feels immense at this angle, impossibly thick, and each deep, invading push seems even fuller than the last, bringing me to the brink of pleasure and pain.

And I want more. I want all of him. I tilt my pelvis, opening myself wider for him so I can take every hard inch, ever jarring thrust. He's starving for me, too, and the staggering force of his lust is hotter than anything I've ever felt.

Coarsely uttered curses and growled praise for how I feel, how I look, boil out of him in sharp blasts as he fucks me. The sensory overload is too much to contain, and there's no stopping my climax. It roars up on me in a searing flash, filling my vision with stars as the jolting burst of sensation explodes inside me.

Nick's tempo doesn't slow as I shatter apart beneath his powerful thrusts. His hands clamp down tight on my hips as he pounds into me. "Yeah, baby. Let me hear you."

I couldn't hold back my scream of release even if I tried. I moan his name, quivering as the orgasm ripples through me, wave after wave of pleasure. Nick's palm slides up my spine, toward my shoulders. He presses me farther down against the cushion, the motion levering my ass even higher as he powers into me with greater urgency.

I feel the shift in his focus now that I'm spiraling down from my orgasm, my body slack and boneless. Nick's hands return to my hips, clenching harder as he chases his own release. I feel the coiled tension in his cock, the steely length of him swelling larger with every deep pump of his hips. He is as stiff and solid as granite inside me, as hot as molten iron.

He makes a strangled sound as he pistons hard and fast within me. And then his body arcs sharply and he slams home, shuddering and swearing with the force of his release. He keeps moving inside me, releasing my hips to wrap his arms around me instead, folding over me and dragging me tight against his heated chest.

I don't know how long we stay there like that, both spent and slick with sweat and the earthy musk of our lovemaking. All I know is that I don't want to move. I want to feel him inside me all night if possible.

I groan in sullen protest when he eventually withdraws to dispose of the condom.

"Are you all right?" He asks the question quietly, almost hesitantly, as he reaches up to unfasten my bindings and set the rope aside. "I didn't hurt you—"

"No." I shake my head, still drunk on ebbing pleasure as my arms sag onto the cushion, as boneless and fatigued as the rest of my body. I roll to my back and look up at his solemn, breathtakingly handsome face. "No, you didn't hurt me. That was . . . amazing."

"You're amazing," he murmurs. "Being with you is . . ." His words trail off and his gaze cuts away from me. "I wasn't expecting this. I wasn't expecting you, Avery."

He glances back at me and curses low under his breath. Then he bends toward me, taking my face in his hands as he kisses me. Not with fire and urgency this time, but with a tenderness that nearly breaks me.

Because I feel something unexpected with him too. Something I didn't plan for or want. Something I cannot afford to risk.

I need this man. I want him with something deeper than desire. Something more powerful than the obsession we both share for each other. I'm falling fast, and as much as I want to pretend I'll be able to walk away after Claire returns and my reality resumes, I have to admit another surrender to Nick tonight.

My body and my pleasure both belong to him, but the more staggering truth is, so does my heart.

32

Are you sure no one can see us?"

"No one can see us." Nick's grin skims the surface of the sunlit turquoise water as he moves toward me, both of us stark naked beside the boat. "There's no one around for miles. Just you and me. And maybe a small shark or two."

"What?" I shriek my reply and lunge for him in reflex.

He chuckles, catching me in his arms and pulling me against him. "Got you right where I want you now."

"Bastard!" I smack my palm against his shoulder. "Are there really sharks out here?"

His smirk is cryptic, and I decide I don't really want to know. I don't want to escape his arms either. His muscled body feels too good against me, our legs sliding together, tangling below the surface.

It's peaceful out here, just the two of us . . . and the various sea life I prefer not to imagine. A couple of miles away, off the port side of the *Icarus,* Islamorada is a long strip of lush green. Behind us in the distance are clumps of smaller green islands that bristle out of the water.

Although we woke to a handful of neighboring boats moored in the large bay with us, all but a couple had moved on soon after sunrise. Nick and I took our time having breakfast on deck, followed by a lazy few hours of lovemaking in the main cabin. When we crawled out for a breather and refreshments afterward, I quickly found myself being talked into some morning skinny-dipping off the side of the boat.

I loop my arms around his shoulders, reveling in the simple intimacy of the moment as we float almost weightlessly in the warm, crystal blue salt water of the bay.

"This is absolute paradise," I murmur, tipping my head back to look up at the pristine blue sky and a pair of white gulls riding the breeze overhead. "How do you ever find the will to return to New York after spending time out here?"

"My life is in New York. Not here. Hasn't been for a long time."

I lower my head and meet his gaze. "How long?"

He shrugs, nonchalant. "I moved away for good when I was twenty."

"And made your first two million in real estate investments by the time you were twenty-two?" I can't help but gape as I put together the pieces of what he's told me. "That's amazing. I realize you're brilliant, but you must've been a business tycoon prodigy too."

He smiles dismissively. "I got lucky, that's all. When I came to New York, the Iraq War was just beginning. I had some money saved up, and I figured the one thing every war needs is equipment, supplies. So I invested in a few defense contractor companies."

"A smart move."

"And lucrative as it turned out. After about a year, I'd more than doubled my money. Around that same time, real estate in Florida was starting to go crazy. So, I bought up a few properties, flipped them, then reinvested in bigger and bigger developments and put some money into the market as well. I knew it couldn't last, and just before the housing market bubble started to burst, I got out. I dumped everything, sold it all at the peak. By the end of 2008, I was worth half a billion. Since then, I diversified. Stocks, corporate finance. Anything that catches my eye and looks to be a solid investment. Anything I can either turn into something bigger or disassemble and sell off at a profit."

I reach out to trace a dampened wave of black hair that's sticking to his brow. "And now, here you are," I say, utterly impressed by all that he's accomplished.

"Yes. Here I am."

His gaze doesn't leave mine, and in the heat of his penetrating blue eyes, I try to understand how it is that we've ended up together like this. How is it that of all the women he could choose to spend his time with, he is with me?

"Why me, Nick?"

"What do you mean?"

He studies me so intently, I'm sure I must be overstepping. I shake my head, uncertain how to begin now that I've broached the subject. "I'm not asking you to tell me how many other women have been here with you like this—"

"You can ask," he says, though his voice is clipped.

"The answer is none."

"None." I repeat the word dully. I hadn't expected him to answer, let alone say this.

He shakes his head. "Not on board my boat. Not to my place in Miami. Not here, like this. No one."

This revelation is more than unexpected. It's bewildering, and much too gratifying, to think I am the first. The *only*. But still . . . "Then why now? Why me?"

"To be honest, I'm not sure. I hadn't planned for this." There is an edge to his gaze as he looks at me, a hardness that makes me worry that I've ruined our moment. With his silence, the only sound around us is the soft lapping of the water against the boat, and the high-pitched cry of a sea bird. Then Nick shakes his head and utters a curse under his breath. "I've done a lot with you that I haven't with anyone else. You've obsessed me, Ms. Ross. Now that I've opened the door, I don't think it's going to be easy to close it."

"Is that what you want?" I swallow hard. "To close the door on me?"

"No. That's not what I want. I want to throw them all open. I want to be the one to lead you through them."

"I don't understand," I murmur. "You can have anyone, Nick. That night at the gallery, you could've gone home with any woman there. Yet you chose me."

"Yes, I did." His arms drift down my back below the water as we continue to float together. "Unless I'm mistaken, you chose me too."

"True, but I didn't know who you were."

His dark brows arch. "And if you had?"

I recall how bruised I'd been by the rejection of my art. How pissed I was when I learned from Margot that he was not only a reputed player, but Dominion's owner.

"I think I would've told you off rather than spend the night with you."

"Is that right?" A devilish smile quirks at the corner of his lush mouth. "I think you would've gone home with me regardless of that."

Eyes narrowed, I snort a laugh. "How positively arrogant of you to say so, Mr. Baine."

"Tell me I'm wrong."

I can't and he knows it. And as I float in the circle of his strong arms, my argument that I might have been able to resist him—then or now—is quickly losing steam. I cling to the only piece of indignation I have left.

"You don't like my art." Even though my voice is soft, it's an accusation.

"I never said that."

"You told me yourself it wasn't very good. Not good enough for your gallery."

"That's not the same as saying I don't like it, or that I don't think you have talent."

"Do you?" I can't help but ask the question. His professional opinion as the owner of a highly respected gallery cannot be disputed, but it's his personal judgment that has me holding my breath. "Do you think I have talent, Nick?"

He nods. "Clearly, you do. I think it's possible that you could be great."

"But?" Because it's obvious he doesn't think I'm anywhere near that yet.

"You really want to know?"

"Yes. I need to know."

He studies me, as if he's weighing how to say it. "Your art is self-conscious. It's not honest. I look at your paintings, Avery, and I see someone who's either unsure of who she really is, or trying to hide from that truth."

I bristle to hear it, a swift jolt of defensiveness—and alarm—shooting through me. Can he be right about my work? Even more troubling, can he truly see through me so clearly? It's not as if the idea should come as a surprise. From that first night in the lobby of the Park Avenue building, I've felt stripped—exposed to my soul—under Nick's shrewd gaze.

I feel that way now too, and every reflex in my body tenses with the urge to escape. I want to hide. And because he can read me like no one else, instead of letting me retreat, Nick closes his arms around me even more, caging me in his embrace. I glance away from his searching gaze, but he refuses to give me that either, gently catching my chin and bringing my eyes back to him.

"You have a gift, but you're not letting it reach the canvas. I think you're afraid of what you'll see. You're always going to be afraid, unless you find the courage to open your eyes." A dangerous, alluring heat flickers in his fathomless blue irises. "I can open doors for you, Avery. I can lead you through them."

His words from a few minutes ago seem to carry a darker, more sensual meaning while he's holding me captive in his arms and his gaze. "Are we still talking about my art, or something else?"

His mouth curves, but his eyes remain utterly serious. "That's up to you."

It's impossible to ignore his erection as we gently bob against each other in the water. The small waves rippling through the bay push us together in a lazy, sensual rhythm that has me reflecting back on everything we did last night.

Everything I am eager to do with him again.

And because he seems to enjoy provoking me—in and out of his bed—I shift my hips and bring my legs up, wrapping them around his waist. He closes his eyes on a groaned curse as my naked sex gets up close and personal with his abdomen.

"Better be careful, Ms. Ross," he warns as his cock nudges my rear. "You're giving me a lot of interesting ideas."

I laugh and lean back in his arms, levering myself until I'm floating prone on the water. It feels like heaven, drifting suspended in Nick's embrace with endless blue sky above me and a bed of gentle waves beneath me. "I don't want to leave this spot. Can we stay here a while longer?"

"How long do you want to stay? The rest of the day, the rest of the week? The rest of the month?"

He can't be serious. I lift my head out of the water and find him staring at me hungrily, his scorching gaze traveling the arch of my body and the swell of my breasts above the surface line of the water, where my nipples are pink and puckered as the tiny waves lick at them.

"Don't you need to work? Do all of those important things that billionaire shadow moguls do?"

He chuckles. "Most of my business is conducted by email and phone calls. Anything I need to handle can be done from here."

"Well, I'm supposed to be house sitting," I remind him. "Claire's plants will forgive a couple of days without water, but not much more."

"I'll call Manny. He'll make sure everything is taken care of."

"What?" I sit up, realizing he's not joking. "Nick, I'm

sure that's not in his job description."

"No, it isn't. But if I ask, I'm fairly certain he'll be willing to do it."

I gape, suddenly understanding something I suspected that first night we were together. "You don't just own the penthouse, do you?"

He smiles.

"Oh, my God," I groan, but I can't keep from returning his grin. "You're crazy. We can't just disappear for days or weeks on your boat."

"Of course, we can. Whatever we need, we can get at one of the neighboring keys. Food, coffee, clothing, condoms." He smiles wickedly. "All the essentials."

I laugh, realizing I'm practically giddy at the idea of extending this fantasy escape with him. It's wildly romantic, more than borderline reckless . . . and I can't think of anything I want to do more.

I have no resistance—not for Nick's plan, nor for the man himself. Noting my obvious surrender, he cups my nape and drags me to him for a breath-stealing kiss.

I moan when he finally releases me, arousal spiraling hot and tight in my core. "You're going to corrupt me, you know that?"

"Oh, Ms. Ross. I fully intend to."

33

Then, after island-hopping around the keys for three weeks, we sailed back to Miami and spent a couple of nights at his beach condo before flying home to New York last week."

"Damn, girl! That sounds absolutely amazing." Tasha beams, seated across from me at the diner in Queens where we've met for lunch on her day off from Vendange. She's just spent the last twenty minutes listening indulgently while I recapped the highlights of my tropical escape with Nick.

The PG-rated ones, anyway. The rest of the highlights belong to Nick and me alone.

"You look amazing too, Avery. I can't decide what you're wearing better—that killer tan, or the smile that hasn't left your lips since you walked in here."

I tilt my head at her. "What, no smartass remarks about Nick or threats to disown me as your friend?"

"Nope. Not when you look this happy. I like seeing

you finally let down your guard with someone." She takes a sip of her iced tea, then salutes me with the glass. "And for the record, I'd be saying that even if your boyfriend wasn't a drop-dead gorgeous bazillionaire with a yacht and multiple penthouse apartments. But it damn well doesn't hurt that he is."

I return her teasing smile, and go back to eating my turkey wrap and fries. "My boyfriend? I'm not sure I'm comfortable calling him that just yet."

She shoots me an incredulous look. "Are you kidding? Uh, gee, let's review. You've been practically inseparable for the past two months—nearly half of which has been spent alone with him, sunbathing and skinny-dipping your way around the Florida coast on his million-dollar sailboat. Which, by the way, he's never done with anyone else before. He's cooked for you, taken you out to nice places and fancy parties, and now you're sitting in front of me looking like a woman who's not only extremely well taken care of and well-pleasured, but also very possibly falling head over heels for this man. What the heck would you call him?"

"Well, when you put it that way, maybe." I laugh and shake my head. "But I don't know. And I'm not falling in love with him."

God, am I? What I feel for him is intense, no doubt. It's white-hot and consuming. After all the time we've spent together—naked and otherwise—I certainly can't call our relationship casual anymore. He is my first thought when I wake up and my last as I'm falling to sleep every night. Granted, both of those moments are usually spent in his arms, but that doesn't change the fact that there's nowhere else I'd want to be. And despite the fact that I haven't considered where we're heading in just a few more weeks when Claire is due back from Japan, I can't think of Nick and not imagine us together.

Whatever feelings I have for him, I'm getting in deep and I can't deny it. Least of all to myself.

Apparently I can't deny it to my best friend either.

"So where is lover boy today?" she asks as she stabs a forkful of Caesar salad. "I'm surprised he let you out of bed long enough to come see me."

"He's got business meetings with his acquisitions team in London again."

"Oh, back to London *again*?" She sighs melodramatically, her voice effecting a bored tone. "Well, Tony's going to Staten Island tomorrow to head up a new sewer pipe installation with his construction crew. So really, that's like almost the same thing, right?"

"Shut up." We burst into a fit of giggles, and I shake my head at her. "Anyway, Nick left yesterday and he won't get home until a week from Friday." I don't mention that I'm missing him terribly and can't wait for our time apart to pass. Instead, I munch on a fry and glance over at Tasha. "Speaking of work, how are things at the restaurant?"

She rolls her eyes. "Kimmie got promoted last week. Joel put her in charge of the bar, of all things."

"What? She can hardly place a drink order without messing it up, much less mix one."

"You're telling me? Not that it matters. She's an expert at kissing Joel's fat ass, so she's golden." Tasha dumps a sugar packet into her tea, then chases the granules and ice cubes around with her spoon. "I'm supposed to be training her on the inventory and the register in our downtime, which, as you know, is next to nil. So, basically, I'm doing everything myself while she stands around and chats up Joel and the customers."

I wince. "I'm sorry. If I'd known my leaving was going to make things worse for you—"

"No. Don't even go there," she interjects sharply. "I'm glad you stood up to him. I'm glad you got out of there. Believe me, I would too if I had half your guts."

There was a time, not so long ago, that the thought of locking horns with my employer would have been unthinkable, let alone something I'd actually do. But I'm not that person anymore. Maybe I never was. I just never dared to push back before, to let that side of me loose.

Nick has said he thinks I'm running from who I really am—hiding from it. I've been turning those words over in my mind ever since, and although he made that observation in connection to my art, I can't help thinking that he is right. There is so much about me that he's gotten right. So much that he's unlocked, set free.

I can open doors for you. I can lead you through them.

The truth is, he already has. Even if our relationship ends tomorrow, I know I can never go back to the person I was before he entered my life.

Where exactly that leaves me now, I haven't quite figured out yet.

"So much for my bartending career," I mutter, giving Tasha a wry look. "Vendange was the only restaurant I've worked in since I came here, and it's not like Joel is going to give me a reference."

"Oh, please." Tasha dismissively waves her hand. "Who needs references when you're Dominic Baine's mystery girl?"

"His what?"

"You haven't seen it?" She draws back, giving me a surprised look. "Oh, that's right. I forgot—you're allergic to the Internet. Yes, you and your maybe-sorta boyfriend were all over the society pages after the mayor's gala last month."

She wipes her hands on her napkin, then digs in her purse for her phone. I feel uneasy and confused, waiting as she brings up a website page on her browser. She turns the screen toward me and wiggles her brows.

"See? There you are."

It's the gossip page of a big New York City newspaper. There among the dozens of paparazzi shots of socialites and business magnates attending the mayor's fundraiser are two photos of Nick and me. One is the snapshot taken of us through the windshield of Nick's limo. The other was captured as we made our way past the photographers and police barricades into the hotel for the event.

"'A rare public appearance tonight by billionaire businessman and philanthropist, Dominic Baine, arriving with his guest, Ms. Avery Ross,'" Tasha recites for me, adopting a faux snooty inflection that normally might make me giggle along with her. But not now. Not over this.

"Let me see that."

I take her phone and look at the photos, groaning because I know how Nick values his privacy. Hell, I value mine, too, and it's with no small amount of alarm that I realize these photos—and my name—are now in the public domain. They must've gotten my name off the registry when Nick and I checked in that night.

I glance down at the social media stats at the bottom of the article and feel some of the color drain from my face. "Are you shitting me? Tasha, this article has more than a million views."

"Congratulations," she says cheerfully, unaware of the growing knot of unease that's coiling in my stomach. "You're officially famous, girlfriend."

~ ~ ~

I'm in a restless mood when I arrive home from brunch with Tasha, and I can see it in the painting I'm working on in my makeshift studio in Claire's living room. The landscape I'd been trying to perfect for so long without success currently sits abandoned against the wall, along with the crated works I haven't bothered to open since I brought them home from Dominion a couple of months ago.

On my easel now is something all new, a piece inspired by my getaway with Nick. I began working on it secretly after we arrived back in New York. In the weeks since, it's been my obsession. As I add the last of the shading on the silvery feathers that are the heart of the piece, I'm so engrossed, I barely register the ringing of my cell phone on the end table beside me.

Although I'm waiting on a call from Nick after texting him when I got back from brunch, I'm not surprised to see the Pennsylvania area code on the caller ID display. After a favorable interview with the parole board a couple of weeks ago, my mother's excitement for her pending case review next month is practically all she talks about now. I'm excited, too, praying with an almost desperate hope that the state finally shows her some mercy.

Setting down my brush, I quickly wipe my hands on a paint cloth and grab for my phone. I swipe the lock screen and wait to hear the automated operator.

But the familiar message doesn't come.

The line is connected, but all I hear is empty air . . .

And the faint sound of breathing on the other end.

"Hello? Is someone there?" I wait another second, then pull the phone away from my ear and check to see if the call has dropped. No, it hasn't. And now I swallow on a suddenly arid throat, even as I assure myself that I have no reason to feel afraid. "Hello? Mom, is that you?"

The line goes dead.

I'm still holding the phone in my frozen fingers when it rings again. Whether it's been a few seconds or a several minutes, I'm not entirely sure. All I know is the rapid pound of my heart beating in my chest, and the chill dread that squeezes me in its fist as I nervously glance at the screen again.

Nick.

Relief pushes the air out of my lungs on a heavy sigh, but my nerves are far from steady as I swipe my finger across the phone to answer his call.

"Hi." My voice comes out thin and quiet, almost breathless.

"Hi, yourself." He gives me a low, sensual groan. "Why do you have to sound so damn sexy when I'm thirty four hundred miles away?"

I smile despite the adrenaline still coursing through my veins. Hearing Nick's voice always has a comforting effect on me, and now is no exception. Besides, I'm sure the other call was nothing. Probably someone from the prison administration or the public defender's office calling my number unintentionally. Just a harmless butt-dial. No reason to start looking for ghosts or jumping at shadows.

Instead, I reach for a tether to bring me back to the

real world. "How was the meeting with the aerospace people?"

"Profitable. We closed on the acquisition before dinner tonight." He sounds genuinely excited, even proud.

"Nick, that's fantastic. Congratulations."

I can practically hear the grin in his reply. "The capital we're injecting into the operation's going beef up production schedules by twofold. If everything goes well, by this time next year, Baine International will be the third largest entrant in the private spaceflight market."

I'm astonished, but not surprised. Nothing about this man's ambition and drive, nor his intellect, shocks me anymore. He is a force to be reckoned with, and I doubt he's ever met a challenge he couldn't conquer—on this planet or any other, evidently. "If you keep dominating markets outside our orbit, you're going to have to seriously consider new letterhead. Baine Intergalactic has a nice ring to it."

He chuckles. "I'll take it under advisement."

"I'm excited for you, Nick. I wish we could celebrate in person."

"So do I. And we will, as soon as I return." Then his voice takes on a deeper timbre. "Until then, I can think of some interesting ways to celebrate together long-distance."

"I'm sure you do." I laugh, even as my body quickens with interest. "And I want to hear every wicked one of them, but . . . that's not the reason I wanted to talk to you. I met Tasha in the city today. While we were talking, she showed me a gossip page article about the mayor's gala last month. There were photos of us together as we arrived. Apparently, they've gone viral on the Internet."

"Ah." He doesn't sound pleased. Then again, he doesn't sound surprised either. "I suppose that was to be expected."

"You already knew?"

"I employ enough people who'll bring these kinds of things to my attention if I don't see them for myself first."

"So, you're not upset that we've been photographed together?"

"Of course I'm upset. But I'm used to the press constantly buzzing around in search of their next meal. They might've fed on us for a lot longer if we hadn't left the city when we did and for as long as we did."

"Oh." A pang of disappointment stings me as he explains. "I hadn't thought of that, but you're right, Nick."

Dominic Baine is nothing if not a shrewd man. And, as I've learned, he is always in control, always one step ahead of everyone else drifting through his orbit.

So, I really can't fault him for thinking that far ahead, for taking steps to protect his privacy. I shouldn't feel disappointed if his motivation for whisking me off on the fantasy getaway of my life was more pragmatic than it was spontaneous.

"Hopefully, things have died down by now," I murmur.

And I can't help thinking that our escape from the press's eye was beneficial for me too. One of the things I love most about New York is the sense of anonymity it provides. It's easy to blend in here, easy to vanish into the masses. Here, it's easy to start over. Unlike back home, where nothing is ever forgiven or forgotten.

"If things haven't died down," Nick says, "we'll just have to find another place to explore."

"Sure, why not?" I reply, pushing away my grim thoughts and trying to keep my tone as light as his. "Although, it's going to be hard to top three weeks on the *Icarus.*"

"How do you feel about Paris?"

Thankfully, he's not here to see me gape. "I don't know how I feel about it." I drift over to one of the sumptuous sofas and sink into the corner of it, tucking my legs under me. "I've never been there."

"Never?" He says it as if I've just confessed to a crime. "Every artist owes it to their work to spend as much time as possible in Paris. How does your schedule look next month?"

I close my eyes, wishing I could play along with this game. But next month is when Claire is due back from Japan. Next month, she'll be sitting here in this beautiful apartment again, and I'll be looking for work and someplace cheap to live. "I'll have to check with my secretary and get back to you."

"I'm serious, Avery. I want to take you to Paris."

"I don't have a passport," I say, grasping for the closest excuse that isn't an outright lie.

"A minor detail, which I can take care of for you in less than a day. You'll only need to be available to go. You can do that, can't you?"

I exhale softly and gaze out at the view that doesn't belong to me. Nick and this glittering, jet set life I'm enjoying with him doesn't belong to me either. It's been all too easy to ignore that fact, but very soon it's going to come crashing down on my head.

"Ask me again next month, and we'll see."

He's silent for a moment, and the weight of his contemplation is palpable. "All right, then. I will ask you again next month, Ms. Ross. In the meantime, I'd like to explore some of those long-distance celebration options we left open for discussion."

I smile. "Is that right, Mr. Baine?"

"Yes. You can start by telling me what you're wearing."

34

For the remainder of the week, I throw myself into my work. Creatively, I am on fire as never before, but a big part of my obsessive hours at the easel is the fact that I'm missing Nick.

We've talked every day this week, and even though hearing his voice and receiving his frequent, often wickedly dirty, texts has helped make the week apart more bearable, by the time he is finally due back from London, I am practically giddy with excitement to see him.

Any hope I have of playing it cool vanishes completely when he calls me from the tarmac at JFK Friday afternoon.

"We just touched down," he tells me and I can hear the anticipation in his voice too. "I'll be at the Park Place building within the hour. Be ready for me."

"I've been ready all day," I tell him. "And Nick? I'm not wearing any clothes."

"Jesus, baby." His deep voice turns to roughened gravel. "In that case, I'll be there in half the time."

I don't want to consider how he actually manages to cross the city so quickly, but, true to his word, Nick is standing outside the fifth floor apartment door in record time. I make good on my promise too, opening the door to him naked and utterly shameless.

He steps inside, looking urbane and handsome in his dark gray suit and white business shirt. His attire may be boardroom sophisticated, but the look in his stormy blue eyes is pure animal.

"Hi," I say, smiling up at him. "What took you so long?"

His answer is something close to a growl. He drops his leather bag on the foyer floor and kicks the door closed behind him. As soon as he's all the way inside, I lose all patience for my game. I just need him. I launch myself at him and he catches me in his arms, holding me aloft as I wrap my bare legs around him and attack his mouth in a desperate kiss.

He carries me like this, kissing me with equal ferocity as he effortlessly navigates the hallways of the apartment, bringing me into the guest bedroom where I've been staying since I began living in Claire's place. Nick's hands are firm under my ass, his expensive suit soft and silky against my bare breasts and torso. He is strong and protective and utterly in control, yet I can feel his measured discipline burning away under the fever of our joined mouths.

His eyes are turbulent with passion when he finally tears his lips away from mine. "I can't go slow right now."

"Don't," I say, as much a command as it is a plea. I

moan with the force of everything I'm feeling. "Nick, I need—"

"I know, baby. Me too."

Tossing me onto the mattress, he quickly strips out of his clothing. Then, gloriously naked, he steps toward the bed where I watch him, reclined on my back and levered up on my elbows. He looks so beautiful, so magnificently male, it makes my mouth water and my sex clench hard and wet with desire.

After a week without seeing him, now I gorge my senses on the sight of his muscled body and smooth, suntanned skin. I know every inch of his powerful physique. I have traced each honed plane and valley, memorized the taste and texture of every delicious inch. His clean, spicy scent is imprinted deep within me, so much so, that just the faintest inhalation now wrings a whimper of unabashed need from my lips.

He doesn't make me wait a second longer. Thank God.

Retrieving a condom from the box I now keep in the nightstand beside the bed, he takes the packet between his teeth and climbs on top of me, straddling my hips. His erection juts high and proud and immense from the dark thatch at his groin. He is virile and gorgeous, and, right now, he belongs solely to me.

"This time, let me do that," I tell him when he starts to open the condom.

He hands it over and I reach out to roll the protection over his length. My fingers slide down his thick-veined shaft with the condom, and I can't resist cupping the heavy sac beneath. My touch draws a moan from his lips and a shudder of pleasure from his body.

I love that I have this effect on him. I love that he

makes me believe he is as wild for me as I am for him.

I love . . .

Oh, God. I love so much about this man.

I glance up to his face and find him staring at me—staring through me, as he's managed to do from the moment we first laid eyes on each other. Can he see what he means to me? Can he possibly know how hopelessly I'm falling for him?

"Lie back," he commands me, his voice gruff.

When I obey, he draws back from me, positioning himself between my legs and parting me wide. I'm already soaked and ready for him, but he bends to kiss my sex as if it's a temptation too strong to resist. He strokes me with his tongue, penetrates me, sucks at my clit in a deep, urgent rhythm that has me writhing beneath his mouth.

Just when I think I can't bear another second of pleasure and torment, he releases me and guides his cock to the slick opening of my body. I cry out as he enters me, my sheath gripping him tightly as he pushes inside, plunging to the root in one delicious thrust.

I gasp his name and then I am lost, overcome by sensation as our bodies crash together in a desperate, almost violent tempo. All the weeks we've been apart, the hours of longing, are obliterated by the intensity of our joining now. I've missed him, missed this fierce intimacy that connects us.

Nick's hot gaze holds mine as we rock and claw and strain together, both of us surrendered to the enormity of our hunger for each other. I let go first, unable to stop the massive wave of pleasure as it rolls up on me. Moaning under the force of it, I spiral over the edge in a shattering orgasm.

Nick's control is stronger than mine, but I can see in the savage beauty of his face that he's losing the battle too. A ragged shout boils out of him and he drives into me again and again, each thrust harder, deeper, until the pressure is too great, even for him. He comes on a wordless roar, a sound that's raw and unhinged, beyond erotic.

"Fuck, I needed that," he utters hoarsely against the side of my neck as we lie there together, our bodies still connected. He lifts his head, frowning as our gazes meet and hold. "I needed *you*, Avery."

Whether he means it as an accusation or admission, I can't be sure.

"You have me." It's the truth, and I can't deny it from him. Not even when all of the warnings I've been given about getting too close to him clamor in my head like alarms. I reach out and caress the rigid slope of his cheek. "There's nowhere else I want to be."

His frown deepens in his answering silence, but his gaze does not break mine. And for the briefest second, I see what he cannot—or will not—put into words.

I matter to him. I've gotten inside.

If only for this moment, I've slipped through his forbidding walls.

But then he blinks and those emotional shutters of his fall back into place as firmly as an iron gate. He rolls off me, out of my reach.

"Stay here," he says, removing the spent condom as he gets out of bed.

I watch him walk into the adjoining bathroom, trying not to feel abandoned to my feelings and the swiftly cooling sheets. After disposing of the condom, he walks out of the bedroom, back toward the living area of the apartment.

He returns a moment later holding something behind his back.

I sit up near the edge of the bed, folding my legs beneath me. "What are you doing?"

Naturally, he doesn't tell me. "Close your eyes," he says as he approaches.

"Nick—"

"Close them." I obey on a huffed, impatient sigh. "Now, hold your hands out in front of you. Palms up."

I comply, waiting to feel him place something in my hands. But he doesn't. Instead, he wraps a length of something sleek and cold around my wrists. I gasp at the sensation, my mind working to process what I'm feeling. Small, cool spheres press against my skin in a long strand, clicking softly as they are wrapped and twined around my crossed wrists.

"Beads?"

Nick doesn't answer. Remaining maddeningly silent, he continues to bind my hands together. The bond is tight, but not so much that I couldn't break free if I wanted. And the cool beads have now begun to warm from my body's own heat.

"You can open your eyes now."

My lids lift and I glance from his hooded gaze to the gleaming strand of pearls that are wound no less than half a dozen times around my wrists. I don't have to ask if they're real. This is Nick, after all. But even with my limited firsthand experience with fine things, I can tell the creamy pearls are authentic. And must have cost a small fortune.

"A little something I picked up for you in London."

"You can't be serious."

And yet he is. His expression is enigmatic, but his eyes study me intently. "I hope you like them."

Like them? I'm wearing easily multiple tens of thousands of dollars' worth of gemstones as casually as if they're the rope line off the *Icarus*. "They're . . . incredible, Nick. They're too much."

"As soon as I saw them, I knew I wanted to see them on your naked skin." His smile is decadent. "And now that I have, I can think of several other interesting ways I'd like to see you wearing them."

Just the suggestion sends a rush of heat to my core. "You're crazy." I shake my head, overwhelmed by his gift, and the fact that he would lavish this kind of luxury on me. "I don't think I can accept—"

"Yes, Avery. You can. And you will, because it pleases me to see them on you."

He reaches out, gathering my face in his hands. Leaning toward me, he takes my mouth in a slow, searing kiss. I melt into him, helpless to do anything but bend to his will now. As I shift on the bed to meet his possessive kiss, the pearls slide against one another. The thought of damaging the gems is almost too much for me to take.

"I'm afraid they'll break."

"They won't." He smoothes a strand of loose hair from my face. "So long as you're honest with me—and with yourself—these pearls are stronger than any rope. They're stronger than steel. Like trust, Avery, the only way they'll break is if you pull away from me."

Trust. Honesty. Two things I've never been able to give another man—not to anyone in a very long time.

Nick has my trust. He has my honesty, too, at least when it comes to the passion we share. The obsession we both feel for each other is real. I've never been more honest about something in my life.

In bed with him, I have no barriers. And I want it all. I want to give him everything too. I won't let myself think about all of the things I can never have with him.

Not now, when I'm one shaky breath away from weeping with the force of everything I feel for this darkly compelling man.

He joins me on the bed and kisses me again, easing me back onto the mattress with him. My bound hands rest on my stomach, and it's all I can do not to reach for him as he lavishes my belly and breasts with a trail of hot kisses and fiery licks of his tongue. I'm shivering with need and anticipating the many clever ways I know he'll have me at his mercy now.

I can do nothing but submit as he takes hold of my bound hands and guides my arms over my head. His fingers trace slowly down my sides, raising goose bumps in their wake and wringing a shaky sigh from my lips.

He claims my mouth with renewed ferocity, while his fingers skim between my thighs. My cleft is soaked with my own juices, still hypersensitive and swollen from before. Nick delves inside me, at the same time thrusting his tongue deep into my mouth to stroke and spar with mine.

We kiss as if we haven't just had each other moments ago, as if we will never get enough.

Nick strokes my sex, rubbing my clit with his thumb and sinking his fingers deep into my sheath. I moan, feeling my body contract around him, greedy for more. As I arch and writhe in time with his thrusting fingers, he plunders my mouth with urgent, bone-melting kisses.

I don't notice that he's withdrawn his fingers from within me until I feel him turning my hips in his strong hands, guiding my lower body onto its side. Then his touch glides slickly over my anus. I tense at the first stroke of pressure, pulling against my bonds. It's unexpected, but then so is the jolt of excitement that arrows through me as Nick's fingertip rims me, pushing in a testing rhythm against my tightness.

I open my eyes and find him staring down at me. He says nothing, but his gaze doesn't leave mine for a moment as he strokes me more intimately than ever. Touching me in ways I've never wanted anyone to before him and never knew I could crave so fiercely.

His thumb on my clit is making me wild with need, and the slick finger toying with my ass is enough to push me to the razor's edge of madness. I bite my lip at the delicious pressure of his touch as he gently penetrates me. My pussy is drenched, coating his fingers and the tight hole of my anus as his digit thrusts inside.

The intensity of my arousal, and my need for release, is too much. When combined with the restraints that trap my hands and prevent me from touching Nick, the depth of my need is almost unbearable. I moan and writhe, mindful of my bindings, yet desperate to come.

"I know, baby," he murmurs against my parted lips. "I'm going to give you what you need."

He pivots to reach for a condom, his fingers never leaving me, never slowing their sensual assault. Holding the packet one-handed, tearing it open with his teeth, he deftly rolls it onto his erection then pivots back to me.

"On your knees, beautiful."

He withdraws from me only long enough to help me flip onto my stomach. As soon as I do, he gives my ass a playful smack. The broad head of his cock slides through my folds, then with a powerful thrust, he cleaves deep. I cry out at the pleasure of him, my sex gripping him tightly, already rippling in waves of mounting release as he pistons behind me.

My orgasm roils, sweeping me up swiftly. And then, as if he understands what will push me over the steepest ledge, Nick draws his finger through our wetness and finds my anus again. He pushes inside, his finger penetrating my ass as his cock surges to an even stronger presence within the pulsating walls of my sex.

"Oh, God. Nick."

A hard groan erupts out of him. "I know, baby. Feels so fucking good."

"Yes." I'm panting now, about to shatter.

"Let it go," he urges me. "Let it go, baby. I've got you."

I come on a keening cry, shameless and raw. Pleasure swamps me, drowns me. I succumb without a fight. I let the ecstasy sweep me away, trusting I can because Nick's hold on me is firm and steady. My safe mooring, no matter where he takes me.

I've never felt so free, so protected. So thoroughly possessed.

I've never felt so intimately connected to someone.

And when his own release starts to crest and he clutches me tightly against the heat and strength of his body, I don't know how I'm ever going to learn to live without this kind of passion and connection in my life.

I don't know how I will ever learn to live without him.

35

"Any more pad kee mao left over there?" I gesture with a chopstick to one of the half-dozen Thai takeout containers sitting on a large tray at the end of the bed.

Nick grins. "The lady has an appetite."

"The lady had quite a workout."

His dark brows arch. "Ready for another round?"

I laugh, but I have no doubt he's serious. "You're completely insatiable, aren't you?"

"Yes. I thought that was one of the things you like about me."

"Utterly shameless too," I add, smiling as I pop my last bite of sauce-slathered noodles into my mouth. Holding up my near-empty plate, I indicate our decimated food supply with another jab of my chopstick. "More, please."

He leans over to kiss me. "Baby, *more* is one thing you never need to ask for with me."

We're both seated on the bed naked—or partially naked in my case. I'm wearing the string of pearls again, although in a more traditional manner now. Looped twice around my neck, the long strand falls over my breasts and down my belly, pooling in the V of my crossed legs. Each slide of the silky gems over my nipples or against my nude sex is a decadent reminder of the hours of pleasure I've shared with Nick tonight.

We've hardly left the bedroom since he arrived hours ago. When our stomachs started complaining, we finally showered and called for food delivery, neither of us interested in getting dressed to go out when we could extend our naked reunion into a likely all-nighter.

As I watch him stretch to grab one of the food containers off the tray, my body stirs all over again in lustful appreciation for this gorgeous, intriguing, endlessly seductive man who feeds every hunger I have.

When Nick pivots back toward me to spoon the last of the drunken noodles onto my plate, his gaze catches mine. He pauses, tilting his head. "What?"

"I just remembered we were supposed to celebrate your London deal when you got home."

"Isn't that what we just did?" He empties the container, then sets it back on the tray, licking his fingers. "I think this should be the new standard in celebrations. You, me, hours of uninterrupted sex. A week's worth of takeout for the lady and her alarmingly massive appetite afterward."

"Oh!" I gape in venomless outrage, setting my plate down so I can lunge for him. "My massive appetite? You ate just as much as me, you bastard."

Chuckling, he takes me down with him, my body sprawled across the front of him on the mattress. I hardly even care that we've upset the tray at the end of bed. I'll worry about a little spilled rice later. Right now, the only thing that matters to me is the firm warmth of Nick's body beneath mine, his mouth hot and consuming as we fall into a slow, sensual kiss.

His cock presses thick and steely against my abdomen. I'm already wildly turned on and aching for him, and the erotic feel of the string of pearls crushed between us makes my desire ratchet even higher.

With some effort, I draw back from his kiss. "Just for that smartass remark, I shouldn't tell you that I have a bottle of champagne in the refrigerator. I was saving it for when you got back, but now I'm not sure you deserve it."

He smirks at me. "That's not what you would've said earlier tonight. How many times do I have to make you come?"

I shrug, pretending to consider. "At least once more. Twice, if you really want to impress me."

He laughs, his eyes dark with erotic promise. "I always strive to impress, Ms. Ross."

As if to demonstrate, his hands drift from my ass to the crevice of my body. He strokes my cleft, plunging two fingers inside my sex without warning. I arch into his intimate touch, a sigh hissing through my parted lips. "Nick. Mmm . . ."

He withdraws much too soon for my liking, giving me a light spank. "Let's go get that champagne I'm going to earn."

We head out of the bedroom together, me in my pearls and nothing else, and Nick looking godlike as he strides into the living room where my easel is set up atop a blanket of paint-speckled sheets. My newly finished painting is still on the stand, but covered with a cloth drape.

I pause at the threshold of the kitchen as he approaches the piece.

"What are you working on?"

"Oh. Um, nothing really. Just playing around, trying something different."

He turns a curious look on me. "May I?"

"No." I shake my head, worried he won't like it. I'm terrified he'll think this new piece is just as awful as my others—or worse, that it will negate even the small amount of talent he claims to see in me. "I'm not ready to show it to anyone, Nick."

Least of all him since he was the reason I painted it in the first place.

"You don't trust me?"

I drift over to where he stands, subtly inserting myself between him and my easel. "I'm not ready."

I don't think he can possibly understand how many ways that statement is true. I'm not ready to show him my new work. I'm not ready for his criticism or his praise. And I'm not ready for the way I feel toward him . . . the way he makes me want so many things I can't possibly have.

Not with him, not with anyone.

"If we don't have trust, Avery, we don't have anything. Haven't we covered that?"

He reaches for me, taking hold of the pearls that dangle between my breasts. He winds them around his fist, the tension drawing me inexorably toward him. I can no more fight his pull now than I could any other time we've been together. I take a step, then another. Until his pearl-wrapped fist is the only thing between us.

His eyes search mine. I can see the demand in those deep blue depths, the challenge. This is no longer about my painting. We both know it. And I can see from the rigid determination in Nick's handsome, hard face that he will not be denied. Not this time.

"I want to see every part of you, Avery. That's the only way this is going to work between us. No fear. No hiding. No barriers, remember?"

"Nick, I . . ." I shake my head miserably. My throat is dry, clogged with all of the words I cannot say. Things he should know about me and my past—things that are far more shameful than any of the half-truths I've fed him about my life since I've come to New York. "Please, don't," I murmur thickly. "I just . . . I can't."

I watch something dim, then darken, in his piercing gaze. The mouth that has kissed me so tenderly, worshipped me so pleasurably today and every other time we've been together now hardens in a stern line.

"Nick, I know you don't understand why—"

"Then tell me." Clipped words. A harsh command that hits me like a slap. "Make me understand what you're afraid of. Is it me? Have I hurt you, Avery? Have I frightened you?"

"No. Never." It kills me that he would think that. It breaks my heart to see him trying to make sense of my withdrawal. "You've never done anything wrong, Nick."

"Then why are you pulling back from me?" His voice sharpens. "What are you hiding from? *Who* are you hiding from? Damn it, Avery, what won't you say?"

I shake my head. My voice has left me entirely now.

He doesn't say anything either. His expression unreadable, shuttered to me, he lets go of the pearls and lets the strand drop. It sways against my bare torso, the heat from his hand swiftly fleeing the gems.

He steps back, and his distance creates an even bigger chill in me. I shiver from the coldness I feel opening up between us, and from the impenetrable ice of his gaze.

As we stand there, locked in our miserable impasse, the apartment intercom buzzes with a call from the lobby. The sound punctuates the tension between us, making our unbearable distance widen with each passing second. For a long moment, neither one of us moves.

Nick is the first to break the awful silence. "Go find out what Manny wants."

He strides away, back into the bedroom, leaving me alone and naked, wracked with an uncontrollable shudder. With emotion dammed up in my throat, I pad over to the intercom and answer the doorman's call.

"Yes, Manny?" My voice is shockingly steady. Then again, I was trained a long time ago how to act as if my world isn't crumbling all around me.

"Miss Avery, one of your friends is down here. She says she needs to talk to you."

The announcement is so unexpected, it takes me a second to answer. "Who is it?"

"Tasha Lopez, ma'am."

Confusion burns through my haze of despair. It's Friday night, just past nine o'clock. Tasha should be at Vendange. "She's here? In the building?"

"Yes, ma'am." Manny lowers his voice discreetly. "If you don't mind me saying, she seems very upset. Shall I put her on the phone?"

As much as my heart aches for what I've likely lost tonight with Nick, my concern for Tasha has me snapping to attention. "No. Don't put her on the phone.

Tell her I'll be right down."

When I pivot to hurry to the bedroom for some clothing, Nick is standing behind me, dressed in his dark suit pants and buttoning his white shirt. "What's going on?"

"I don't know. Tasha's downstairs. Manny says she's upset."

I duck past him to get dressed, my heart caught in my throat for the fact that Nick doesn't even try to stop me, and my stomach twisting with worry for my friend.

36

I don't expect Nick to follow me, but he steps into the elevator with me a few moments later, each of us taking up opposite corners of the car as it descends silently to the ground floor.

Tasha is waiting in the empty lobby, seated on one of the white leather and chrome chairs near the main entrance. Dressed in her black pants, deep-V shirt, and heels, she looks like any other chic Manhattanite who might step into this building on a Friday night. But as she spots me approaching and vaults from the chair, I see the stress in her face immediately.

Her mouth is drawn, deep lines bracketing her lips. Her normally sparkling brown eyes are puffy and bloodshot, as if she's been crying recently.

As soon as I realize her distress, I break into a panicked jog to reach her. "Tasha? Honey, what's wrong?"

She throws her arms around me, just as a jagged sob

rips from her throat. "I didn't know what to do, Avery! I didn't know where else to go."

"It's okay," I soothe, but I feel her trembling against me. "You're all right. You're safe. Just tell me what's going on."

"Joel." She chokes his name like a curse and my blood runs a little cold. "He tried to—" She lifts her head, and I am stricken by the true fear I see in my friend's face. "He said if I wanted to keep my job, I'd have to—"

She doesn't finish, her words cut off by fresh tears.

"That son of a bitch." Fury erupts from somewhere deep inside me, as bitter as acid. I am stricken by the thought of anyone hurting my friend, especially someone like Joel. I pull her out of my embrace, holding her at arm's length so I can clearly see her face. "Tasha, did he . . . did he touch you?"

She shakes her head. "No. I ran out of there before he had the chance. I just grabbed my purse and I ran. I didn't know what else to do."

"Who's Joel?"

Nick's deep voice is a dark demand beside me. When I swivel my head to look at him, I am met with a stormy blue gaze that is a mere shade away from violent. He's heard everything Tasha said, and his reaction seems as visceral as mine.

"Joel's the manager at Vendange, a restaurant over on Madison."

He nods tightly, disapprovingly, but he remains silent as Tasha launches into the details of what occurred.

"I was straightening out an order that Kimmie fucked up, and Joel comes over to me, telling me I've got customers waiting to cash out. I lost it. I told him they wouldn't be waiting if it wasn't for his useless girlfriend making extra work for me. I guess I finally had enough of his overbearing bullshit, you know? I didn't think anything would come of it, but he was pissed. When I went to the storage room a little while later, he followed me inside. He locked the door." She swallows hard, then blows out a sharp sigh. "He told me if I wanted to keep my job, I would have to make it up to him somehow, and that I could start right then and there."

"Jesus Christ," Nick mutters.

My own outrage is on full boil too. I never had much regard for Joel and his oily tactics, but what he's done to Tasha tonight is beyond disgusting. "What about Tony? Does he know this happened?"

"No!" Her eyes go wide with alarm. "Are you kidding? I didn't dare tell him. You know my husband. He'll want to kill Joel for even thinking of touching me."

She's right about that, I have no doubt. Tony's devotion to his wife is immutable. If he saw her like this, tearful and trembling, he'd put Joel in either the hospital or a body bag.

Based on the undercurrent of menace I feel radiating off Nick, I have to wonder if he's struggling with the same impulse.

Tasha sniffles and wipes her tear-streaked face. "I'm sorry to put this on you, Ave. It's not your problem. I just didn't know where else to go."

"It's okay," I reassure her. "You're my best friend. Of course this is my problem too."

She shakes her head. "What am I going to do? I can't go back there now. I won't. I'd rather flip burgers at a damn fast-food chain than go back and grovel for my job with Joel."

I'm not about to let either of those things happen to her. "You're absolutely not going back to work for Joel," I tell her sternly. "We'll figure this out, honey. But right now, I need to get you home. And you need to tell Tony what happened."

She nods weakly. "Okay."

"Come on. My purse is upstairs. Let me grab it and we can go catch the subway."

We turn to head for the elevators. Nick stands in my way. "I'll drive you where you need to go."

Considering we left the apartment barely speaking to each other, I'm sure taking Tasha and me to Queens is the last thing he feels like doing. I'm not too enthused by the idea either. It hurts just to look at him now and feel the distance growing between us. I really don't want to prolong my own torture by sitting beside him in his car, knowing he's only helping out of obligation.

"We'll be fine, Nick. You don't have to—"

"I'll drive," he repeats, his tone as firm as his stare. "Get your things, Avery. I'll wait for you down here."

~ ~ ~

Nick is on his cell phone when we return to the lobby a few minutes later. While upstairs, Tasha fixed her mascara and I hastily threw my hair into a ponytail before grabbing my purse and heading back down to meet him.

We step off the elevator, and, for one brief second, I am transported to the first night I saw him in this same lobby. His stare still seems to look right through me. He still unsettles me, makes me achingly aware of myself as a woman and of him as a man.

I want to rush over to him now. I want to feel his arms wrap around me and hear him tell me in that sensual, deep voice of his that everything is okay between us. I need to know that, even though I don't deserve those reassurances. All Nick has asked for from me is honesty, trust. Today he understands, perhaps for the first time, that I am incapable of giving him either one.

"I didn't ask if the deal was going to be easy," he says to the person on the end of the line, glancing up as Tasha and I approach. "Just do what you have to and make it happen, Beck."

He tone is curt, final. I can't help feeling sorry for whomever he's speaking to, since I'm all but certain Nick's impatience is spurred by his irritation with me. He slides his phone into his pants pocket.

He glances at Tasha in brief concern, then his gaze slides to me, unblinking. For the first time since we met, I don't feel heat when Nick is looking at me. I feel chill remoteness. I feel anger, although he's too polished a negotiator to truly let his emotions show. But I've come to know him too well, too intimately, for him to hide it from me.

"All set?" he asks, his tone flat, all business.

We take the elevator down to the garage where his BMW is parked, then proceed to make the drive to Queens in a strained silence.

At Tasha's house, we're met with confusion and concern and the predicted outrage from her husband upon hearing the reason for his wife's early return from work. Nick and I hang back to let Tasha explain the situation to her family—her mother-in-law, who comes out with a basket of clean laundry under her arm, and Tony, who's working on construction invoices at the kitchen table when we arrive.

Although Tasha held it together on the ride to Queens, now that she's safe at home, her voice wavers as she relays what happened at Vendange.

"That motherfucker," Tony grates out furiously. "That fucking son of a bitch!"

"It's okay," Tasha reassures him through her tears. "He didn't touch me. I didn't give him the chance. I just got out of there as fast as I could."

He's obviously still fuming with violent rage, but he tenderly gathers his wife into his arms and holds her close. I don't doubt that the only thing keeping the big man from getting into his truck and racing back to the city to kick Joel's ass is his more immediate worry for Tasha.

"Good girl. You did the right thing, babe. You forget about that asshole, all right? You're done there and it's over. You're safe now." He kisses the top of her head as Tasha buries her face in his broad chest and clings to him. "As for that cocksucker back at Vendange, he better hope I never see his face anywhere or I'm gonna fucking break it."

Tasha looks up at him, smiling through her tears. "I love you too, babe."

He lowers his head and kisses her, as sweet a kiss as I've ever seen them share. I have to will myself not to look at Nick as I glance away from Tasha and Tony to give them their moment. I know if I meet Nick's eyes now, my misery is going to be written plainly in my face.

I miss him as if we're not even in the same room

now. I miss him as if the space that's opened up between us earlier tonight is becoming impossible to cross.

In the awkward quietness that's settled over us all, Tony's mother clears her throat. "Why don't I make everyone some tea?"

Without waiting for our answers, she shuffles over to the stove and busies herself with putting on a pot of water.

Nick holds his hand out to Tony. "I'm Nick, by the way."

"Oh, sure. Right. Good to meet ya." Tony nods vigorously as the two men shake hands. "I figured you were Avery's new boyfriend when I saw that sweet M6 you drove up in."

I immediately feel awkward, both for the reference to Nick belonging in any way to me, and because I didn't think to make introductions. Neither of the men seem to notice or care.

"Can I get you a beer, Nick?"

"No!" Tasha and I both say in unison.

Then, just like that, all of the stress and tension from Tasha's ordeal tonight is lifted as she and I look at each other and burst into laughter.

"No beer for Nick, Tony," she admonishes her husband.

Nick glances between us and his eager host. I subtly shake my head at him in warning, but all it earns me is a questioning look. "Actually, I'd love a beer."

Tony grabs a couple of homebrews from the refrigerator while his mother serves tea to Tasha and me. The older woman doesn't join us at the kitchen table, instead bids us all goodnight and takes her laundry off to another room.

Nick takes a seat across from me. With a murmured thanks, he accepts his opened beer from Tony, who drops into the chair at the head of the table for six, next to his wife.

"You doing okay, babe?"

She nods. "Better now that I'm home."

Nick lifts his bottle to take a drink, but pauses when his phone chimes with an incoming call. *Saved by the bell.* He glances at the screen. "Will you all excuse me? I need to take this."

He steps out of the kitchen to speak privately, and I'm half tempted to knock his full bottle of beer off the table while he's gone, if only to spare him from actually tasting it.

Tasha nudges me after Nick's out of earshot. "What's going on with you two? I can't tell if I'm feeling massive sexual energy or a cold war brewing between you guys."

I let loose a defeated sigh. "Some of both. I think I'm messing things up with him, Tasha."

"Well, cut it out. He's really into you in case you haven't noticed."

"You think so? Even now?"

She rolls her eyes. "Duh! Every time he looks your way, I can feel the air crackle with heat."

Tony tugs one of her brown curls. "Kinda like us, eh, babe?"

This time, Tasha doesn't come back at him with a smartass quip or a dramatic eye-roll. Turning to her husband, she tenderly strokes his cheek. "Yeah, baby. Just like us."

Nick walks back into the room as they share a sweet kiss. "Sorry about that." He slips the phone into his pocket. "A business matter I needed to tend to."

Tony grins at him. "You buy another hotel over in London or Dubai or something?"

"Tony!" Tasha smacks his biceps. "That's none of your business."

"It's all right," Nick says. "Nothing like that this time. Something more local."

I eye him, picking up on his cagey answer. And I know him too well to miss the faint glimmer of amusement in his eyes.

He clears his throat as he sits back down at the table. "So, did you like working at Vendange, Tasha?"

"Yeah." She glances at him and shrugs. "I mean, I wasn't doing rocket science there or anything, but it was enjoyable enough. The place is always busy, and I enjoy doing lots of different things there—tending bar and looking after inventory, training other employees on the computer and the menus. So, yeah. I liked it."

Nick contemplates her. "Sounds like you know what you're doing."

Tony grins, pulling Tasha affectionately under his arm. "You kiddin' me? My girl right here is smart as fuck, Nick. She knows that restaurant inside and out. She could run the damn place. Practically does already. Ain't that right, Avery?"

I nod, feeling the weight of Nick's gaze slide toward me now. "Tasha's amazing. She's driven, hard-working. She can do anything she sets her mind to. The customers love her too."

"Well, listen, you guys," she says. "I appreciate this love-fest and all, but none of it matters because I'm never going back to Vendange. Not if I have to get within a hundred yards of Joel."

Tony grunts. "Damn right you're not. We'll get by for a while until you find something else, babe. I don't want you worrying about it, all right?"

"What if Joel wasn't there?"

All three of us look at Nick, confused.

"What do you mean?" Tasha asks. "Like, if I press charges or something? Get him arrested and have his ass fired?"

"It's up to you if you want to press charges." Nick's tone is even, but there is something cryptic in his expression. "If he was gone from Vendange for good, would you want to work there?"

"Yeah. Of course."

"How would you like to manage it?"

I gape at him, frowning. "Nick, what are you saying?"

"I'm saying as of tomorrow morning, Vendange is under new management. Mine."

"What?" I can't believe what I'm hearing. "But . . . how? And when did this happen?"

"I spoke to my lawyer about it before we left Manhattan."

Of course. The curt conversation about a deal Nick wanted handled. This is what it was about?

He glances to Tasha. "If you're interested, my attorney, Andrew Beckham, will meet you at the restaurant tomorrow morning at seven A.M. to go over some paperwork."

"What about Joel?" I ask.

"Beck has already informed him that the restaurant has a new owner and that his services are no longer required. Joel was escorted off the premises a few minutes ago."

"That was the call you just took?" I'm incredulous, and not a little impressed. "You just made all of this happen in a matter of a couple hours?"

Nick nods as if buying businesses on a whim and making a clean sweep of their toxic assets is something he does every day. Which, yeah, of course, it probably is.

Tasha seems even more astonished than I am. "I can't believe you did this. I can't believe you're offering me this chance. Are you seriously offering me the job?"

"Very serious. Vendange is a thriving business from what I've gathered tonight. I think, with better management, it could be a very lucrative investment. For everyone involved." He holds his hand out to her. "So, what do you say? Are you in?"

She beams at him, nodding enthusiastically as they shake hands across the table. "I'm in."

Tony tilts his bottle toward Nick. "Well, hell. I'll drink to that."

37

I can't believe you drank Tony's homemade beer." I brave a glance at Nick from the passenger seat of his car, looking for some way to break the ice between us. We only left Tasha's house ten minutes ago, but it feels like days because Nick has barely spoken to me. "One sip of that awful home brew was enough for me the day I tried it, but you actually drank the whole bottle."

He shrugs, slanting me a brief look. "Not a fan of hops soaked in old gym socks, I take it?"

A laugh bursts out of me. "I know, right? God, it was terrible. You really didn't have to drink it, you know."

"No, but if I hadn't, I would've insulted my host." Another shrug, but this one is accompanied by one of his crooked, boyish smiles that makes my insides melt. "I'll survive. For the record, I've been offered worse in the name of hospitality."

"Really? I can't imagine."

He grunts in acknowledgment. "Did you know there's a beer in Japan that's made with milk?"

Repulsed, I wrinkle my nose. "No, I did not know that."

"I wish I could say the same. Do yourself a favor and stay away from it."

My mouth curves wryly. "I'll be sure to do that."

I relax into my seat as Nick navigates the BMW into the fast lane and speeds ahead of the other cars. I'm nursing a small glimmer of relief as I watch him drive. Maybe we can end the evening on a lighter mood than it began. I hope so. I'm praying I still have a chance to build a bridge across the crevasse I dug between us back at the apartment. The kindness he showed my friends tonight seems like a promising start.

"Thank you for being here with me, Nick. And for what you're doing for Tasha too. I mean, buying Vendange? Getting rid of Joel? That's an incredibly generous thing for you to do. You're a good man."

"No, Avery. I'm not a good man." He's quiet for a moment, then he glances at me, his expression unreadable in the dim light of the dashboard. "What I am is a good businessman. The restaurant is a solid investment. If Tasha is as competent as you and Tony believe, then hiring her to manage the place only seems sensible."

I nod, but inside I'm deflated. "Well, you made a good decision where she's concerned. Tasha won't let you down."

Unlike me, I can't help thinking, as the silence between us stretches long again.

I gaze out the car window, seeing none of the zooming traffic or the glow of the city that surrounds us.

I see sunny blue skies and miles of crystalline water. I see Nick smiling at me on the deck of the *Icarus*, looking at me with the same kind of insatiable hunger that I have for him.

I see the long strand of creamy pearls coiled around my wrists while he shows me pleasures I never dared dream I could want.

Trust, he told me as he presented his extravagant gift to me.

Honesty.

The only way they'll break is if you pull away from me . . .

Nick's words are still echoing in my mind after we make the rest of the drive into Manhattan. We ride up in the elevator together, not to the penthouse, but to the fifth floor. He steps out with me and walks me to the apartment, hanging behind me as I fumble the key into the lock. My hands are not cooperating, probably because of the mist of tears threatening to fill my eyes.

I flinch when Nick's large hand closes over my fingers, warm and strong. "Here. I've got it."

Reaching around me, he opens the door, but neither one of us makes a move to go inside.

"Nick," I murmur, uncertain what I mean to say to him. There is so much I want him to know right now, but the words all jam in my tightening throat.

I'm sorry.

I'm scared.

I'm sick with the thought that we might be over. If not here and now, then very soon. When Claire comes home and I have to tell Nick that I'm homeless, jobless . . . a liar who's strung him along this whole time, pretending I belonged in his world.

And I'm damaged. Not only from my stepfather's

abuse, but from the violent aftermath of that horrific, explosive night nine years ago. The consequences of those final hours he was alive will stay with me forever—even if my mother finally does get her freedom one day. My shame and my secret are scars I'll never lose.

Nick needs to know that I'm a coward. This is the confession I truly need to give him. It's the only one I might be able to make him understand.

"Nick," I say again, my voice a threadbare whisper as I turn around to face him in the threshold. His eyes burn into me, unblinking, expectant. It's a struggle to hold his gaze, but I force myself not to look away. "Nick . . . I've been basically on my own since I was sixteen years old. It's not easy for me to trust. It's not . . . it's not easy for me to let someone in."

"What happened when you were sixteen?" His eyes hold me, both tender and demanding. "Tell me."

I swallow, wishing I could glance away, but his gaze won't release me.

"Why were you on your own that young?"

I watch a tendon pulse in his jaw as he speaks. I've seen him haunted before, and it's there in his eyes again. Shadows that shield whatever torment he's been made to endure. Dark, private secrets he guards well—maybe as well as I guard my own.

"You're asking me to tell you something I've never told anyone before, Nick." I shake my head, feeling us slip back to where we started earlier tonight. "You're asking me to tell you something that can't be taken back."

A scowl furrows his brow and that tendon that was pulsing before now begins to throb under the hard clench of his jaw. "I'm not here to hurt you. I'll keep you safe, Avery."

But he can't. No one can. My mother did her best to keep me safe, and it cost her dearly. I can't drag Nick into my past. At first, I couldn't allow it because I didn't know him, didn't trust him. Now, I can't let him in because I care too much.

I'm falling in love with him, and he's asking me to tell him the one thing that could shatter that to pieces.

I cut away from his penetrating stare. It's too painful to see the displeasure, the cool emotional retreat, settle over his handsome face.

"I've got business matters to handle in the morning," he announces crisply. "If you want to continue this conversation, text or call me and let me know. I want to give you time, Avery, but I'm not a patient man."

I nod, but inside, my heart is twisting painfully. When I speak, my voice sounds choked and small. "I don't want this to be goodbye, Nick."

"Then don't let it be. I'm giving you the choice."

I understand how much this offer is costing him. Dominic Baine is not a man who surrenders control to anyone. Yet he's handing it over it to me. I want to accept it as the gift I know it to be, but my fear keeps me silent.

Instead, I reach up tentative to caress his cheek. He lets me touch him, a small concession that I latch on to like a life line. He's disappointed with me, even angry. But our physical connection isn't broken. Not yet, anyway. Not unless I am willing to throw it away.

It's the last thing I want to do. But he's asking me for the one thing I cannot give him. Not now. Not ever.

He stands stock-still, his expression guarded, schooled to a dangerous calm as I trace my fingers over the dark shadow on his jaw. Then he draws back, out of my reach, and places the apartment key in my hand.

"Goodnight, Avery."

38

After a restless night without much sleep and half the morning spent drifting around the apartment like a boat cut away from its anchor, I'm relieved to get a text from Tasha inviting me to swing by Vendange before the start of the lunch rush.

Seeing my friend is just the medicine I need today. God knows, I need some kind of diversion from my thoughts and my own miserable company.

Be there in twenty.

Great! she replies. *Also? I totally adore your boyfriend. Don't tell him I said that!*

As I sign off, my smile is automatic, even if it hurts. Tasha's excitement and gratitude toward Nick give me a fresh stab of regret for just how badly I left things with him last night. I don't know how I'm going to fix the mess I've made. I'm not even certain that I can.

If he can forgive that I've lied to him about my work and living situation all this time, I doubt he'll be as willing to overlook the rest of my secrets. Not when he can have any woman he wants. Women who don't come with my baggage and the complications they would bring to our lives.

He doesn't need that kind of burden. And I can't ask him to bear it for me.

Nine years ago, I put a monster in a box. I locked it up tight and threw away the key, and I can't open it ever again. Not even for Nick. God, especially not for him.

He would never look at me the same again.

No one would.

Shoving the ghosts of my past back where they belong, I shower quickly, then pull my damp hair into a ponytail and brush on some mascara and lip gloss.

It's so warm and sunny outside, my impulse is to slip into one of the summer dresses Nick bought for me in Miami. But today it doesn't feel right to touch any of the gifts he's given me. They don't belong to me. Not anymore—if they ever truly did. And wearing any of them now would only worsen the ache inside me.

Instead, I toss on a pair of jeans and flats and top the outfit off with a breezy linen blouse. I grab my purse and cell phone, then catch the subway to Midtown.

Tasha is at one of the tables on the main floor going over schedules with a couple employees as I walk in. She waves, then says something to the crew before they all get up and go back to work.

"Hey, girl!" She hurries over and pulls me into a tight hug. "I'm so happy to see you."

I return her smile, feeling genuinely pleased for her. "How's it going?"

"Awesome." Her brown eyes are wide with enthusiasm and energy. "Nick had his attorney call everyone in early this morning to tell them about the changes. They're all being really cool about the fact that I'm managing now. I don't think anyone's sorry to see Joel gone."

I nod, taking in the busy, but less harried, vibe in the place today. And I can't help but notice that the dress code is already improved too. No more low-cut tops and high heels on any of the female servers. Like Tasha, the other women are dressed in black pants and tops, but with decidedly less cleavage on display.

As we're talking, Kimmie comes out of the kitchen area carrying a crate of bar glasses, still steaming from the dishwasher. Her blond hair is limp and drooping in her face as she schleps the heavy glassware to the bar and begins racking it up for the day's use.

Tasha catches my amused look and shrugs. "I demoted her to kitchen runner. She might be the only one who'll have trouble adjusting to the new world order around here."

I shake my head, unable to tame my smile. "You're bad."

"Hey, I just want the work done right. And I'll be fair about it. I told Kimmie if she works hard and does a good job, I'll consider putting her back on the floor at some point."

I laugh, feeling overwhelmed with joy for my friend. I have no doubt she's going to make Vendange an even bigger success. "I'm glad this all worked out for you, Tasha. You deserve this."

"I don't know if that's true, but I'm going to do my damnedest to make you proud." She grins. "I don't suppose I could talk you into coming back to Vendange, now that Joel is gone?"

"Ah, probably not a good idea." I don't tell her that the new owner likely wouldn't clear me for hire anyway, especially since that Nick and I aren't on speaking terms. "I appreciate the thought, but I'm sure you'll do fine without me."

"You know what's really amazing? I get to hire a night manager in a couple of months after things smooth out. Not only do I have this great opportunity with better pay, but I'll get to spend more time at home with Zoe too." She's beaming, practically glowing with happiness. "I owe all of this to you, Avery. Well, and to Nick, of course. Speaking of our favorite bazillionaire, where is he today?"

"I don't know." I try not to sound as dejected as I feel, but I can't escape Tasha's narrowed stare. "Last night when he dropped me off, he said he had business to handle this morning. I haven't seen him. I'm not sure we're speaking at the moment."

"Oh, Ave." Her brow creases with a worried frown. "What happened? Do you want to talk about it?"

I do, but at the same moment, I see a very attractive black man in a white dress shirt and tie and light gray slacks come out of Joel's former office with a tablet in hand. High cheekbones and close-trimmed hair and beard set off pale eyes and a lush mouth. Even though my heart and all the rest of me belongs to Nick, it's hard not to stare.

Tasha glances back at him, following my arrested gaze. "That's Andrew Beckham."

"Nick's attorney?"

"Yep."

"Oh."

She wiggles her brows at me. "Yeah. *Oh* is right. You

haven't met? Come on, let me introduce you."

I start to protest, but it's too late. The young lawyer approaches us, his mouth curved in a polite smile.

"Mr. Beckham, this is my friend, Avery Ross."

His chin lifts slightly in acknowledgment as he extends his hand to me. "Ms. Ross. Nice to meet you. And please, both of you, call me Andrew. Or Beck. I hear *Mr. Beckham* and I get a little twitchy, expecting to see my dad in the room with me."

I smile and shake his hand, feeling awkward and relaxed at the same time. It's obvious Nick has already mentioned me to him in some capacity. Good or bad, at this moment I don't know. Thankfully, Beck is too professional to point it out.

The three of us chat for a few minutes about the restaurant and trivial things, then Beck's phone chimes and he excuses himself to take the call. I don't have to guess if it's Nick he's speaking to. Andrew Beckham may be an outstanding lawyer, but he's no match for my intuition.

Just knowing Nick is on the other line now puts a knot of misery in my breast.

"I should go," I murmur.

"So soon?" Tasha looks crestfallen. "You just got here."

I shrug lamely. "I have some errands to run. And you need to get back to work, boss lady."

She stares at me for a long moment, then pulls me into a quick hug. "I don't believe you, but I'm gonna let you slide for now. You call me later. But first, you go tell that man you love him and that whatever is wrong, you want to work it out."

"Tasha, you don't understand—"

"I don't understand what? That you're falling head over heels and are miserable without him, or that you're too chicken-shit to admit it?"

I glare at her, but, dammit, she's right. On all counts.

"Look," she says. "We've been friends for a while now. I know it's not easy for you to take advice, but I'm going to tell you anyway. Don't let this one get away. I'm not saying that because he's crazy rich and hot as sin besides. I'm saying it because last night I saw the way you two look at each other."

"Tasha—"

"He needs you, Avery. Maybe he won't say the words to you either, but they're right there in his eyes. And you need him too."

I purse my lips as she finishes. "May I speak now?"

She gestures for me to go ahead.

"You're the best friend I've ever had, you know that? Thank you for caring about me. Not just now, but ever since I walked into this place looking for work and you made sure I got interviewed ahead of anyone else." I pull her into a hug. "I love you."

"I love you, too, girl." She draws back, holding my upper arms and giving me a stern maternal look. "Now go tell him how you feel."

One of the other employees calls for her from behind the bar, and I take the opportunity to edge toward the door.

"Call me afterward," she says. "I mean it. I'm working until eleven tonight. I want to hear from you before I go home."

I nod as I step out onto Madison Avenue. As I head toward Grand Central under a cloudless blue sky, it seems as if years have passed since the last time I made this trek, not a handful of weeks.

It's been almost three and a half months since I first laid eyes on Dominic Baine in that lobby elevator.

It's strange how different everything seems to me now.

I used to feel as though this city and I were at constant odds with each other. I used to think New York sensed me as an interloper in its domain and wanted me gone—that each obstacle I met with since I moved here had been thrown into my path by some cosmic force conspiring to defeat me at every turn.

But it isn't the city or anything else blocking my way.

It's me.

Tasha is right. And isn't that what Nick has been trying to tell me too?

Isn't that what he's been teaching me every time he touches me . . . each time he shows me what I truly crave but am too afraid to admit, let alone ask for?

Last night, he knew how badly I wanted to let him in. He promised I could trust him. He is giving me the chance to reach for what I want most of all—him.

Us.

My breath leaks out of me raggedly. My feet slow to a halt in the middle of the busy sidewalk.

"I can't do this. I can't shut him out. I can walk away."

I hardly feel the bumps and jostles of the other pedestrians pushing past me as I dig in my purse for my cell phone. As I pull it out, I see the light is blinking with a new voice message.

Maybe Nick heard I was in Vendange and tried to call me?

I tap the icon, my heart throbbing in my chest.

A man's recorded voice comes on, but it's not Nick.

"Ms. Ross, this is Walter Stadler."

What would my mother's public defender want with me? Unless it's about my mother's parole board review. God, no. I brace myself to hear there's been another delay or some other wrench thrown into the already slow-moving cogs of justice.

But it's not about my mom's parole.

It's something much worse.

"I'm afraid there was an incident at the prison today. Your mother's been injured. She's in the infirmary, about to go in for surgery. Please call me as soon as possible."

39

I startle awake for what must be the fifth time, the beeping of medical monitors piercing my light doze. At first, I think I'm dreaming. I pray that I am—even as I open my dry eyes and see the green walls of the Muncy State Prison infirmary.

But it's not a bad dream. After a dangerous fall down a flight of stairs during her morning work shift in the prison laundry, my mother is now only an hour out of surgery for multiple broken bones and a pierced lung. I am seated on a hard plastic chair, my arms folded under my head like a pillow on the lowered side rail of her hospital bed while she rests on an oxygen tube and medically sedated. I try not to notice the handcuff that shackles her left arm—her only limb without any fractures—to the bed. The prisoner recovering from surgery across the room from my mom is also restrained to her bed.

The door to the room is open. As I lift my head and

blink away my exhaustion, the public defender quietly steps inside.

"Is there any word from the doctor?" I ask, sitting up to speak to him.

Stadler nods. "I've just come from meeting with him now. Surgery and a couple of titanium pins took care of her femur fracture, which was the worst of the breaks. The others should heal up in time. They'll be starting her on a physical therapy program as soon as her lung is recovered."

A tear rolls down my face as I glance at her in the bed. I swipe my cheek, hating that she's here, knowing that she doesn't deserve this. None of it.

"What does this mean for the parole board review?"

Stadler runs a hand over his balding head. "The doctor wants her under observation until her lung is healed, which he said could be up to a week."

"The parole meeting is in a few days," I remind him. "She's counting on it. She'll be devastated if that appointment doesn't happen."

"I know she's going to be disappointed. We'd all like to see her plead her case for the board, Avery. And she will. Let's focus on getting your mother strong and back on her feet first. We can reapply with the parole review board once Brenda is ready."

I want to scream at him that she's ready now. My mother would wheel herself to the meeting in this hospital bed if she were given the chance. Hell, I would roll her in there, too—assuming she'd permit me anywhere near the judicial system to try to help win her freedom.

She likely won't be happy to know I'm here now either.

She's been protective of me all my life, but even more so after she realized what her second husband had done to me. She's sacrificed everything to keep me safe, to keep me shielded from any pain. It breaks my heart that there is so little I can do for her now.

Stadler checks his watch and awkwardly clears his throat. "Unfortunately, visiting time is ending in about ten minutes, Avery. I've got to get going, but if you need a ride somewhere—"

"No, thanks. I drove down from the city. My rental car is in the visitor lot."

"Well, you have my number if there's anything you'd like to discuss. I've got another client meeting across town, so I really should be going."

I stand up and shake his offered hand. "Thank you for letting me know about this."

"I'll keep you informed," he tells me as he heads out the door. "Your mom's a tough lady. And she loves you more than anything."

I nod, knowing it's true. And I love her more than anything too. There was a time when I'd have said I love her more than anyone else in my life . . . but that was before I met Nick.

Just thinking about him puts a cold ache of longing in my breast. And regret.

I haven't spoken to him since we parted last night. After Stadler's call this morning, my primary concern had been my mom. I left Vendange and raced to the nearest rental car agency, then drove more than three hours to Pennsylvania.

I haven't spoken to anyone since I arrived at Muncy. The prison policy prohibits visitors from bringing in all manner of things when visiting an inmate, so for the past several hours, my purse and cell phone have been secured at the registration desk.

I know I need to call Nick and tell him where I am. I need to tell him what happened.

I need to ask him to forgive me for all of the things I've kept from him, fearing he wouldn't want me once he knew my truths.

Now I'm terrified that I've lost him because of everything I haven't said.

Especially that I love him.

I can only pray he'll still be willing to listen.

One of the prison guards stops by the room to inform me that it's time for me to leave. Reluctantly, I kiss my mother's forehead and head out, collecting my belongings at the desk. My phone light is blinking with several missed calls. Nick's number, I see as I quickly scroll through the log. He didn't leave any messages. And his last attempt to call me was several hours ago.

He's given up on me. Of course, he has. I've all but ensured he would, haven't I?

I rub my sternum as the ache that took up residence there earlier now feels like an icy abyss.

It's raining when I exit the infirmary building. I hardly even notice the cold, wet drops as I walk out to the visitor lot. My rental is near the back and I walk to it feeling adrift, uncertain where I'm going or where I belong anymore.

As I reach the white compact car, my gaze snags on the vehicle parked in the space beside it. The sleek black BMW's engine is running, thin gray exhaust steaming in the drizzle.

My feet stop moving. At the same time, Nick emerges from the driver's side.

At first, I can't find my voice. Torn between elation and dread, I can only stare at this beautiful man who means everything to me, shocked to see him. Horrified that he's come here, to the very place I never wanted him to see.

"I had to know if you were okay," he says. "When you wouldn't answer my calls, I had your GPS tracked. And it led me here." I can't read his expression. Standing with me in the rain, he looks as uncertain and wary as I know I must to him.

"Nick." The impulse to run to him—to bury myself in his arms—is nearly overwhelming. But I don't know if he'll reject me. I wouldn't blame him if he did. I stand frozen in place, unsure what to say to him now that he's standing in front of me. "I wanted to call you. I would have. I planned to . . ."

He doesn't seem interested in my excuses now. He gestures at the women's prison behind me. "So, I'm guessing this is where your mother's been since you were sixteen."

Not a question he needs me to confirm, but I nod. "Nick, I don't want to do this here—"

"We didn't have to, Avery. You could've told me long before it came to this."

He's right, and I won't even try to argue. I start to shiver, though it's not the rain that's making me so miserable.

"Get in out of the cold," Nick says, his tone level, devoid of emotion. "We'll talk in the car."

Woodenly, I open the passenger side and climb in. He slides into the driver's seat, the soft thump of his door making me flinch. For a long while, there is only silence in the car.

Finally, the words just start tumbling out of me. And once they start, I can't stop them.

"My daddy, Daniel Ross, died when I was very young. He was a good man, and we were happy—me, my mom and him. When I was seven years old, he had a massive heart attack. He was gone, just like that. And everything changed. My mom eventually met someone else—a man named Martin Coyle. He worked at a school the next town over. He seemed nice. He was nice, but then he married my mom and things started to change. He would say mean things to her sometimes—then, once, he hit her. He promised he never would again, but that promise didn't last. None of his promises or apologies were worth a damn. And then, after I started getting a little older, he began looking at me in ways that made me uncomfortable. He started trying to touch me when my mom wasn't there. I learned to avoid him, to leave the house if I knew he was home alone. Finally, when I was sixteen, he did more than touch me. And, that time, I wasn't able to stop him."

Memories of that day crash down on me as I speak. All my life, I've shut them out, banished them to a dark corner of my mind if only so I could survive. So as not to let them own me. But, now, I let them flood in. The dam is breaking and I need Nick to understand.

"I couldn't get away that day. He . . . he raped me."

Nick stares at me. "And then your mother killed him."

"Yes. She shot him." I swallow the regret—and the guilt—that's lodged in my throat. "She killed him to protect me."

Although it's my personal horror, Nick looks stricken by what he's heard. "I didn't know, Avery. I'm sorry." He slowly shakes his head, and when he speaks, his voice is softer than I've ever heard it. "I told you that you could trust me. I told you that the only way this would work—the only way *we* could work—was without barriers or inhibitions. But if I'd known about this—"

"That's right," I say softly. "If you'd known about this, you would've looked at me differently. You would've been different with me. Or worse, you would've stayed away."

He doesn't deny it, and strangely, that gives me strength.

"There's more I haven't told you, Nick. I've been lying to you about a lot of things these past three and a half months."

I tell him how Claire Prentice isn't a friend of mine at all, that she hired me to housesit. I tell him how my 'public relations' job was actually bartending with Tasha at Vendange, and how I'd been two weeks away from being homeless because my apartment had been sold out from under me and I couldn't afford to move somewhere else.

He listens, stoic, silent. Giving me no indication whether he forgives me or despises me.

"Nick, please say something."

He blinks, then glances away from me, staring at the rain-sluiced windshield. "Has anything you've told me the past hundred days been true?"

"Yes." The word cracks in my throat, thick with emotion. I'm desperate to make him understand, to make him believe me now. "Everything I've said about us, about the way you make me feel . . . about what I feel for you . . . Nick, it's all been true. Every word. Except I didn't tell you everything."

His gaze locks on me, hard with suspicion. It twists my heart to see the edge of rawness in his eyes when he's looking at me now.

I lick my lips. "I should have told you something else before now. Nick, I'm falling in love with you."

I've caught him off guard completely. I see the telling flicker of surprise in his expression. But then it's gone, replaced with something steely, something stronger than denial.

I smile nervously. "Is this the part where you cut me loose because I've been fool enough to get too close to you?"

"Is that what you think I'll do?"

"I don't know. Other women—"

"Never compare yourself to other women." His reply is clipped, firm. "I've never compared you to anyone. This is about us. There's no room for anyone else."

I nod, swallowing thickly. "Then where do we go from here? Tell me what I can do to make this right between us again."

I watch him contemplate, a tendon pulsing in the side of his cheek. When he looks at me, his blue gaze is steady, unyielding. "One hundred nights."

"What?"

"One hundred nights in my bed." He leans toward me, those arresting eyes refusing to let me go. "You've had a hundred days on your terms, Ms. Ross, now I want the same on mine."

My breath catches, and while part of me fears the kind of control he's about to demand, there's another part of me that can think of nothing I want more. "What are your terms, Mr. Baine?"

"For the next one hundred nights, I want you open to me—anywhere I want, whatever I ask of you. No limits, no barriers, no hiding any part of yourself from me. And, Avery, I will demand more from you than I ever have."

"That's it?" I shake my head, hope and elation streaking through me like licks of fire. "That's all you'll require of me?"

He leans forward and cups my face in his strong hands. "That's a good beginning."

"Yes," I agree, as he pulls me into a sensual kiss. "That is a good beginning."

~ ~ ~

Nick arranges to have my rental car picked up from the prison lot and we decide to stay overnight in Pennsylvania rather than make the long drive back to the city. Besides, I've just entered into an agreement with a formidable negotiator, and both of us are eager to get started hammering out the fine points as quickly as possible.

The nearest hotel is a cheap chain a few miles away, and Nick runs to check us in while I wait in the car. I can't take my eyes off him as he strolls into the hotel and walks up to the desk. Will I ever tire of looking at him? Will he always make my pulse quicken and my body melt with desire?

I suspect so, and I intend to spend the next three and a half months testing the theory.

I'm enjoying watching the young reception clerk flirt with my man when my cell phone rings with a local call.

Thinking it's Stadler or the prison calling with an

update on my mom, I swipe the screen and answer. "Hello?"

"Hello, Avery."

The male voice is thin, but sharp as the edge of a blade. I can't place it immediately, yet my body's reaction is visceral, as if I've just taken a face full of frigid water.

"Shame about your mother, huh? 'Course, all things considered, that fall coulda been worse. A helluva lot worse."

"Who is this?"

An airless chuckle grates across my ear. "Oh, come on, now. I think you know. But I'm guessing your rich boyfriend in there doesn't."

Dread forms a cold knot in my gut at the mention of Nick. And, yes, I do recognize this voice now. The fact that I do makes the dread I felt a moment ago corrode into something vile. Something poisonous and deadly.

How did he find me after all this time? The question no sooner burns through my thoughts than I recall the photo that was snapped of Nick and me at the mayor's gala. The photo that went viral online. *Dammit.*

Anxious, I chance a look back at Nick now. He's still at the reception desk, having just signed for our room. The young clerk smiles at him as he takes the key from her, then starts to turn in my direction.

"We need to talk," says the voice on the other end of the line. "I'll be in touch."

The connection is cut, and I'm left holding my phone in trembling hands. I drop it into my purse before Nick returns to the car.

He's grinning as he climbs in and hands me the room keys in their little paper sleeve. "Honeymoon suite was all they had left. Hope you don't mind."

"No." I force a smile that feels tight on my lips. "I don't mind."

He cocks his head at me, frowning. "Something wrong?"

"No." I try for another smile, a stronger one that draws on years of practice in pretending nothing is wrong when, in reality, my life is coming apart at the seams. "Everything's fine."

~ * ~

Nick and Avery's story continues in these suspenseful, scorchingly sensual novels of the series:

FOR 100 NIGHTS
FOR 100 REASONS

Plus, an all-new novel coming soon!

FOR 100 FOREVERS

The 100 Series is also available in eBook and Audiobook editions. Look for the individual novels and the digital boxset at your favorite eBook retailer today.

Never miss a new book from Lara Adrian!

Sign up for Lara's VIP Reader List at
LaraAdrian.com

Be the first to get notified of Lara's new releases, plus be eligible for special subscribers-only exclusive content and giveaways that you won't find anywhere else.

Sign up today!

ABOUT THE AUTHOR

LARA ADRIAN is a *New York Times* and #1 international best-selling author, with nearly 4 million books in print and digital worldwide and translations licensed to more than 20 countries. Her books regularly appear in the top spots of all the major bestseller lists including the *New York Times*, USA Today, Publishers Weekly, The Wall Street Journal, Amazon.com, Barnes & Noble, etc. Reviewers have called Lara's books "addictively readable" (Chicago Tribune), "extraordinary" (Fresh Fiction), and "one of the consistently best" (Romance Novel News).

With an ancestry stretching back to the Mayflower and the court of King Henry VIII, the author lives with her husband in New England.

Visit the author's website and sign up for new release announcements at **www.LaraAdrian.com**.

Find Lara on Facebook at
www.facebook.com/LaraAdrianBooks

You met Baine International security chief and combat veteran Gabriel Noble in the 100 Series. Discover his hidden scars and forbidden cravings in this all-new novel!

Run to You

Available Now

Look for this 100 Series standalone novel in ebook, trade paperback and unabridged audiobook

You met brilliant artist Jared Rush in the 100 Series. Unravel his darkest secrets and desires in this all-new novel!

Play My Game

Available Now

Look for this 100 Series standalone novel in ebook, trade paperback and unabridged audiobook

Love paranormal romance?

Read Lara's bestselling Midnight Breed vampire romance series

A Touch of Midnight
Kiss of Midnight
Kiss of Crimson
Midnight Awakening
Midnight Rising
Veil of Midnight
Ashes of Midnight
Shades of Midnight
Taken by Midnight
Deeper Than Midnight
A Taste of Midnight
Darker After Midnight
The Midnight Breed Series Companion
Edge of Dawn
Marked by Midnight
Crave the Night
Tempted by Midnight
Bound to Darkness
Stroke of Midnight
Defy the Dawn
Midnight Untamed
Midnight Unbound
Claimed in Shadows
Midnight Unleashed
Break The Day
Fall of Night
King of Midnight

Discover the Midnight Breed with a FREE eBook

Get the series prequel novella
A Touch of Midnight
for FREE at LaraAdrian.com!

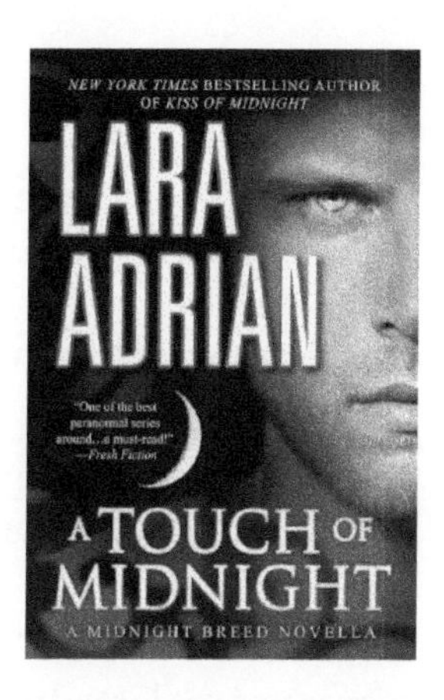

After you enjoy your free read, look for Book 1

Connect with Lara online at:

www.LaraAdrian.com

www.facebook.com/LaraAdrianBooks

https://www.bookbub.com/authors/lara-adrian

www.goodreads.com/lara_adrian

www.instagram.com/laraadrianbooks

www.pinterest.com/LaraAdrian

Milton Keynes UK
Ingram Content Group UK Ltd.
UKHW040224271124
3129UKWH00003B/277

9 781939 193421